WALKING DEAD

WALKING DEAD

GREG RUCKA

BANTAM BOOKS

WALKING DEAD
A Bantam Book / May 2009

Published by
Bantam Dell
A Division of Random House, Inc.
New York, New York

Book design by Glen Edelstein

Bantam Books is a registered trademark of Random House, Inc., and the colophon is a
trademark of Random House, Inc.

Library of Congress Cataloging-in-Publication Data

Rucka, Greg.
   Walking dead / Greg Rucka.
      p. cm.
   ISBN 978-0-553-80474-4 — ISBN 978-0-553-90648-6 (ebook)
   1. Bodyguards—Fiction. I. Title.

PS3568.U2968W36 2009
813'.54—dc22   2008049507

Printed in the United States of America
Published simultaneously in Canada

www.bantamdell.com

10 9 8 7 6 5 4 3 2 1
BVG

FOR BRANDY

NO MAN CAN PUT A CHAIN ABOUT THE ANKLE

OF HIS FELLOW MAN WITHOUT AT LAST FINDING

THE OTHER END FASTENED ABOUT HIS OWN NECK.

—FREDERICK DOUGLASS

WALKING DEAD

CHAPTER
One

People came to Kobuleti to hide. It's why we were there, and it's why Bakhar Lagidze had brought his family there, and I knew it, and I never asked him why.

I should have.

I was awake but unsure of it, my eyes suddenly open, the last whispers of dream vanishing, leaving me with no true memory, just the impression that it had been unpleasant, that I had done things of which I was not proud. Full-moon blue filtered into the bedroom, shadows swayed behind the thin curtains as long pine boughs rocked in the breeze.

Our dog, Miata, an old Doberman with no voice, was pacing at the door. I tried to focus my blurred vision on him as he turned a circle in place, raised a paw to scratch at the door, then glanced back my way. I fumbled my glasses off the nightstand and onto my nose, watched as he repeated the sequence. It had been the noise or the motion or both that had pulled me from sleep, and I knew the behavior for what it was, and it shifted me fully awake, and I put a hand on Alena's shoulder.

"Trouble," I said.

She murmured, refusing to surface.

"Wake up." I'd been speaking in Georgian. I switched to Russian. "Trouble."

I looked to the door in time to see Miata finish another circuit, this time to fix me with a plea in his eyes. Any other dog, I'd have thought he was fighting a weak bladder. I slipped out of bed, felt the hardwood immediately leech heat from my feet. There was a pistol in the nightstand drawer. I put the gun down long enough to pull on my jeans.

"What's going on?" Alena asked.

"Miata's got something."

She looked at me blearily, halfheartedly shook her head, as if unsure she was dreaming this or not. "Not the alarm?"

"I'll check. Stay here."

She was readying a pistol of her own as I left the room.

The two laptops that ran our security system lived in the linen closet beside the bathroom, on the shelf above the towels. I could feel Miata's moist breath against my bare ankles as I checked each. No alerts, nothing had been tripped. Nothing on the video. Nothing in the logs. It occurred to me that Miata was now an old dog, and maybe he really did need to take a leak, nothing more.

Then he bolted away down the hall, paws clacking on the floor. I followed more slowly and caught up with him at the back door. Together we listened to the night, and whatever it was he was hearing, I wasn't. I opened the door, and stepped out after him into the summer darkness.

The air was close to cold, chilled as it came in off the Black Sea, with threads of thin fog hanging in the trees, and it was as dead silent outside the house as it had been within. I thought about going back for a shirt, but Miata had begun cautiously trotting toward the woods that ringed our house, muzzle and ears both raised, and he clearly wasn't in a mood to wait. Two will-o'-the-wisps, dim halos, blinked at me as a car came along the road that cut through the forest in the distance. The sound of the engine followed a second later, but barely, the vehicle easily half a mile away, turning along the road that led to the Lagidze home. The light, then the sound, faded.

I followed Miata to the edge of the treeline, where it bordered our backyard, put a hand on his back to calm him. Alena and I had cut down several of the trees in the past two years to clear sight lines to the perimeter, and we still had four cords of wood split and stacked and ready to keep us warm through the coming winter.

Then I heard the shots.

This time, Miata had to follow me.

Flat run, barefoot, in the forest, in the dark, it took me almost three minutes to cover the distance, and I counted gunshots as I ran. I heard a total of fourteen more, all of them sounding as if spoken by the same weapon. An engine turned as I reached the edge of the dirt road leading to Bakhar's house, and the car it belonged to was already in gear and accelerating, and the lights hit me. The driver's response to seeing me, shirtless, barefoot, and armed, was to floor the Land Cruiser and swerve it in my direction.

My answer was to get the hell out of the way as fast as I could, and when I got to my feet again, the car had already shot around the bend, taillights retreating. Miata burst out of the woods, racing in the direction of the house. I went after him. A second Land Cruiser was parked outside of the darkened house, its tail to Bakhar's beat-up Opel, and I could see three men heading for the larger vehicle. The night stole details, but I saw that two of them were armed, and one of them had a long gun, the distinctive silhouette of an AK, and maybe Miata didn't care, but I sure as hell did.

"Back!" I shouted the command in Russian, and Miata took it immediately, veering off sharply, into the cover of the woods on the right.

I went left, and had just enough time to put a tree between myself and the AK before the shots came. Whoever was on the trigger knew his business and controlled his bursts, sending three my way in short order. The Land Cruiser started up right after the third salvo. I broke cover to run alongside the road, using the trees, and the AK shouted at me again, and this time I got a fix on the shooter and returned fire, two double-taps that went true.

A door slammed, and the Land Cruiser shot forward, then past, then was gone.

I brought my pistol down, tried to get my heart rate and breathing to follow suit. Miata edged out of the shadows on the other side of the road, followed me as I went to check on the man I'd shot. His legs had folded beneath him where he'd collapsed, the AK lying parallel to his knees. I could see he was Caucasian, probably Eastern European, which was hardly a surprise, considering that was where we were. I found a wallet and a wad of euros on him and took both, stuffing them into my own pockets. I picked up the AK, gave it a quick check.

The night had gone quiet again.

I looked toward my friend's house. The front door was ajar, perforated with shots. Moonlight dropped a shadow that filled the entrance with darkness.

"Bakhar?"

I didn't get an answer. I didn't expect one.

I already knew what I was going to find.

CHAPTER
Two

The first thing Bakhar Lagidze had said to me was, "You run like someone is chasing you."

Then he laughed.

This wasn't the first time I'd seen him, but it was the first time we'd exchanged words. He, his wife, daughter, and young son had moved into the neighboring house the previous spring, and in the interest of exercising due diligence, Alena and I had taken discreet notice. It wasn't that neighbors were a danger, per se, but any change in the status quo, by necessity, had to be viewed as a potential threat. Theoretically, we were as safe now as we were ever likely to be, living under carefully established cover that we had each come to embrace. But theory and practice continue to be two different things, and there were people who knew what we had done, and what we could do, and who, despite their promises to the contrary, might one day decide not to leave well enough alone.

So we had made it our business to know who these new neighbors were, if only to be certain that they posed no threat to us.

It would have been easy for me to have ignored him, then, to have pretended to be too absorbed in my run to have heard him. But we'd passed each other on this road before, me running back up from Kobuleti's one main street, heading home, him walking with his fishing pole and tackle box down to the beach. It wasn't simply that it would've been rude; better to be known and accepted in the community, to belong, and thus turn the community itself into another layer of security.

So I slowed, then stopped, then turned back to face him, maybe twenty feet between us. He was watching me, head cocked to the side, the edges of a smile visible beneath his thick mustache.

"You're always going so fast," he said. "Every time I see you. Sprinting."

"Tail end of the run," I explained. "Last push."

He nodded, then used the fishing pole to gesture up the road, at the woods. "You and your wife, you're in the little house, right?"

I crossed the road closer to where he stood, nodding. It was easier than using words, and I was somewhat breathless, and it gave me a few more seconds to think things through. Alena took her run in the afternoon, preferring to leave it before dinner, and it was as likely as not that he'd seen her taking the same route I did.

He used the pole again, this time to gesture in the direction of his home. "We're in the Party house, the old Russian's place. Fucking Russians, we had to tear out half of everything just to make it into a home."

"Yeah, we're always working on our place," I said.

He nodded, commiserating with a lifetime commitment to home improvement, then set down his pole so it leaned against his side and offered me his hand. "Bakhar. Bakhar Lagidze."

"David," I lied. "David Mercer."

We shook hands.

"American?"

"Canadian," I lied, again. "You're local?"

"Born in Tbilisi. You speak our language very well."

"My wife taught me."

"She's Georgian, too?"

I nodded. The lies were so practiced they didn't require any thought on my part. "But she grew up in Moscow. She used to dance."

Bakhar Lagidze's eyes lit up. They were blue, deep set in his lined face. His mustache, mostly black, had strays of gray emerging. I put him in his early forties, maybe five years older than I was.

"She should meet Tiasa! She's my daughter, she wants to dance, like the Bolshoi. Your wife teaches, right?"

"A little," I admitted. Alena had begun taking on students, only a handful of them, since we'd last returned from the U.S. She'd posted flyers in the cafés in town, initially as a means of reinforcing our cover, establishing a meager supplemental income that we didn't really need. It was my suspicion that she enjoyed teaching, though she had yet to admit as much to me. "You should bring her by."

"Maybe Ia will bring her over."

"Ia?"

"My wife." Bakhar's smiled broadened, showing stained

teeth and genuine pleasure. "Wonderful to meet you, David. Nice to meet the neighbors."

"Good to meet you, too," I told him.

It wasn't until I was home, under the needle-spray of the shower, that it occurred to me that Bakhar Lagidze had most likely done to us what we had done to him. He'd checked us out, just enough to be sure his neighbors didn't pose him a threat.

He'd been right.

The threat had come from another source entirely.

I stepped in blood when I stepped into the house. There was a lot of it, and I could smell it, along with the lingering of gunpowder. The moonlight outside wasn't enough. I was going to have to turn on a light.

When it came on, I could see the puddle, spent brass glittering in and around it. The blood broke into a smear, leading down the hall. Like our home, Bakhar's was only one story. Unlike ours, it was large, as befitted a family of four. On entry, the hall opened to a common room that doubled for dining, and then, off that, was the kitchen. Following the hall led to the master bedroom, and then the corridor went ninety degrees to the left, to the bathroom and the two other bedrooms.

Miata snuffed at the air behind me, hesitating.

"Home," I told him, and pointed the way. He looked at me sorrowfully, then dropped his head and went.

The smear ran straight to the master bedroom, its door wide open. I tried to be careful where I stepped as I followed the trail down the hall. My blood-covered soles dried on the carpet, and for a second I thought they might be a problem later, but then I thought about the general state of law enforcement in Georgia in general, and Kobuleti in particular, and admitted that I was most likely worrying about nothing. Forensic science hadn't ever been high on the national agenda, and since the war in South Ossetia and the subsequent Russian stranglehold on the country, it had fallen even further.

A table lamp had fallen in the bedroom, its light still on, and it illuminated from below. Somehow it made the scene inside the more horrible.

The blood had been Bakhar's, but I'd already guessed that, and maybe that was why I thought I'd find less of it in here. I was wrong. There was more.

There was a lot more.

He'd been shot in the hall, through the front door, perhaps as he'd come to answer it. I hadn't seen a gun anywhere on the floor and I wasn't seeing one in the bedroom, so if he'd been expecting trouble and had come to answer it with some of his own, the men who'd killed him had taken the weapon. They'd hit Bakhar in the chest, perhaps as many as four times from what I could see. Then they'd entered and taken hold of him, likely by his hair, and dragged him to the master bedroom, where they'd propped him on his bed.

At that point they'd gone to work on him with a knife.

He was still recognizable to me, but barely. Stabs and slashes covered his face, chest, and groin, though I couldn't see any on his arms or hands, nothing that resembled a defensive wound. It would have been nice to believe that meant he'd already died before they brought out the blade, that he hadn't tried to defend himself because there'd been nothing left of him to defend. But it was just as likely that he'd been dying instead of dead, and from the two Land Cruisers I knew there had been at least four of them who had come for the killing, and certainly two could've held his arms while a third set to carving.

The knife had been entirely unnecessary, and the savagery of it spoke clearly of cruelty and rage. His neck had been cut so badly it seemed now barely able to keep his head with his body. Blood, brain, and flecks of bone glistened in the macabre light. I could see the pearl gray of his cervical vertebrae in the mass of red meat that had been his throat.

This wasn't simply murder.

This was looking at hatred, pure and plain.

"Dancers," Ia Lagidze said mildly. "Very flexible."

This was perhaps a year ago, sitting in the small kitchen of our house, the tail end of winter outside, rain pelting the windows. We'd built a freestanding gym about fifty feet from the house to suit our own needs, but it doubled as a dance studio, and that was where Alena gave lessons. She was in there now with Tiasa and maybe two or three other girls from town.

I tried to keep from spit-taking my tea, instead forced it down without choking, and stared at Ia, sitting across the kitchen table from me. She gauged my reaction with a smirk that blossomed into a self-congratulatory grin.

"Don't tell me she isn't, David," Ia said, giggling. "You and Yeva must be at it all the time, just the two of you here." She glanced over at her son, Koba, who was sitting by the cast-iron stove, playing pinball on my laptop as a reward for finishing his homework while they waited for Tiasa to finish. The boy didn't acknowledge that he'd heard his mother, and even if he had, being seven, he was hopefully oblivious to such innuendo.

Ia leaned closer, putting a friendly hand on my arm, adding conspiratorially, "Baki and I used to be like that all the time, before the children came."

"Flexible?" I asked.

Ia laughed, sitting back, taking her tea up again. "That and other things." She sipped through a smile, memory perhaps, and then her face lit again. "Oh! Bakhar has tickets for the Dinamo game this weekend in Batumi, he's taking Koba and he has an extra, he wanted me to ask if you cared to join them."

"Who're they playing?" I asked, more out of reflex than interest.

Koba answered without pausing from his game. "Spartaki!"

"We're all going down," Ia said. "Tiasa and I are going shopping, then we'll meet my boys after the game for dinner. You should come! Yeva should come! She could go shopping with us!"

"I'm sure she'd like that," I said, thinking that it was the last thing Alena would want to do.

The bed Bakhar and Ia slept in would've been called a super king if it'd been in the UK, just a king if it'd been in the U.S. It sat with its foot to the door, headboard against the wall opposite, with enough space on each side for a dresser. On the left side, as you faced it, was a nightstand, and the lamp had fallen from there. On the right there was nothing, and when I finally could bring myself to look up from Bakhar, I saw his wife, or rather the top of her head, the streaked blonde hair that she paid twice a month to be carefully dyed and styled in one of the salons near the beach. She was slumped in the corner, between what had been her side of the bed and her dresser.

Ia had fallen on her knees, or perhaps been forced to them. She was wearing pajamas, a billowy satin top and companion pants, turquoise and violet beneath a pattern of red roses, as gregarious as she had been. The three buttons on her top were missing, though the shirt had fallen closed when she'd collapsed, a comic nod to modesty in the obscenity of the room.

The entry wound was behind her right ear, the pale skin

blackened and puckered from the point-blank shot. Pieces of her stuck to the wall from the exit wound.

They'd made her watch, I realized. They'd made her watch as they mutilated her husband.

Then they'd forced Ia Lagidze to her knees, and taken her fear, and everything else, away from her.

Koba asked me to teach him English.

"You're not learning it in school?" I asked.

He bobbed his head from side to side, not quite shaking it to say no. His shoulders raised and lowered in time, making him look like a gangly marionette. He was tall for his age, or at least I supposed he was, and very thin, and at the age of seven he already needed glasses, which we both took as a symbol of unity.

"Not much."

He kicked a pass to me, sending the soccer ball bounding over the uneven ground of what passed for our backyard. It was summer, and I'd been surprised when he'd shown up, accompanying his sister for her biweekly lesson. This time of year, this time of day, most of the kids his age would be down at the beach, playing in the water or trying to scam treats from the tourists. But the request served as the explanation.

The ball took a bounce at the last second, nearly hitting me square in the crotch, but I got my thigh up and managed to trap and land it.

"I want to play in England," Koba told me, by way of confession. "I'll have to know how to speak it."

I tried to remember what it had been like to be seven and fearless and a dreamer.

"Sure," I told him. "If it's okay with your parents."

■   ■   ■

I left Ia and Bakhar in their bedroom as I'd found them, turned the corner, passing the bathroom. Koba's room was on my left, but I didn't need to look inside it to find him.

He was lying in the hallway, facedown, just outside his sister's room, one hand extended, as if reaching out to her. His glasses, broken at their bridge, rested a few inches from his head.

He'd been shot in the back.

Eight years old, and they'd shot him in the back.

They'd shot him in the back six times.

"Yeva says you dance, too," Tiasa said to me, some six months after she'd begun her lessons.

Unlike most of the other kids who took dance from Alena, Tiasa had demonstrated that rarest of all commodities, commitment. Twice a week, rain or shine, she came for her lessons, while the other students often seemed to find the obligation of showing up just once a week to be a superior challenge. Some days after school she would simply appear with her ballet slippers in hand, asking if she could use the studio to practice. We always said yes, and if Alena was around, she'd stand by and observe, granting the equivalent of a free lesson.

Today, Tiasa had come while Alena was in town seeking fish for our dinner. I'd let Tiasa into the studio-slash-gym, turned to leave, when she'd spoken.

"Alena said that?" It surprised me. It wasn't like her to offer anything personal, or at least, nothing that was both personal and accurate.

"She says she taught you."

"I wouldn't call what I do dancing." It wasn't false modesty.

I'd been practicing ballet for almost six years at that point, and while the physical conditioning and control it had granted me were certainly worthwhile, I'd yet to achieve anything that I would, even at my most charitable, describe as art.

Tiasa began stretching at the barre. Like her brother, she was tall, but unlike him, she was growing into it, beginning to form the body of the woman she would be. Her hair was black, and she'd neglected to tie it back today, and it flopped about as she bent and twisted, loosening up. I realized that she was styling it the same way Alena did, and wondered when that had happened.

"We don't have any boys who dance," Tiasa said to me, as she started practicing her positions. "Only girls take lessons."

"There's Jarji," I said.

"He stopped coming." She fixed me with a stare, then looked away. Like her father, her eyes were blue.

"You want me to dance with you?" I asked.

Suddenly shy, she mumbled her response.

"All right," I said. "I'll dance with you."

Like all the others, the door to Tiasa's room was ajar, and once again, I saw only darkness within. I used the barrel of the AK to push it further open, stepped inside, reaching out for the switch and finding it.

I didn't want to see what they'd done to her.

I didn't think I had a choice.

I threw the light, and, in its way, it was worse than everything I'd seen before.

There was no blood. There was no body.

Tiasa Lagidze was gone.

They'd taken her.

CHAPTER
Three

The regional head of the police in Kobuleti, Mgelika Iashvili, was in his late forties, tall and broad and thick through the neck and shoulders. Georgian pride runs to many things: their wine, their tea, their nearly four-thousand-year history. Stalin. They're also very proud of their weight lifters, and the rumor was that Iashvili had trained as a powerlifter for the Soviets back in the day, before everything had changed. Whether he still kept with it was unknown, but it did nothing to detract from his thuggish air, one that was well earned.

"And neither of you heard anything last night?" he asked. "Anything at all?"

Alena, at the stove and preparing tea, shook her head. She

let her lower lip jut just enough beneath her upper to indicate both sincerity and bewilderment.

"I sleep very deep," she lied. "Just ask David."

"Like a log," I agreed. In fact, the previous night had been the only one I could ever remember when I'd had difficulty waking her. "Are you going to tell us what this is about, Chief? Did something happen?"

Iashvili kept his eyes on Alena, watching her. He did it not so much because he suspected she might be lying, I thought, but rather because he liked looking at her. It wasn't unusual. A lot of people did, and if they noticed that she was sometimes a little slow, sometimes seemed to favor her right leg over her left, they still watched. Given that once upon a time, she had excelled at being someone who was barely noticed, I think Alena had come to even enjoy it.

The chief turned his attention reluctantly to me. After a moment for thought, he said, "You'll hear soon enough. Bakhar Lagidze, his whole family—they were murdered last night."

Alena dropped the teacup she was about to fill. The crash of it shattering in the sink was enough to turn Iashvili's attention back to her. I was grateful for the misdirection. It gave me an extra handful of seconds to set my reaction.

"Jesus Christ," I said.

"The children?" Alena asked softly, her voice thickening.

"All of them," Iashvili replied. "I'm very sorry. They were your friends?"

I thought about the word. In Georgian, "friend" was *megobari*, which, loosely translated, meant, *I will take your place in times of danger.*

"Yes," I told him. "They were."

"I was teaching her to dance," Alena said. "Tiasa."

"I have to ask," the chief said. "Did you notice anything unusual? Strangers in the area? A change in Bakhar's behavior?"

"No, nothing," I said. "Everything was . . . everything was fine. I talked to Bakhar the day before yesterday, we were going to take Koba to the football game in Batumi next week."

"Do you know if he'd bought the tickets?"

"I was going to buy them. I was going to get them today."

The chief frowned. At the sink, Alena began gathering pieces of broken crockery.

"I'm sorry to say this," Mgelika Iashvili said. "It looks like Bakhar killed his family, then himself."

Alena walked him to the door when he left, waiting there to watch as he drove away. I stayed in the kitchen. Miata trotted over from where he'd been taking the sun through the windows, and I gave him a scratch beneath the chin, stroked his neck. Alena returned and fixed me with a stare that was almost accusatory.

"He's lying," I said.

"Of course he's lying," Alena said. "He's been bought."

"Then he knows who killed them. Maybe he even knows why."

"He certainly knows who paid him."

"And maybe where Tiasa is."

"It's not our problem."

We stared at each other. I understood her anger, though the intensity of it surprised me. I knew what she was thinking. I knew why she was thinking it. I didn't like it, and I didn't go to any great length to hide that fact.

"What you did last night was foolish," she said.

"I didn't go over there planning to find the house soaked in blood. I went to help."

"I know that. I know why you went. Just as you know you shouldn't have."

"I'm not going to apologize," I said.

"I don't want an apology. An apology does us nothing. We have a home here, we have built a life. Do you want to have to leave, to run, to find somewhere new and to start again? To spend the years it will take us to rebuild? Do you want to lose all of this?"

"The only thing I fear losing is you," I said.

That stopped her, at least for the moment. Affection was still difficult for her, probably always would be, the way it dogs most survivors of abuse. Even though she knew my sincerity, believed it, speaking of it could bring her to moments of confused silence. Love was still a fragile thing for her, despite all its strength.

"You should never have gone over there at all."

"I didn't know what I would find," I said.

"It's not a question of what you found! You shouldn't have *done* it, Atticus!"

The mere fact that she'd used my real name was proof of how upset she was. I got out of my chair, went over to her, rested my hands on her arms. When I kissed her forehead, she closed her eyes and put her arms around me.

"They were our friends," I said, holding her.

"Yes, they were," she whispered. "And now they're gone."

We spent the rest of the day going about our routines. I made my daily check of the security arrangements, the alarms, did yoga for an hour with Alena, then went for my run, leaving her to work out in the studio.

I covered eight miles, down to the water, along the beach. It was hot and growing humid, even by the waterfront, and the beach was beginning to fill. It was tourist season, and the influx had easily doubled Kobuleti's population, though that was down from the previous years. Another by-product of Russian pressure on the economy.

I passed the Gio, a café that, like so many others in town, turned into a bar-slash-nightclub after dark during the summer months. One night, the summer after we'd returned to Kobuleti, Iashvili had been dining there with a couple off-duty members of the force, celebrating a junior officer's impending marriage. A group of laughing teenagers attracted the policemen's attention. Iashvili thought he and his fellows were the source of amusement. The fight that followed ended with the chief shooting three of the boys in the foot. There was no official record of the event. Even the hospital where the boys had been treated refused to document the case.

Democracy was wheezing its way into the Republic of Georgia, but it still had a very long way to go. The Russian Army still maintained a presence in both Poti, further north on the coast, and in Gori, restricting traffic to Tbilisi. In the open land between the Black Sea and the capital, brigands still lurked the roads. The declaration of independence in both South Ossetia and Abkhazia made Moscow's shadow fall long and cold throughout the country.

I looped back, this time following the main street, waving at the people I knew and exchanging brief good-mornings as I went past. I no longer got the stares I once did, but the amusement at my commitment to exercise still remained. I made my way back up the road toward the house, digging down for extra speed, feeling my lungs starting to burn. At the fork in the road, I went right, heading toward home, telling myself there was nothing in Bakhar Lagidze's house that I needed to see again.

■   ■   ■

The rest of the day passed in tight silence. Late in the afternoon, when Tiasa would've come for her lesson, Alena went out to the studio again. I was working in the yard on an old Dnepr motorcycle I'd bought a couple of months earlier, Miata lazily watching me as I tried to make sense of the schematics I'd downloaded from the Internet. Alena and I had only the one car for the two of us, a forty-year-old Mercedes-Benz diesel sedan that took five minutes to start during the winter, and that could easily double as a light tank in an emergency. The Dnepr, once repaired, would hopefully serve as more reliable, if smaller, transportation.

The music in the studio came on, one of the more energetic pieces that Alena used for warming up. She'd left the door open, and the noise kept Miata and me company. After a few minutes there was a quick silence, and then the sound of John Lennon's voice as she switched to her Beatles playlist. Alena had loved the Beatles for as long as I'd known her, and she frequently danced and taught to their catalogue.

So when "Golden Slumbers" came on, I barely noticed, occupied as I was with trying to remove the dead battery from the bike without tearing my knuckles open. It's a short song, hardly a minute and a half long, and so when it repeated, I missed that, too. But somewhere around the fifth time through I registered what I was hearing, and when the song ended, and then began again almost without pause, I got to my feet, wiping my hands on my jeans. Miata lifted his head to see what I was doing, then went back to watching the squirrels.

The song had ended and begun again when I stuck my head through the doorway. Most of the space was cleared for dancing, mirrors on the barre wall. At the far end was our heavy bag, the stack of weight plates and barbells. The stereo sat in the opposite corner.

Alena was on the floor, her back to the mirror, facing the

stereo. She sat with her knees drawn to her chest, arms holding them close, head buried, and now that I was inside, I could hear it. In all the time I'd known her, I'd seen her cry only once. Tears weren't something she cared for, nor were they something she offered readily. And even when I had seen her cry, it had been nothing like this.

The sobs wracked her, making her shake, and it was obvious she was trying to control them, to control herself, and that she was failing, but yet unwilling to surrender. It was so utterly unexpected, so unlike her, that I spent an instant unsure of how to react. Then I went to her side, and she heard me coming, and tried harder to hide her face away. I sat on the floor beside her, the mirror glass cold against my back, and carefully put my arms around her, waiting to see if she'd resist. She didn't; she slumped against me, her whole body shaking.

She continued to cry, and I continued to hold her, and Paul continued to sing, and I wondered if this was grief, or something more.

I couldn't leave it alone.

The next morning, when I reached the fork in the road, I went left instead of right.

There wasn't much sign of crime scene investigation as I approached the house. The front door still hung open, the splintered and burst wood from the rounds that had torn through it all the more garish. Bakhar's car remained where it had been the other night. I slowed to a walk, feeling sweat dripping off me into the dust. A dark brown puddle had dried on the dirt road, where the man I'd shot had bled out. When I listened, I could hear the buzzing of flies from inside.

There was no police tape, nothing saying that I could not enter, not that the presence of an official sign would've stopped me. There was a curious sense of déjà vu when I stepped inside, triggered, perhaps, by the shift in the illumination, the transition from bright sunlight without to the shadows within. A cloud of flies, swarming over the still-tacky puddle in the entryway, scattered and then almost as quickly re-formed, ignoring me.

The house had already had one full day to cook in the summer heat, and it reeked. Whatever tracks I may have made had been obliterated by the multiple police boots that had tromped up and down the hall since the discovery of the bodies. I wondered, idly, who had called the crime in to the police, how they had been notified. Conceivably, it could've taken days before anyone noticed what had happened here.

Unsure of what exactly all my questions were, I started searching for answers in the kids' rooms first.

I spent nearly five hours on the search, with a couple of breaks in between to grasp some fresh air and clear my head. In Koba's and Tiasa's rooms I found nothing extraordinary, only sad. Koba had an eight-year-old's collection of detritus, scraps of paper covered with drawings of spaceships and football players. He'd taped a crude family portrait he'd drawn on the inside of his bedroom door, the house small in comparison to the figures. In it, he'd drawn himself biggest of all, smiling with lots of teeth. His sister had been smallest, but not by much, almost as tall as he'd drawn Ia.

Tiasa's room was harder. Books, schoolwork, magazines. A DVD Alena had lent her of a Savion Glover tap performance. A bottle of cheap perfume, and a brand new lipstick. I didn't find a diary. If I had, I doubt I could've brought myself to read it.

It was in the master bedroom that I began to concentrate my efforts. There was nothing in the clichés—no documents taped to the back of the furniture, nothing beneath the mattress or submerged in the toilet tank. In the back of the closet I found a nylon carry-all, the kind of thing to hold towels and swimsuits for a day at the beach. This one held three pairs of underwear, three clean shirts, three pairs of socks, a pair of pants, and a toothbrush. It also held just shy of five thousand euros, a loaded 9mm Makarov, and two passports, one Russian, the other Romanian. The pictures inside each matched Bakhar, even if the names didn't.

There was also a small, tattered address book. When I flipped through it, the entries were all in Georgian, first names and phone numbers. Some of the country codes I recognized—Ukraine, Romania, Turkey, Russia, Germany, England—and some I didn't.

I put it aside, wondering why it was Bakhar Lagidze needed a go-bag.

The only other item of interest I found was in Bakhar's tackle box, the same one he always took with him fishing. Beneath the top compartment, wrapped in an oily rag, was another pistol, this one a small Czech semi-auto. The gun was a cheap one, poorly maintained, and nothing I would have trusted my life to in a pinch. Bakhar clearly seemed to have thought otherwise.

That was all I found.

Alena was in the kitchen when I got home, putting together a salad, and I let her know I was back, though she'd already determined that from Miata's reaction the moment I'd come onto our property. I dropped the go-bag on our bed, stripped and took a quick shower. When I returned, Alena had the contents dumped out, examining them. She shot me an accusing glare as I passed her but said nothing until after I'd finished getting dressed, and then, when she did, failed to deliver the admonishment I'd expected from her expression.

"I have to go to Tbilisi tomorrow morning," she said, tossing Bakhar's Russian passport back onto the pile, and picking up the address book.

"Why?"

"Nicholas is meeting me at the Marriott." She leafed through the little book in her hands, flipping the pages slowly.

"We saw him in March," I said, surprised. Nicholas Sargenti, to grossly oversimplify things, was our banker.

"Yes. I want him to free up some more funds, just in case we need them quickly." She looked up from the book to read my expression, and then added, as if it needed further explanation, "In case we have to run."

I tucked in my shirt, thinking. In the world Alena and I had made for ourselves, Nicholas Sargenti was the hidden facilitator. When Alena had been working, it was he who had arranged contact protocols, had retrieved job offers, passing them along to her through varied and elaborate cutouts and dead-drops. He had been her hidden necessity, able to provide papers and identities on short notice, and all of them entirely legitimate. From his office in Monaco, he had moved the substantial amounts of money required for her to do her job around the world quietly and quickly, deftly funding each cover. While we rarely availed ourselves of his other services these days, Nicholas still handled the majority of our finances.

Alena had never admitted to him what it was she got paid tens of millions of dollars to do, and he had never asked, but he was smart enough to do everything else, which meant he was

smart enough to have figured it out. Which meant he was a risk
to us, albeit a very calculated, necessary one. For that reason,
face-to-face meetings with him were always planned with great
care, their number limited. That Alena had arranged to meet
him only three months after last seeing him concerned me, but
not nearly as much as the fact that she was meeting him in-
country, in the capital. It was sloppy, and that was utterly unlike her.

"I'll come with you," I said.

"Better if you don't. If Iashvili comes back with more questions and we're *both* gone, it will look worse than it already
does."

"It doesn't look bad right now. You heard him, he's calling
it a murder-suicide and putting it all on Bakhar."

"Even so." She indicated the spilled contents of the go-bag
on the bed with her free hand. "Did you find anything else?"

"Bakhar kept a pistol in his tackle box," I said, aware she
was changing the subject. "Piece-of-crap little Czech thing."

"That is not so unusual, that he would bring a weapon for
self-defense."

"Maybe. Wouldn't do him much good at the bottom of a
tackle box."

"That implies a level of tradecraft that isn't evident here."

"He had a go-bag."

"A very bad go-bag. Too many clothes. Not enough cash. No
credit cards. And this." She held up the address book. "If this is
a list of contacts in whatever his business was, this is very un-
professional."

I held up a hand, began counting on my fingers. "Drugs,
guns—"

"It doesn't matter," Alena interrupted, dropping the address book on the bed. "Whatever it was he was into, his sins
caught up with him. Come, dinner's ready."

She walked out of the bedroom. I stared at the scattered clothes, the two passports, the address book, the gun. I thought about my own go-bag, waiting on the top shelf in the front closet, resting beside Alena's.

Wondering how much longer I had before my sins caught up with me.

CHAPTER
Four

Alena took the car, leaving before dawn. If things went well, she could do the drive to Tbilisi in four hours. If things went the way they normally did, it would take her closer to eight, accounting for the appropriate checkpoints and shake-downs. I didn't fear for her well-being. Anyone who tried to take something from her she wasn't willing to give would draw back a bloody stump, and that was only if she allowed them to keep their life.

For my part, I knew Alena left before dawn because I was awake when she did it, and that was because I hadn't been able to sleep. I couldn't stop thinking about Tiasa. Whoever Bakhar Lagidze had been before he'd come to Kobuleti—and clearly he had been someone he was trying to escape, to put in the past—I could imagine Tiasa no more culpable in it than Koba was.

There were a handful of reasons to have taken her alive.

Not a single one of them was pleasant.

Georgians, in the main, are not early risers, and Mgelika Iashvili was no exception. I had been waiting at his office for forty minutes already when he arrived just before eleven. Only a handful of officers were present prior, and many of them I knew by name. I spent the wait with small talk, mostly about how much the tourists were a necessary evil this time of year and how much we all hated the fucking Russians.

A couple years back, the police in the Adjara Autonomous Province, of which Kobuleti was a part, received new patrol cars and new uniforms from the Interior Ministry, as part of President Saakashvili's efforts to stamp out corruption and rebuild the public trust in the nation's police. The money came as trickle-down American largesse, brought about in turn through Georgia's cooperation in the Global War on Terror. In addition to spiffy new duds and shiny new cars, the money also went to training, improving border security, and to aid stamping out corruption in the ranks.

The new uniforms were baby-boy-nursery blue, and less totalitarian looking than the Soviet-era-influenced ones that had preceded them. The cars were white with a navy stripe on the hood. The corruption remained.

Five minutes after Iashvili arrived, he invited me into his office, where a junior officer brought us the ubiquitous hospitality of a cup of tea, leaving us alone behind the closed door after we'd been served. I sipped—drinking tea fast in front of your host is considered an insult, almost, but not quite, as bad as toasting someone with beer rather than wine—and Iashvili and I made more small talk for a bit. By the time he finally asked me why I'd stopped by, I could feel the caffeine crawling in my veins.

"Bakhar didn't kill his family," I told him. "He didn't kill himself."

Until then, Iashvili had been smiling, friendly. Not so much now. "We're saying he did, David."

"And I'm saying that I know he didn't."

"And how would you know that?"

"It doesn't matter how I know. What matters is that you understand three things. I know he didn't do it. I know Tiasa—his daughter—wasn't killed, at least not at the house. And, most important, that I'm *not* asking you to prove otherwise."

The hostility that had been growing on his face froze, then shifted to confusion. "You're not?"

"No, I'm not. I understand your position, Chief, I really do. I'm not asking you to make trouble."

"You're looking to make trouble yourself."

"Maybe. But that's my business."

He considered that. "You and Yeva, you've lived here four years now?"

"About that."

"Never any problems from you two. Everyone likes you, everyone likes Yeva. Everyone even likes your damn dog."

"We like it here."

"What I don't like is trouble, David. You remember that thing with the kids, couple years back? You remember?"

"I remember."

"You know I shot them?"

"So I heard."

He turned his chair, took another sip of his tea. On the wall he was facing was a photograph of six men, all wearing red leotards, in a line. Each held a barbell above his head with what looked to be a couple hundred pounds in weight plates on each end. Neck muscles strained, and even in the faded color, I could see the flush of exertion in each face. The second one from the left bore a striking resemblance to the man sitting opposite me.

"That was stupid of me," the chief said. "That could have been very bad for me."

I sipped my tea, waited.

He swiveled back to look at me. "I could have lost everything, you understand? I could have lost it all."

"I want to find the girl." I shifted in my chair, pulled the bundle of euros I'd taken from Bakhar's go-bag. I set them on his desk, between us. "I just want to find the girl."

The chief stared at me for several seconds, then looked at the bills on his desk, green, yellow, and purple.

"My business," I said. "No one will ever hear me mention your name."

He looked at me again, no doubt wondering if he could trust me. Then he picked up the bills, tucking them into the breast pocket of his baby-boy-blue shirt.

"You should go down to Batumi," the chief said. "The port, maybe on the northern end. Ask for Zviadi."

I nodded, got to my feet.

"If you have friends, David, you might want to take one or two with you."

"Just me," I said.

"You don't even know who he was. You don't know who Bakhar Lagidze *was*."

I stopped at the door. "I want to find the girl. I don't care about the father."

"The father and the girl, they're part of the same thing," Mgelika Iashvili told me.

CHAPTER
Five

I found him having dinner in a restaurant on the Batumi waterfront, maybe half a klick from the working part of the port, at a place called Sanapiro. Dinner appeared to consist of *khinkali*—high-density meatballs—and several bottles of beer. *Khinkali* is something of a national dish, and I knew from experience that one or two were enough to fill the stomach like fresh-poured concrete. If I was reading his table right, he'd already gone through half a dozen already, and showed no signs of slowing down.

"I'm looking for a girl," I told him.

He didn't look up from his meal, giving me an excellent view of the top of his head. His hair was thinning, stringy, black, and long, and the fat at the back of his neck swelled and spilled where his collar failed to contain it.

"Later," Zviadi said. "I'm eating."

I resisted an urge to sigh, took in the restaurant around us instead. It was busy and loud, as almost every Georgian restaurant is wont to be, and nobody was paying us any attention at all. Floor-to-ceiling windows formed the wall along the front of the establishment, and the sunset ricocheting off the Black Sea bathed everything and everyone within in golds and reds. When I looked back to Zviadi, he'd taken up his bottle of beer, gulping from it as he studied the pedestrians and the traffic, resolutely ignoring my presence.

"You're Zviadi?" I asked, though there was no doubt that I had the right guy.

He brought the bottle back down to the table, empty, then renewed his assault on his plate, all without looking at me. His hands were stubby and broad, but surprised me by being clean.

"I'm. Eating."

I dropped a fifty-euro bill onto his plate. It stopped his fork short, and his other hand darted forward, snatching the bill up. He put it to his mouth, sucking the oil and sauce that had begun to collect on it, and as he did so he finally turned his attention to me. Then he nodded, folding the bill one-handed and shoving it into a pants pocket, before gesturing for me to take the chair opposite him. He never let go of the fork in his other hand.

After I'd taken a seat, he resumed eating, asking around a mouthful, "For how long?"

"Depends on if it's the right girl. I'm looking for a specific one."

"I don't remember you. I've never seen you before."

"I don't think she's one of yours." Actually, I was praying

she wasn't one of his. "You were pointed out to me as someone who could help me find her."

His chewing slowed, and the fork came down and a napkin came up, and he cleaned his mouth and his chin, again watching me. He was rightly suspicious, but curious, too, though I suspect he was mostly wondering how many more of those euros I was carrying, and what the most efficient means of parting me from them might be.

I answered without his asking. "I've got money. I'll pay for the help."

A slight nod, followed by a pull from a fresh bottle of beer. "Who gave you my name?"

"I asked around."

"Asked around. Where did you ask around?"

I used my head to indicate the harbor, out the window.

"People talk too fucking much," he muttered. "Tell me about this girl."

In my pocket, I was carrying a printout, a picture of Tiasa that I'd pulled from old security video at the house, and for a moment I thought about showing it to him. But already I wasn't liking where things were heading, what I'd stepped into the moment I'd arrived in Batumi, begun searching for Zviadi around the port. It hadn't taken long to learn that the man was a pimp, and the women who'd pointed me to him had done so only with great reluctance, and only after I'd crossed their palms, their apprehension visible. The girl who had finally told me to check Sanapiro was maybe—*maybe*—sixteen.

"Young," I told him. "Black hair, blue eyes. Tall and slim. Local girl. Pretty."

"How young?"

"Fourteen." I was careful to not betray any revulsion when I said it.

"Sounds like you know her pretty well. You've been with her before?"

"Can you help me find her or not?"

"I got a girl, almost as young. Blonde. Ukrainian."

"I told you, local. If you can't help me find her, then I'll take my money somewhere else."

He waggled his fingers at me, telling me to calm down, grinning. Bits of dinner were visible between his teeth. "Just checking. I tell you what, I'll make a couple of calls, you give me an hour or two, then meet me at Lagoon. You know Lagoon, just down the street, at the corner of Portis Shesakhevi?"

"I can find it."

"One hour, two hours most, okay?" He finished his beer, wiped his hands and face again with his napkin. "Two hundred euros. In advance."

"You've got fifty," I said, not because I wasn't willing to pay that much, but because if I did, he'd have known I was a fool. "You get another fifty if you've got information for me when I see you again."

"Maybe I can't find you this girl," he said, shrugging.

"Then you've already been paid for doing nothing."

Zviadi used a fingernail to clean his teeth, then got out of his chair. His lower body was a surprise, compared with his upper, his legs so relatively slender I wondered how they managed to support him. He trundled out of the restaurant without another word, leaving me to pay for his meal.

The Dnepr wasn't in any condition to drive, so I'd had to take a bus down from Kobuleti, a modified minivan the locals referred to as a *marshrutka*. By the time I'd left Iashvili in his office, gone home, gotten my things together, printed off the best picture of Tiasa I could find, squared Miata away, and actually come back into town to arrange the ride, it had already been late afternoon. It was just before six when I reached Batumi.

I'd taken enough time before leaving home to check Bakhar's address book for anyone named Zviadi, but of course, nothing was going to be that easy, and there'd been no one by his name, let alone an entry with a Batumi number. Ultimately, though, the search for Zviadi hadn't taken long at all.

I'd headed north up Zubelashvilis Kucha from where the battered minivan had dropped me outside the old train station, and made for the port. It was a twenty-minute walk, and I'd actually passed Lagoon along the way. Once I'd reached the harbor, I'd started asking around.

The trick hadn't been in finding someone who actually knew Zviadi. The trick had been in convincing one of his girls that it was safe for her to take my money and to then tell me where I could find him.

Tonight would mark the third night since Tiasa had been taken, and the thought of her having had to spend any of it in the company of men like Zviadi wound my spine tight. That the man would sit in a restaurant—*could* sit in a restaurant—and so casually discuss his business in full view of the world made it all the more grotesque, and it made me feel as if I was the only one who actually gave a damn about his business at all.

I'd wasted time, and Tiasa Lagidze was suffering for it, and I kept telling myself that if I could find her, I could make my inaction up to her. I could free her from the nightmare that had started three days ago in Kobuleti.

If I could just find her in time.

Zviadi surprised me. He was actually at Lagoon when I arrived before ten, and, just as he'd been at Sanapiro, he was easy to spot. The restaurant had a naval theme going, old Russian submarine clocks and ship wheels on the wall, and I thought it was surprisingly busy for a Thursday night. I waited just inside until I was sure he'd seen me, then stepped back out onto the street. The humidity had died down with the sunset, and the air was pleasantly cool. After half a minute, he emerged and began walking toward the water, motioning me to accompany him.

"You're not from here," Zviadi said, checking the traffic as we crossed the road to the waterfront. "Your Georgian is very good, but you're not from here."

"Does it matter?"

"Maybe, maybe not. You an American?"

I shook my head. "I have money. Do you have the girl I want?"

"I think maybe I found her, yeah. Maybe not her, maybe one like her."

"I'll need to see her."

"You need to pay me."

I peeled off another fifty-euro bill and handed it over to his waiting palm. He didn't look at it, just stared at me.

"I told you two hundred," he said. "Two hundred, I take you to the girl."

"You get the rest when I see her. Maybe it's not the right girl."

"But maybe it *is* the right girl," Zviadi said.

I handed over another fifty. When he saw I wasn't giving him any more, he grunted and crammed both bills into the front pocket of his tightly stretched pants, where he'd stowed the other fifty I'd paid him earlier. Then he pulled out a mobile phone and brought up a number, turning away from me as he dialed it.

"We're coming," he told whoever answered. He listened to

the response, grunted, then hung up and replaced the phone on his hip.

"Who was that?" I asked.

"We can walk from here," Zviadi said. He began heading in the direction of the harbor, where the big ships were loading cargo in the sodium lights, not bothering to look back.

I followed him, thinking it was probably a very good thing I'd brought a gun with me to Batumi.

It was creeping past eleven by the time we reached our destination. We could probably have covered the distance quicker, but Zviadi's anatomy made that unlikely. Spindly loading cranes moved containers of cargo overhead, and the sound of the cranes, forklifts, lorries, and men at work was constant and loud. Perhaps a kilometer to the south was a rail yard, and every now and again I could hear the whistle from an engine, pulling out or pulling in, another part of the never-ending supply convoy feeding goods south into Turkey and Armenia.

We pushed further into the docks, passing a line of four giant fuel tanks to the east. The harbor here had been built like an inverted C, opening to the west, with a breakwater formed along the northern side, then mirrored to the east in a similar, though less trafficked, setup. We passed several outbuildings, port offices, more storage, more containers. Sweat shone on Zviadi's face, glistening orange in the lights, and as we moved further away from the main business of the port, as the noise dropped away, I could make out his breathing, labored from the walk.

Our destination was the third of three blue-roofed, Soviet-era structures, what looked to be warehouses from the outside, all of them windowless. The last of the lighting had dropped away some hundred meters back, and most of the illumination now came from the canopy thrown up over the main harbor, magnified by the water vapor constantly in the air. To the north, barely silhouetted against the eastern edge, I could make out the hulks of abandoned ships, beached and corroded. I could taste sea salt and rust.

Zviadi stopped, looking at the buildings, and I watched his tongue creep out over his lips, wetting them as he tried to catch his breath. Then he thrust out his hand to me, palm up. "The rest of the money," he said.

"You think they won't let you have my wallet after they're done with me?"

He blinked. "What? I—"

He was to my left, so I used that leg, brought my foot up and swept his right knee. He tumbled forward, managed to barely get his hands out in time to keep from planting himself face-first into the broken concrete beneath our feet. I used my right to kick him in the side once, and then to flip him onto his back.

Then I put the heel of my boot on his sternum and pressed down, to make certain he understood.

He got the message quickly, and didn't make a sound.

"What am I walking into?" I asked him, and when he didn't answer, I gave him some of my weight. He grunted, more in fear than in pain, I thought. "Who's in there?"

"Nobody!" It came out choked. "Nobody!"

"You're supposed to signal them, is that it? How?"

He stared up at me, then nodded. "I was going to text them."

"Who are they?"

"Some guys. They just want to talk to you, that's all they want."

"Why do they want to talk to me, Zviadi?"

"I don't know."

I moved my right foot from his sternum to his groin and applied pressure. He brought his hands down to try and push my leg away, but he had no leverage, and he wasn't strong enough, and when he did it, I pushed down harder. His inhale was sharp and accompanied by a whimper. I put a finger to my lips to indicate that he wanted to keep it down.

"I called around!" He sounded like he was choking, either on his pain or his fear, both of which would've been fine by me. "For your girl, the one you were looking for! And they asked who wanted to know, and I told them, I told them this foreigner was asking! They said bring you here!"

"Why?"

He shook his head, wincing, cheeks inflating. I wondered how many of his dumplings were threatening to come up the direction they'd entered.

"Why?"

"I don't know! They just said bring you here!"

I looked up from him, at the building. No idea what was inside. Alena would've shat a brick if she knew I was considering walking in there alone.

"How many of them?" I asked Zviadi. "How many are coming?"

"Two, three, I don't know."

So double that, and the high estimate became six. There was no way I was going to take six guys, certainly not if they were who I thought they might be. Low estimate would be four, and even that was too many. Taking four by myself would require a minor miracle.

Nothing in what I had been taught, in what I had learned, either in my first career or my present one, told me that meeting these guys head-on was a good idea. Everything I knew told me that I should walk away, walk away now, and not look back.

Except there was a chance that whoever they were, they knew where Tiasa Lagidze was.

I drew my weapon and Zviadi flinched, hands flying to his face. I let his nuts go free from my boot.

"Get up," I told him. "You're coming with me."

CHAPTER
Six

I wasn't a total idiot. I searched Zviadi first, took his cell
phone and the knife he was carrying, a lean-looking Russian
Army talon. Then I scouted the building, walking around its
perimeter with Zviadi in front of me, my gun pointed at his
back. He tried appealing to me twice. The first time I told him
to shut up. The second time I hit him, and had to pull him to
his feet again before we could resume.

He stopped protesting after that.

The building was, on the outside, everything I had feared it
would be. Three portals total, covering the north and south
sides, facing the water and the port, respectively. The south had
the addition of a garage door. No windows, no ladders, no fire
escapes. Some ten, maybe twelve meters tall, and damaged

enough that I figured I could find the handholds if I had it in mind to try and scale it, which I didn't.

When we came around again to the south side, I told Zviadi to open the door. Both he and the door did as ordered without hesitating. I didn't take much reassurance from either.

I had to keep Zviadi close once we went inside, because it was dark and I didn't want him trying to escape. The fact that I didn't like him or his business made manhandling him easier. The fact that it was his own damn fault he was here with me in the first place only added to that. It took a few seconds of him fumbling in the darkness with the pressure of my pistol at his back before he found the light.

The bunker, it turned out, was a garage, or had been before port operations had moved further west and south. Now all that remained were the pieces that couldn't be relocated or the things that no one had wanted responsibility for. There was a hydraulic lift, left at three-quarters raise, the pit for work beneath. A dozen or so rusted-out fifty-gallon oil drums, pieces of metal, shavings, and rat feces.

I gave Zviadi back his phone, put my gun to his neck, and said, "Text them. Show me first."

He tapped out a simple message, the word NOW, and with a nod from me, sent it out. I took the phone back.

"Now what were you supposed to do?"

"I was supposed to leave." Either stupidity or gall made him put hope in his voice.

"Yeah," I said, imagining him running as fast as his mismatched legs could carry him, far enough to reach a phone or intercept his friends. "Yeah, Zviadi. That's not going to happen."

I dragged him over to the oil drums. Used motor oil filled most of them to the brim, fetid and thickened. One was mostly empty, and merely disgusting and rank. I told him to climb in.

He hesitated.

"You want to live through this," I told him, "you'll get in the fucking barrel. Otherwise, I've got no problem shooting you, and *then* putting you in the fucking barrel."

He didn't like it, and he was almost too fat to fit, but he got in the barrel. When I moved to place the lid back on it, he found his voice.

"Please," he said. "Don't."

I shook my head, tucked my pistol away long enough to take the top with both hands. "Don't move. Don't speak. You'll know when it's over."

I put the lid on his barrel, leaving enough room for air to leak in. He could push it off with no effort, but it was either that or kill him, and despite everything, I didn't want to do that. It's one thing to put down the shooter trying to light you up; that's survival, and when it comes down to survival, anything goes. But it's something else entirely to put a round in a man who's been rendered defenseless, who poses only a *potential* threat. Yes, Zviadi could make things difficult for me when his mates came through the door, but he could be smart and stay quiet, too. I had to give him the benefit of the doubt, no matter how vile I found him, no matter how dangerous it might be.

I had a good idea what Alena would've said about that, too.

Lid on, I made another quick survey of the space, looking for anything I'd missed, anything I could use. There was a rusted fuse box on the west wall, near the broken mounts where some heavy machine or another had once been secured, and I followed the conduits running off it with my eyes, tracking them. The trunk line dropped into the foundation, as was to be expected, but the two others running from the box ran up to the ceiling, then separated at a junction, sending out power to the rest of the building. The lights were high-hanging fluorescents, set in naked fixtures, half of them dead.

I checked the doors, first the southern one, from which we'd entered. It opened inward. I paused at it, listened, and then resolved myself to the fact that I wouldn't be hearing anything anyway through the concrete and steel. I cracked the door, looked out, and as I did so saw a set of headlights approaching, maybe fifty meters out, and if headlights could look familiar, these certainly did.

I shut the door and sprinted across the space, to the northern access. They'd arrived faster than I'd thought, probably waiting on Zviadi's call. Hell, we could've easily walked past them on the way here and I'd never have noticed, because I hadn't been certain at all what I was looking for. I checked the north door, and this one opened inward, too. I scanned the floor, found a rusted length of pipe that I thought would serve, stepped outside far enough to prop it quietly against the wall. I heard car doors slamming, the echo amplified by the concrete all around. The water's edge was only twenty, maybe twenty-five meters away, but it was all open ground between here and there, with no place to hide. I closed the door quietly, counted my steps back to the hydraulic lift, had almost reached it when the door to the south opened and they entered.

There were four of them, which was better than six, but not nearly as good as one, and they all had the swagger that comes from being predators feasting in an ocean of prey. Each was Caucasian, the same Central-to-Eastern European stamp on his face. Maybe Russian, or Ukrainian, or Georgian, or Albanian, or Romanian—I couldn't tell and doubted they'd answer if I asked. The weak fluorescent light grayed each of them out, made their pale skin paler, their dark hair darker.

The first one through the door was the biggest of the crew, and not in the way Zviadi was big. His hands, surprisingly, were empty, and when he saw me, he saw the pistol I was holding parallel with my thigh, barrel down. His expression didn't even flicker. I was a threat that didn't rate.

Which made sense, because the second and third guys through the door were carrying their pistols in hand, much the way I was, and the last of their party had brought a shotgun with him. The door swung closed after him, heavy metal meeting concrete, and the echo rang off the floors and walls.

"Tiasa Lagidze." I kept my voice even. "Where is she?"

The one to the left spoke softly in Russian, and the leader canted his head slightly, to listen. None of their eyes left me. Shotgun and the second pistol began to spread out slowly, trying to keep from bunching up.

"That's the guy," the one on the left was saying. "That's the guy who dropped Gorda."

The leader righted his head, then nodded, barely. His whole expression was as dead as when he'd entered, his stare empty, with nothing for me to read in it.

Then he turned away, saying, "Kill him."

At least I'm pretty sure that's what he said, but I could be wrong. Everything after the word "kill" was lost when I started laying down fire.

I put my first two at the shotgun, and the double-tap hit him before he could bring his gun to bear. By then I was already moving back and left, counting my steps as I shifted my aim right. Second pistol got a shot off as I lined him up, but he rushed and it went high, and I was still counting steps when I drilled him with another two, then swung the pistol back left.

The leader had moves, already behind the nearest hard cover he could find, the two oil drums closest to the south door. I didn't linger on him. I was firing 45-caliber jacketed hollowpoint, and there was no way it would penetrate both walls of the barrel to hit him. I continued bringing my weapon around to find first pistol, the one who'd spoken, who'd identified me. He was going for a set of oil drums himself, the same cluster of them that held Zviadi, and he was firing blind as he went, and his shots were hitting the floor and the walls and not me.

I shifted aim past him, and hammered the fuse box with five of the six rounds I had left, dumping them off as fast as the trigger would let me. Somewhere around bullet three I broke through, and the lights went, and without windows, the building dropped into an absolute darkness. I finished my count, and the heel of my left foot hit the door behind me.

I went outside, yanking the door closed behind me to give them the noise, checking my corners. No one was waiting to spring on me. With one hand, I grabbed the pipe I'd placed and slid it through the handle, leaving six inches of overlap on the wall, effectively barring the door from the outside. Then I sprinted for the eastern side, coming around and making for the southern door as fast as I could. I'd brought two mags with me, and I switched them out as I ran, slowed at the corner, then rounded strong, my weapon in high-ready. I saw the car, the same damn Land Cruiser, parked fifteen meters off to the side.

The door burst open. I'd thought it would be the leader who came out first, because he'd been the one closest to it, but instead it was the first pistol who emerged, raising his gun, and I realized too late that I was too close. I got a forearm up and under his weapon as he came in, forcing his gun away from me, and he fired anyway, for all the good it did him. Even as he did that he was barreling into me, and we went down together, each of us trying to get our weapons to bear, twisting like kids in a playground fight.

The fall trapped my weapon beneath him, denied me any useful shot. He didn't have the same problem. He fired again despite my grip on his arm, this time dangerously close to my left ear, and the report hurt like a motherfuck. I sacrificed the gun, went for the knife I'd taken off Zviadi, and doing it cost me my leverage, and we tumbled. He ended up on top of me, fighting viciously against my grip to bring the barrel of his gun in line with my head.

He was still fighting to do it when I punched him twice in the side with the knife. He made a soft and awful sound of surprise, then cut it short when I quickly drove the blade into him a third time. Then I pulled it free and stabbed again, fast, this time coming down into the side of his neck, where it met his shoulder. He turned to dead weight.

Then something heavy and hard skittered on the pavement my way, and a fucking hand grenade bounced out of the darkness of the doorway straight toward me.

The last time I'd dealt seriously with hand grenades had been in the Army, and that had been a lifetime ago, and all the training options that flashed through my mind came back as no-go. There was no way I could get into a pencil position in time, and even if I could free myself from the body, the nearest hard cover was ten meters behind me.

But I had soft cover.

I heaved myself and the dead weight off the ground and onto the grenade. Then I lunged back, losing the knife but heading for my gun, twisting to hit the deck on my belly, trying to get into the pencil position anyway. I managed to get my feet together and my mouth open and my hands up to my ears when the explosive detonated.

The dead man's body absorbed most of the blast, but overpressure still slapped at me, first from the explosion, then from the vacuum as air rushed to return to the detonation zone. Opening my mouth had helped, and my eyes didn't feel like they bulged too much, or at least, they stayed in my skull. Even with my hands over my ears, the concussion shot pain through my head, further traumatizing my left ear. I lost my body long enough to realize it, had to force myself back into play.

I reached for my gun, rolling clumsily back to my feet and staggering to the side. The leader had used the grenade to clear his exit, but he'd had to wait until after it had detonated to leave for fear of eating his own blast. I just hoped he didn't have a second grenade. Or a third.

Then he made his move, coming out with his gun at high-ready, pure Russian-military-style. Maybe he thought the body on the ground was mine, but it drew his attention and his aim first, and it gave me the half-second to pick my shot. I needed a live one, and he was the only one left.

The round punched him just inside the hip, shattering his pelvic girdle, and he dropped hard with his legs suddenly unable to support him. When he fell, he fell forward, and I closed on him as fast as I could manage. He was cursing in Russian, trying to bring his pistol around, but my boot found his hand, knocked the weapon free and sent it bouncing a couple of meters.

I holstered my gun, then dropped a knee onto the base of his spine and began to search him. It wasn't direct pressure on the pelvis, but it was close enough, and the pain kept him occupied. He had a pack of cigarettes, a lighter, a wad of bills, a knife of his own, a set of keys for the Land Cruiser, and a phone. He also had a wallet, and the wallet had an ID card, and the ID card had his picture and a name, Vladek Karataev. I put the money, the keys, the wallet, and the mobile in a pocket, then flipped out the blade on his knife.

He was hissing out deep breaths, hands clenching and unclenching, trying to control the pain. I came off his back, rolling him. His breath caught when I moved him, the shattered bones in his hip grinding and shifting. I waited until his eyes focused on me again, then showed him the knife.

"Tiasa Lagidze," I said. I used Russian. "Where is she?"

"Go fuck your mother." The strain of keeping pain out of his voice made it sound very sincere.

Fucking Russians, I thought. *Always proving how tough they are.*

After a half-second for thought, I stabbed him in the thigh. He yelled, cursed me, tried to grab for my hand and immediately fell back in the agony the movement caused. I yanked the blade out, wiped it on his shirt, then closed and pocketed it. I straightened up, then put my foot on the wound I had just made, pressing down hard. From my pocket, I brought out his phone. It was a BlackBerry, one of the new ones.

"Vladek," I said. "That's your name?"

"Fucking cunt, fuck you!"

"I just cut your femoral, Vladek," I told him. "You can't walk. You can barely crawl. Your friends are dead. We're far enough from the port that no one heard a grenade go off, which means we're far enough that no one will hear you no matter how loud you yell. Right now, my foot is the only thing keeping you from bleeding out."

Then I showed him his phone.

"You want this back, you talk to me."

It was all across his face how much he hated me and my offer. He was sweating now, and he licked his lips once, twice, and I knew his mouth had gone dry, knew he was going into shock.

"You're running out of time," I told him.

He swore again, then said, "Tourniquet. Put a tourniquet on it first."

"No."

He swore once more, but this time it was quieter, and more at himself and his position than at me.

"She went out yesterday, before dawn," Vladek Karataev said. "On the boat to Trabzon. She's already in Turkey."

"Why there? Why'd you send her there?"

"She went with the others."

"What others?"

His eyes focused. "What's it to you? Who the fuck are you?"

"A friend of Bakhar's," I said. "What others? Why did you send her to Turkey?"

He began coughing, and it must have hurt like hell to do it with a shattered pelvic girdle, but he didn't stop. After a moment, I realized he was laughing, not coughing, and he was laughing at me. Then pain caught up to the joke, and his noises subsided.

"That shit had it coming," Vladek told me, and he smiled. "He fucking sold us to the police, Bakhar got what he had coming. Gave it to his daughter, too. We all did."

I didn't say anything.

"You won't find her." The smile turned into a grin. One of his incisors was missing, another was gold. "She's pretty and young. She's already been sold. Some fat Arab sheikh already has her wiping his floors and sucking her own shit off his cock."

My arm felt cold where it was covered in blood, like it had been dunked in a bath of ice. My head pulsed with pain, my left ear still ringing sharply. The backs of my thighs and shoulders throbbed, and for the first time I was aware that what I thought was sweat running down my back probably wasn't sweat at all.

He really loved the reaction he got, the look on my face that I couldn't hide, and didn't bother to try to.

"What the fuck you think this is?" he asked, as if assessing me for brain damage. "You fucking think Bakhar was living in that shithole town because he liked the beach? Coward, fucking coward was *hiding* from us, he knew what he had done. So we paid him back, we paid him in full."

I still didn't speak, but this time it was because I didn't think I could.

"He sold them, too, you understand me? He sold more girls than you've ever seen, and then the fucking Americans leaned on Tbilisi, and Tbilisi leaned on us, and he sold us out. Your *friend*. Fuck you! That was your friend!"

He was shouting at the end, furious at Bakhar, at me, at his wounds and the injustice of a world that would punish him like this. I watched his chest heave as he tried to replace his spent breath, glaring at me, the hostility as naked as it had been on Bakhar's body.

I moved my foot off his thigh, watched the blood begin to flood out of the wound I'd made, spreading beneath his leg.

"Give me a name," I said. "The captain of the boat, the contact in Turkey, something. I want a name."

The glare stayed as before. He knew the way that I knew that he would never get a tourniquet or the phone. He knew he was done, and he knew that giving me anything more wouldn't change that.

I took out my gun.

"You'll never find her," Vladek Karataev said.

"You'll never know," I told him, and shot him twice in the face.

CHAPTER
Seven

Halfway back to Kobuleti, after crossing the Supsa River, I took the Land Cruiser off-road, heading inland, headlights off. It was closing on two in the morning, the moon beginning to move toward setting, but there was more than enough to see by as long as I drove slow. I followed the riverbank for four kilometers, passing farms and their distant houses, before reaching woodlands. Then I turned the nose of the car to the river and parked. When I moved to get out of the car, I realized that my shirt had stuck to the seatback as well as to me, and when it came free I felt my back start bleeding again.

I opened the doors and the rear, then found a rock big enough to weight the accelerator, put the car in gear, and let it go into the water. The Land Cruiser did pretty well for itself, got about six meters into the Supsa before stalling out, and it was already turning slowly in the current, beginning to drift, when I turned away and headed for home on foot. I followed E&E procedure as I moved, staying away from the roads and anything that advertised people, going through the woods.

It required concentration, and that was good, because it meant that I didn't think about Bakhar, and who he was, what he had done, what he had been. It meant I didn't think about Tiasa, what had happened to her, what was being done to her right now.

It was dawn when I reached home, and Miata came to meet me, licking my hands and following close to heel when I went indoors. Alena hadn't returned yet, and even though that was expected, it was also profoundly disappointing. I needed her.

I checked the security, rearmed the system, then went to the gun locker and reloaded my gun. I put everything I'd gathered on my trip in Bakhar's go-bag—the money, the two knives, and the BlackBerry, along with its battery, which I'd removed before leaving the road. Then I went into the bathroom and started the shower. I stripped down at the mirror, twisting around in an attempt to catalogue my injuries. There were bruises and scrapes acquired from the fistfight and the desperate motion before and after. Most of my blood was from the grenade, minor shrapnel mixed with pebbles and dirt that had carried enough velocity to penetrate cloth and skin, but none too deep. I picked what I could out of my body, got my legs clean, but there was a spot on my upper back that I just couldn't reach. Fresh blood leaked out of me where I reopened my wounds.

Then I got under the shower and watched as blood, mine and others', spiraled down the drain. After a couple of minutes

I got the shakes, and decided that sitting might be a better idea, so I slumped down in a corner and tried to ride it out. Then I got the dry heaves.

It was to be expected. The only thing that surprised me was that it had taken this long for everything to catch up.

I was asleep when Alena returned home, deep in a bone-tired coma, and she woke me with a touch, saying my name. She was sitting beside me on the bed, a hand on my back, and I had a vague sense that she had been there awhile, but perhaps it was only a dream. The lamp was on, but otherwise, the room was dark.

"Welcome home," I said.

"I'll get the kit," Alena told me. "Stay still."

She rose and left the room, and I decided that staying still didn't mean I couldn't reach for my glasses. I had them on when she came back carrying one of the two homemade first aid kits we had in the house. They were closer to the jump bags you'd find on an ambulance than the kind of thing you could buy in a store, filled with bandages and tape and gauze, even two liters of Ringer's solution. Alena opened the kit and came out with a clamp and a set of forceps, set them aside and went to work dumping Betadine on my back.

"Tell me," she said.

I told her.

When I had finished, so had she, smoothing the last of the tape down across the bandage. The three fragments of shrapnel she'd dug out of me sat on the open gauze wrapper, black and sharp. She scooped up the paper, crumpling it before setting it aside, then checked my legs, her fingers careful as she examined the rest of my wounds.

"Superficial," Alena said. "Fortunate."

"Are you finished?"

"Yes. You should drink something, try moving around."

She took the kit, rising, and I got myself off the bed, feeling muscle-sore but unimpaired. The ringing was gone from my ear but my head still ached, though it might have been dehydration as much as anything else. I pulled on a shirt, feeling the tape on my back pull and flex, then followed after her, down the hall.

In the kitchen, Alena handed me a glass of water, then put the kettle on. She avoided looking at me.

"How was Nicholas?" I asked.

"He was fine. It was a short meeting."

"No trouble?"

"With him? Is there ever?"

"I meant on the trip."

"I was stopped on the M1, outside of Gori, by the Russians. They wanted to search the car, but it was a shakedown. I had to pay twice, going and coming."

"Money."

"Yes." She looked up from where she'd been watching the kettle. "You think something else?"

"Nothing you would give them," I told her. "Doesn't mean they didn't want it."

She shrugged. "The same everywhere."

I finished my water, watching her. She was right, it was the same everywhere, all around the world, first to third, and certainly here in the former Soviet states. At almost every border crossing, at almost every checkpoint, someone, always male, had his hand out. Most of the time, money would do it, because most of the time, the people manning such checkpoints and crossings were desperately poor, despite their uniforms. But if you were traveling with a woman, or if you were a woman alone, most of the time it wasn't money they wanted.

"You're thinking about Tiasa."

"Trabzon's maybe two hundred and fifty kilometers," I said. "We take the car, leave by midmorning, we should be there before evening, even with all the stops."

"No."

"The other option I'm thinking is to go back to Batumi, take a boat. It'll take longer, though, and I don't want to lose the time. And we'll need to arrange transportation on the other end."

She shook her head. The light in the kitchen turned her copper-colored hair orange, turned her complexion sallow. "I'm not talking about the route. I'm saying no, we're not doing this."

"Tiasa—"

"I know." She held her look on me for a fraction longer, then reached for the canister of tea, began digging a spoon out of the utensil drawer.

"If this is because you think the information is—"

She cut me off. "I doubt he lied to you."

"Then Trabzon—"

"No."

I tried again. "She's fourteen, she's—"

"I *know*," Alena said, sharply, spooning too much tea into the pot.

"I can't abandon this," I said.

The utensil hit the counter with a clatter. "Tiasa is gone. Like her family. We have to forget them."

"You trying to convince me or yourself?" I asked, after a second.

"Yes, both of us, yes." She straightened, squared her shoulders, fixing her posture, all her little tells that I knew meant she was struggling with her emotions. When she was ready, she looked at me again. "Those men in Batumi, they will have friends, friends who found Bakhar. They can find you. They can find us."

"All the more reason for us to go."

"This is our home. I will not leave it."

"You know what's happened to her, what's going to happen," I said. "Someone has to find her."

"Then let someone else do it. Not us."

My frustration finally broke. "I don't understand. You liked Tiasa. Forget about the rest of them for now—Bakhar, who he was, what he did, it doesn't matter. This is about Tiasa. You adored her."

"I love her."

She said it softly, without hesitation. Considering that "love" was hardly a word she was ever willing to speak aloud to me, it was surprising.

I said, "There's no one else. You know that. We can't just sit here and hope some NGO is going to discover her, free her, and we both sure as hell know some Good Samaritan won't come to her rescue."

"I know."

"I can't forget this," I insisted. "I have to go after her. I can't let this sit."

She inhaled, and her eyes shifted aside for a moment, pained. Her eyes were hazel, and beautiful, and since I'd first met her had become more and more expressive. There'd been a time when reading her was next to impossible, quite deliberately so on her part, something she'd been taught that had turned as autonomous as breathing. Survival had hinged on being able to hide not only her thoughts but her feelings. While I'd become better at it, she'd become worse; it was another of the trades we had made by joining our lives.

"You'd leave me here alone?" she asked.

"It's not like you can't take care of yourself."

"Don't. Don't go."

"Come with me."

"I can't." Behind her, on the stove, the kettle began to rattle, spilling steam. "I can't."

"What aren't you telling me?" I asked her. "What's going on?"

She shook her head, brushing past me as she left the room. I heard the back door open, then close, hard.

I stood in the kitchen alone, listening to the chattering kettle.

After a minute, I went to the bedroom and began to pack.

CHAPTER
Eight

My second night in Trabzon I met a man named Arzu Kaya, who promised me all the pretty girls I could ever want.

"How much?" I asked.

"Two hundred, you get one all night," he answered.

I stopped myself from laughing. "Maybe for two. Two hundred for two girls."

"Two hundred *yeni*?"

I shook my head. "Euros."

He bit his lower lip, sucking air through his teeth. "You got my name from Vladek?"

"Last week. In Batumi."

Arzu went after his lip again, thinking. He was a Turkish

national, possibly even a Trabzon native from the way he spoke his Russian—there was a large Russian expat community in the city, and had been for decades—and younger than I'd expected, only in his early thirties. His clothes and manner were better suited for Istanbul than the more conservative eastern part of the country. There, like here along the northern Black Sea coast, Islam was both omnipresent and traditional. Yet Arzu's clothing didn't particularly mark him as out of the ordinary. I'd seen plenty of similarly Western-attired folks about and around since I'd arrived the day before. Women dressed modestly, at least in public, and the men I'd seen went clean-shaven.

"Wait here a minute, okay?" Arzu sprang from his chair opposite me, grinning. "I'll send one of the girls down, keep you company."

I checked my watch. "I've got other places to be."

"Won't take me long." He was already crossing the lobby, such as it was. "Just wait for me."

I watched him disappear up a set of stairs, turning out of sight. The hotel we were in was off the northeastern edge of Atatürk Alani, the kind of place that guidebooks charitably listed as "budget," except that the kind of guidebook that would list this place you'd never find in a bookstore. Like countless other similarly grimy lodgings around the world, the hotel doubled as a brothel.

A handful of seconds after Arzu disappeared, a young woman in a halter top and shorts that were too tight and too short came into view, descending the stairs. She saw me immediately, and started on a beeline. I gave her my don't-fuck-with-me face, and it stopped her in her tracks, but only for a second. Then she glanced over her shoulder, back the way she'd come and Arzu had gone, and resumed crossing to me. When she reached where I was sitting, she tried to sit in my lap.

"No," I told her, in Russian, pushing her gently away.

"Free," she said, and tried it again. "For a friend of Arzu Bey."

She was pale, her hair a filthy blonde, with a face hidden beneath heavy makeup. She might've been pretty once, before she'd come across the Black Sea from Russia or Ukraine or Moldova, the same way she'd had a name. Now she was just another *natasha,* like countless other girls who, one way or another, had been trafficked across the water expressly to be used for sex.

I let her sit in my lap, and when Vladek Karataev's BlackBerry began to vibrate in my pocket, I had a damn good idea who it was who was calling. The girl looked down, feeling the phone shivering against my thigh, then looked at me curiously. I smiled at her.

"What's your name?" I asked.

"Natasha," she said. There was no irony in it, no humor, and no pause.

"I'm David." The BlackBerry in my pocket went still again. "I should check that."

She shifted off my lap so I could get the phone, and I pulled it free, slipped the back cover off and dropped the battery out, then replaced the cover and put both the phone and the battery in my pocket. She watched me with disinterested curiosity.

I'd let her back into my lap when Arzu appeared again, bounding down the stairs.

"Sorry, just had to take care of something," he said. "Let's go upstairs, we can talk somewhere more private. You like her, huh?"

"She's very nice," I said.

"Yeah, she's a good girl." He turned his attention to her, still on my lap. "Get off him."

She slipped off me, immediately moving to the opposite end of the couch. Arzu waited while I got to my feet, then led the way. He took the stairs as before, two, three at a time, full of energy. Another two women were in the hall when we came off the landing, smoking cigarettes, and both looked down when Arzu passed, followed me with their eyes when I did. They looked as wasted and tired as the girl who'd taken my lap, and I didn't want to guess how young they were, or how long they'd been here, and found that I couldn't help myself.

We went into one of the rooms, a small shoebox of a space that had been turned into a private lounge, with a television, a couch, a couple of chairs. The television was on, broadcasting local news that I didn't understand. Arzu indicated the couch, offering it to me, and I thanked him and sat. A Nokia phone was sitting on one of the chairs, and he picked it up, checking it, and I saw the frown flash across his face for an instant before he tucked it into a pocket of his own. Then he maneuvered the chair around to face me before taking a seat.

"You talked to Vladek?" I asked.

He grinned. "Don't worry about that. You wanted to talk about some girls. Two hundred euros."

"Two hundred for two girls. But that's not what I really want to talk about."

"No?"

"I'm looking to buy, to set something up further south."

"How far south?"

"Gulf region. Depends on what my partners come back with. Can you help me?"

"How many?"

"Four to start. More later if it goes well. But the girls have to be young, and I'll want to see them myself."

"Of course, sure. How young?"

"Sixteen. Maybe younger."

Arzu cracked his grin again. "That's more expensive."

"I know. That's why I need to see them. But we'll pay what they're worth."

"So you understand."

"Vladek made it clear," I said.

He did the teeth bit once more, then nodded. "Okay, you're staying in town?"

"At the Zorlu. I'm supposed to leave the day after tomorrow, but I can stretch it until the end of the week if I have to."

"You'll hear from me tomorrow. David Mercer, right?"

"That's right."

He got up, offering me his hand, and I got up and took it. The shake was firm and professional, as cleanly executed as any boardroom deal-closing. He walked me to the door, but paused after he opened it, his expression brightening.

"That *natasha*," he asked. "You liked her?"

The thought of what might happen to the woman if I said I didn't flashed in my mind's eye. "Sure."

"Take her with you, back to the Zorlu. Keep her all night, whatever you want to do to her, that's fine."

"That's very generous," I said to him, and Arzu's smile faltered, hinted at the offense he would take if I refused his gift. "But it's like with the drugs. I never use the product."

For a moment, I was sure I'd lost him. Then he got happy again and clapped me on the shoulder. "You're married?"

"Yeah."

"I'm the same! Why get this when you've got it at home, right?"

"Pretty much."

"I'll call you tomorrow, David," he said, ushering me out the door.

As soon as I was downstairs, I put the battery back in the BlackBerry. I wasn't halfway back to the Zorlu when the phone began vibrating again.

I let it go to voicemail.

It had been just before nine the previous morning when I'd brought the Dnepr's engine to life, and by ten I'd been heading down the coast. Shortly after I'd left Batumi, heading south, I'd passed a billboard, stark and out of place, a PSA put together by the Interior Ministry, most likely with American funds. It showed a grayscale image of a woman, profile shot, framed from the mid-bicep of her right arm to the top of her head, cropped so that she was faceless, but clearly feminine. On the exposed bicep had been tattooed a barcode. The Georgian script, in bright red letters, translated to the phrase *You are not for sale.*

Like she didn't know that already.

It had done nothing for my mood.

By the time I'd finished with my meager packing, Alena still hadn't come back into the house. I'd gone out after her, found her in the studio, music blaring, trying to dance. Her left calf had been badly injured several years ago, hit with a blast from a shotgun that destroyed the anterior cruciate ligament and severed tendons. While the ligament had been replaced by a prosthetic, nothing could be done for the rest, and though physical therapy had brought back much of the agility and balance she'd had before, she didn't have all of it, and was supposed to go easy on her left.

She was not, as far as I could see, going easy on her left.

Both Miata and I had watched for a while, and Alena had ignored us both. Finally I'd shut off the music, and that had forced her to stop. When I'd turned to face her again, she was already on me, and while the kiss was wonderful, it wasn't what I'd come looking for at all. When I tried to explain that to her, she'd told me to shut up, and then clothes had started coming off. She'd pulled me to the floor, and the sex we had reminded me of the first times we made love, when passion had made our hands tremble, and desire and need had been the same things.

After, we'd made our way to bed and slept, and in the morning there had been nothing, it seemed, she could say. That hadn't been the case for me.

"I'm coming back," I told her.

She'd nodded, once, as if believing my sincerity, if not the promise.

The drive itself from Kobuleti to Sarp, at the border with Turkey, was only forty kilometers, but it took me the better part of two hours. I crossed on the David Mercer ID, which was the only one I'd brought along, something I was certain would become a problem for me later. While I had other IDs, they'd stayed behind, in my go-bag where they belonged. In my backpack was a change of clothes, Bakhar's address book, Vladek Karataev's BlackBerry, a smattering of toiletries, and my laptop. The only weapon I carried was a small flip knife, thinking that would be easier to explain if I found myself searched at a checkpoint or the border.

As it turned out, I probably could have brought a rocket launcher with me. Fifty euros seemed to be the going rate for just about anything illegal these days, and in Sarp it bought me a visitor's visa, and papers for the Dnepr. I took the opportunity to refuel the bike, and then it was just a question of following the coast another two hundred kilometers or so until I reached Trabzon.

It had been almost midnight when I'd reached the Zorlu Grand Hotel, the city's finest accommodations, and checked myself into my room. I'd picked the place not out of a desire to live large, but to present a cover if I needed one. The ride had given me plenty of time to think, and thinking had given me the frame for a plan.

Sex was for sale everywhere. It was just a question of knowing where to look.

My first day in Trabzon, the day I met Arzu, I woke early, did yoga for half an hour, then ordered room service. The food arrived just after my shower, and I ate while going through Bakhar's address book, this time looking for numbers with a Trabzon exchange. There weren't any, which left me the BlackBerry, and while I was violently suspicious of the device, or, more precisely, of who might have Vladek's number and be tracking him through it, it gave me a window into his life and his business. All I needed to do was access the information.

The Zorlu had wireless, so I set up the laptop to download the software I needed, then went down to the lobby and got directions from the concierge to the nearest store selling mobile phones. It was a three-minute walk, but they didn't have the USB cable I needed. I bought two prepaid international SIM cards from them, anyway, then got directions to another store, which did carry replacement cables. I bought another two SIMs, and the cable, and headed back to the room. Then I ran the software I'd downloaded, plugged the BlackBerry into my USB port, and cracked open a very disturbing window into Vladek Karataev's life.

His address book, like Bakhar's, exercised discretion. While this time there were both first and last names to be discerned, there were no addresses provided, only phone numbers. It looked like Vladek had made a point of clearing out his emails and text messages regularly, and I was only able to find a handful of each. It would have been simple enough to recover the deleted communications, I suppose, but all the methods I knew of required additional hardware, none of which I had, and none of which I could think of a way to acquire quickly.

So I worked with what I did have, started searching, and the laptop made that easy; all I had to do was run a find. "Trabzon" didn't kick back any results. "Turkey" got the same negative result. When I tried the country code for Turkey, though, three hits came back, and one of those looked like it was for Trabzon, or at least close by—a man named Arzu Kaya. I checked against Bakhar's book, and lo and behold, he had an Arzu, too.

I skimmed the rest of the BlackBerry entries while considering how to proceed. There were numbers for phones in Georgia, Ukraine, and Russia, and it looked to me like Vladek had kept his business local, though I found two out of Western Europe— one in the Netherlands, the other in Germany.

The mail and text messages got my attention next. Almost all of the emails were in Cyrillic, which was a minor headache, as I could speak Russian much better than I could read it. It took me a while, even though they were universally terse. Vladek had been circumspect, carrying on what little correspondence remained in open code, with references to "deliveries" and "stock" and "items." It might've referred to anything, guns or drugs as much as people. It might've referred to Georgian wine.

Of the text messages, the most recent had been the one sent by Zviadi at the point of my gun. The only other sequence was a short exchange of messages sent the night Tiasa had been taken, between Vladek and Arzu. The exchange had run in Russian.

BUYING?

HOW MANY

5. 16 16 17 19 AND 14.

WHEN

TOMORROW NIGHT. CALL TO DISCUSS PRICE.

Which meant that Vladek had planned on selling Tiasa even before he and his pals had murdered Bakhar.

For a while, that was the worst the BlackBerry gave me.

Then I found the pictures.

And the video.

The photos had been taken on the phone itself, and the most sinister thing about them was that they were so very mundane. Mostly headshots of different women, different girls, one after another. In a couple, the subject was actually smiling. In a couple, the subject was crying. If I'd seen them in any other place, had known they were taken by any other person than Vladek, it would have meant nothing.

But sitting at the desk in my hotel room at the Zorlu Grand Hotel, looking at them, I could only see them as the record they undoubtedly were. The women he had taken and trafficked, one after another, kept for posterity on his phone.

There were thirty-seven of them, and I made myself look at them all.

The last picture was of Tiasa. She looked at the camera with tears running down her face, snot leaking from her nose, clearly trying to stop crying.

Vladek had taken the picture after he'd raped her. I knew that, because he had the video of it, taken the same way he'd taken the photograph. Some dirty room in a dirty building with a mattress on the floor and four men taking turns with a fourteen-year-old girl who couldn't defend herself and had nowhere to run.

In Batumi, with a puncture in his femoral, Vladek had told me what he'd done to her, and I'd known he was telling the truth, but I had hoped he wasn't. I'd hoped he was throwing spite and hatred at me, trying to deliver wounds with the only weapon he'd had left. That's what I'd hoped.

I turned off the video before I saw more, but I'd already seen too much.

I should've known better than to hope.

The day after I met Arzu, he called me at the hotel. It was twenty-two minutes past four in the afternoon.

"David," he said, "I think we're in business."

CHAPTER
Nine

There were three women in the room, and if you added
all their ages together, you could probably break fifty years old.

Barely.

None of them was Tiasa. Two sat on a couch, at opposite
ends from each other, strangers bound by common fear. The
third one sat on a rickety chair in the opposite corner, almost in
profile, watching me without turning her head. All of them
wore clean, if worn and used, clothes, and all of them looked
fed, and all of them looked bewildered and haunted by their circumstance.

"What do you think?" Arzu asked.

I forced my eyes to linger on the women, and in doing so

absorbed more details. A broken fingernail. A bruise around one wrist. A clenched jaw. Finally, I looked at Arzu, and showed him a grin to demonstrate my pleasure. Then I put the grin away, so he could see that, too.

"They're all older than I was hoping," I told him.

He looked sincerely apologetic. "These are the youngest I could get. Give me another week or two, maybe I can find others."

"And I asked for four, not three."

"Yes, you did, my friend. And here are three of them less than twenty-four hours after you asked me, all of them ready to start work. Give me until tomorrow night, the day after at the latest, I'll get you a fourth, I promise."

I considered, or pretended to, looking back at the women. The one in the corner had shifted her head slightly to watch me and, when she caught me looking, turned it back again. She was the smallest of them, and perhaps the eldest, black hair and an olive complexion, and I caught sight of the swelling at her lip before she hid her face. Her eyes were as dark as her hair, and she couldn't conceal the hatred in them.

"What happened to her?" I asked.

"You know how they are," Arzu said. "Sometimes they need it explained to them."

I nodded, because I didn't trust myself to speak.

"Let's go." Arzu put a hand on my shoulder. "We can talk business someplace more comfortable."

He guided me out of the room and into the next, where two partners or acquaintances or brothers or who the hell knew were sitting around a small table, eating their dinner. Each one of them had a pistol resting next to his plate of mezes. The one nearest us got to his feet and locked the door we'd just exited. Arzu said something in Turkish, without breaking stride, and the response followed us out of the apartment and into the early evening. Arzu took the lead, down the flight of stairs to the street. It wasn't quite evening yet, but the apartment was close enough to the mountains that the sun had dipped out of sight behind them, and the shadows were growing long as the air grew cooler.

"You talk to Vladek?" Arzu asked me.

"Recently?"

"In the last day or so."

"He's not one for chatting unless it's about business, and right now my business is with you."

Since I'd last seen Arzu, he'd left four voicemails on Vladek's phone, and sent two texts, the most recent just after nine this morning. I'd reviewed the lot, and they'd all been pretty much the same, with Arzu asking about David Mercer, trying to confirm the contact. The last one this morning had added, at the end, ALSO, ANOTHER 14?

I'd considered responding to the texts, but had discarded the idea as quickly as I'd found it as one that would only make trouble for me. If Vladek was capable of responding to a text message, after all, why wasn't he answering his phone? Best to let it lie.

"That's true. That's very true." Arzu motioned toward a black Honda CRV parked nearby. "Let me drive you back to your hotel, David."

I waited for him to unlock the car, climbed into the front passenger seat. He snapped his seatbelt into place, started the car, then immediately reached for the radio, silencing the blast of hip-hop suddenly pouring forth. I made a mental note of the street we were on, the number of the apartment block, then put my attention on Arzu. It might have been his mention of Vladek, but I was having trouble reading him, suddenly. There was no doubt that, by now, Vladek Karataev and his friends had been discovered in Batumi, which meant there was no reason not to assume that Arzu had learned that Vladek Karataev was dead. It would certainly explain why the calls and messages had stopped.

Whether or not Arzu suspected me for it was something I couldn't hazard. Based on what I'd just seen, combined with the last text he'd sent, I was sure that Tiasa was long gone, that Vladek had been correct and that Arzu had already trafficked her someplace else.

Just like in Batumi, I had lost time, and Tiasa was gone. Unlike in Batumi, I didn't have the first idea as to where.

Showing Arzu a picture of Tiasa Lagidze and asking him what he'd done with her, asking him where she was, wasn't going to work. Even questioning him about her in the most general terms would be problematic. The women Arzu dealt with weren't people, they were merchandise. Any assertion on my part to the contrary wouldn't just raise suspicion, it would mark me as his enemy. Right now, he believed we were alike.

I needed him to believe that. Unless I was willing to do to him what I'd done to Vladek, it was the only way I would get a lead on Tiasa. I needed Arzu to believe that I was willing to be his friend, rather than someone who wanted to use his head to shatter all the windows on his car.

But dammit if I wasn't thinking about doing it anyway.

We'd gone all of a kilometer, winding down out of the mountain terraces that faced the Black Sea, when I asked him if he had paper for the women.

"We have their passports," Arzu said, almost absently. "Took them when they arrived, you know."

"If I'm going to move them, I'm going to need clean paper. Can you arrange that?"

"I'll give you their passports."

"You're not hearing me," I said. "Clean paper. I don't want some customs official in Rome wondering why a sixteen-year-old girl from Romania has entry stamps for Ukraine and Turkey in her passport, each of them less than a month apart. They're cracking down on this stuff, you know that."

"They *say* they're cracking down on it. We both know they're not." Arzu slowed for a light, letting the car coast to a stop. "Where are you taking them? Kuwait, right? Or Abu Dhabi?"

"Maybe."

"You're being like that with me? Don't you trust me?"

"I trust you completely, Arzu Bey. It's the people around you I don't know that I don't trust."

"Just us here in the car."

"Kuwait," I said.

Arzu laughed. "You're worrying about bullshit!"

"That's easy for you to say. I'm the one who's got to move them. You'll already have my money."

"Just bribe someone, David," Arzu said, starting the car rolling forward again. "That's what I did with the last one I sent that way. You'd have liked her, she was young. Very pretty, not like these others. I should've kept her."

"She went to Kuwait? You got someone I can deal with there? That would be very helpful."

"I'm sorry, no," Arzu said. "It was Dubai, she went with a couple of others. But no paper needed on any of them, just money put in the right hands, you know what I'm saying."

"Dubai isn't Kuwait."

"It's all the same, wherever you go. Europe, America, UAE, whatever. Always someone you can bribe."

I thought about what he was saying, the likelihood that Tiasa was now in Dubai. "It can get expensive that way."

"What's the saying, you have to spend money to make

money?" He laughed. "Most of these girls, once they've been taught, you can make the money back in a night, two at the most."

"Speaking of money," I said.

Arzu laughed again. "Okay, I'll give you a price. Say, twenty thousand."

"That's not a price. That's a joke. Ten. Maybe."

I caught Arzu's smile from the side, realized that he was pleased with my counteroffer, pleased that I was willing to play the game. That we were haggling over human beings the way I'd haggled over the Dnepr clearly bothered him not at all.

"David, you're trying to rob me! Perhaps I can do nineteen thousand."

"Twelve."

"Eighteen."

"Fifteen."

"Seventeen. No less, I just can't, even for friends."

"Seventeen," I agreed, and I thought about it, then. I didn't have nearly that much on me in cash, but I could get it. One call to Nicholas Sargenti and a wire transfer and I could put the money in Arzu's hand before tomorrow noon. In exchange, I would take possession of three lives.

Then what? Tell them to run for it? Give them a bundle of bills and wish them good luck and Godspeed? Send them to Georgia? To New York? London? Pay for them to make their way home? And all the time, let Tiasa get further away from me; all the time, let her hours of suffering increase.

Never mind the fact that I would be paying Arzu for three lives, putting money into his pocket for trafficking in slaves.

We'd pulled up outside the hotel, Arzu letting the engine idle. I unfastened my seatbelt.

"You want a wire transfer or cash?" I asked him.

"Cash is best, if you can do it."

"You'll have the other girl by tomorrow?"

"Sure."

"Call me when you're ready," I told him. "I'll have the cash."

He nodded, wished me a good night, and I got out of the car and headed into the lobby. He hadn't asked for any money in advance, and I understood that was because he didn't actually need it as security. Even if the deal we'd made fell through, he'd easily find another buyer.

A guy like Arzu would always find another buyer.

The Zorlu had a bar off the lobby, done up like an English pub, and I went inside and ordered myself a whiskey, a double, neat. I hadn't had liquor in almost five years, since before I'd taken up with Alena, and I'd never been much of a heavy drinker prior to that. In Kobuleti, we would occasionally share a bottle of wine, but even that was infrequent.

When my drink came, I slammed about half of it back, then took the remainder more slowly. By the time I'd finished, it had been twelve minutes since Arzu and I had parted company.

I paid and headed back into the lobby, checked with the concierge for the phone number I wanted, and then assured him it was not due to a problem with the Zorlu that I wanted it. Then I went outside, and pulled Vladek's BlackBerry from where I'd been carrying it in my jacket pocket. His SIM card was still in it, and I liked that irony.

I called the police. I spoke only in Russian. I gave them the address of the apartment building I'd left less than an hour earlier, and I gave them Arzu Kaya's name, and I told them there were two other men there, and that they were armed. I told them about the three women. When they asked me, I told them my name was Vladek.

Then I hung up, popped the battery out of the BlackBerry,

and pulled the SIM card. I broke it between my fingers, tossed it in the gutter, then went back inside and up to my room. Packing took all of four minutes, and within ten I'd checked out and was on the Dnepr. I headed to the Trabzon airport in search of another hotel, thinking about Tiasa, wondering how in the world I was going to find her in Dubai, if she was even in Dubai. Thinking about the three women I'd seen, and the little help I'd been able to give them.

It wasn't enough, not nearly enough.

But it was the best that I could do.

CHAPTER
Ten

I called Alena from Atatürk International Airport just before ten the next morning, which put the clock approaching noon back in Kobuleti. We had long ago worked out a communications protocol to follow if we were separated, a system that had one or the other of us checking in every third day at a prearranged, but shifting, time, so we would know when to expect the call.

I was calling early, for two reasons. The first was that I'd be in the air en route to Dubai when the scheduled time came. The second was because I missed her.

The phone rang three times before she answered, saying, "This is Yeva."

"It's me."

"What's happened?"

"No trouble, I'm just going to be in transit later, thought I'd get the call in now." I listened to her exhale. "Nothing to worry about."

"Transit. Not coming home?"

"Heading to Dubai," I said. "We're going to need a new motorcycle, I had to leave the Dnepr in Trabzon."

"Dubai. You have a location?"

"No."

"Where'd the information come from?"

"The guy who moved her."

"He gave you specifics?"

"I was loath to question him directly."

"That was probably wise. Turkey is not Georgia."

"How're things there?"

I heard the hesitation before she answered. "We're fine."

"Miata's taking care of you?"

"I'm taking care of him. How are *you*?"

"I've been better," I said. "I've been a lot better."

"Then maybe you should come home."

"I can't, not yet."

"After Dubai, then."

"Depends on what happens."

There was another silence, and then Alena asked, "Have you really thought this through?"

"Probably not," I admitted.

"Perhaps it's time you should."

"Just say what you want to say."

"Don't be angry at me. If you do not consider these things, I must."

"I'm not angry at you. I'm tired and I'm frustrated, and neither of those things are your fault."

"If you find nothing in Dubai. What then?"

"I keep looking."

"Yes, but for how long? Another week? A month?"

"As long as it takes."

"It might take never."

"I'm going to text you a couple of numbers," I told her. "I should be reachable through them if something comes up. I should get any messages you leave me. Otherwise, expect me to call according to schedule."

"Come home," Alena said again.

"I'll call you in a couple of days," I said.

She was saying something as I hung up, but I missed it, hearing her too late, already killing the connection.

After lunch, I hunted up a place to plug in the laptop, then paid the fee to get online. I did some quick research on Dubai, using my David Mercer Amex to make a reservation at the Four Points Sheraton on Khalid bin al-Waleed Road. I booked for three nights, to make it look good.

Then I put my last clean SIM in the BlackBerry and dialed up an international dating service based out of London. The service was called Singles Internationale, and you could hear the "e" they put on the end. The recorded greeting was by a woman with a sophisticated English accent, and I bypassed her as quickly as I could, navigating the menus until I'd accessed the mailbox I wanted. It was for a fifty-seven-year-old bi-curious divorcée from Bristol whose username was "Alone & Anxious," a profile that I was reasonably certain didn't get a lot of hits. I left my current number, asking for a call back. Then I hung up, stowed the laptop, and found myself an unoccupied corner of an empty gate to wait. I'd barely had time to start counting takeoffs and landings when my phone rang.

"Michael?" Nicholas Sargenti asked.

"Hello, Nicholas. Thanks for calling so promptly."

"I do hope you weren't waiting." He spoke in English, his accent slight, an odd mixture of French monotone married to Italian lilt. "It is only that the service notified me of the message in the box a few minutes ago, and I thought it best if I waited until I was somewhere quiet before returning your call."

"Not a problem," I told him.

"What can I do for you?"

"I'm traveling on business, heading to Dubai. I'm meeting a couple of colleagues at the Four Points Sheraton on Khalid bin al-Waleed. David Mercer, Danil Joshi, and Anthony Shephard."

"David Mercer, Danil Joshi, and Anthony Shephard," Sargenti repeated, and I knew he was committing the names to memory rather than writing anything down. "You've spoken of Mr. Mercer before, but these other two, this is, I think, the first mention you've made of them, Michael."

"Danil's a Georgian," I said. "I think he's from Tbilisi, but I'm not sure, to be honest. Anthony's out of Montreal."

"Hmm. Have you known them long?"

"No, not long at all. Anthony gets around, though. Danil's not much of a traveler."

"I see. Both gentlemen are aware they need an entry visa to visit Dubai, I take it?"

"Anthony's already taken care of his. Danil might have some difficulty, being from Georgia."

"I'd think he can get in on an EU provision. I'll look into it, if you'd like."

"That would be very helpful, thank you," I said.

"And you're meeting them when?"

"My flight doesn't get in until after midnight, so I doubt I'll be seeing them until late tomorrow. Morning of the day after at the latest."

"If either of them needs my help, I hope you'll consider mentioning my name."

"Goes without saying. There's one more thing."

"Of course."

"Elizavet talked to you about freeing up some funds. If you can earmark two hundred or so for this trip, that'd be great."

"I'm sorry?"

"Shouldn't need more than that," I said.

"No, no, that will pose no problem," Sargenti said. "What did you say about Elizavet?"

"You saw her last week."

"We spoke, yes. I've seen neither of you since we were in Prague together, at the end of March."

"Sorry," I said. "I meant call, not saw. Jet lag, you'll have to forgive me."

"Of course. I remain, as always, at your service."

"Which we both appreciate."

"Please give my regards to Messrs. Mercer, Joshi, and Shephard. I hope your business with them brings much success, Michael."

"Yeah," I said. "You and me both."

I hung up, went back to watching the planes taking off and landing. It was a bright day outside the airport, a vivid blue sky and heat distortion rising off the tarmac. After a while, I swapped out SIM cards again, and then sent a text message to Alena's mobile, with the phone numbers I'd promised. Less than a minute later, she sent a reply.

RECEIVED.

That was all. That was all there should have been. Certainly nothing more, certainly nothing sentimental. Certainly no explanation as to why she'd deceived me about meeting Nicholas in Tbilisi, where she'd really gone, what she'd really done. No justification for lying to me.

At twenty-three minutes past midnight, after ninety minutes in line, I cleared customs and entered the United Arab Emirate of Dubai.

CHAPTER
Eleven

The second night, for nine hundred dirham, I brought a hooker back to Danil Joshi's room at the Marina Palais Royale Hotel, which was as luxe an establishment as the name implied. I walked her openly past the security guard at the door the same way I'd seen countless other male guests do. We didn't touch, and we kept a reasonable distance between us, and no one looked at us twice, even though everyone on the staff knew what she was and my intentions with her, and never mind that sex outside of marriage was against the law. I was a business traveler, she was my guest, and in the end, weren't we only helping the economy?

Her name was Kekela, which means "beautiful" in

Georgian, and it suited her. She was tall, almost Alena's height, tanned and fit, with black hair that dropped in a glossy cascade to only a few inches above her hips, held away from her face by a pair of pearl-inlaid hair clips. Her features were sweet, even innocent, and she knew how to apply makeup for best effect, highlighting her cheekbones and drawing out her auburn eyes so they shone with anticipation and passion.

Once inside my room, Kekela went straight to the couch, kicking off her high heels on the way. The shoes were black and shiny, part of her nightclub ensemble. I fixed the locks on the door, and when I turned around again she was already lounging, one long leg extended on the cushions, the other curled beneath it. The pose made her skirt ride up, revealing the top of one stocking and the elastic from the garter belt that held it secure. The stocking was black and sheer, the garter belt black and lace. With her right hand she pulled the clips from her hair, tossing each onto the coffee table, while her left worked the buttons on her blouse, unfastening them one after the other. As I watched, she teased her top open. Her bra matched the garter belt.

"I'd like something to drink, Danil." She spoke in Georgian, using the same husky register that had made me strain to hear her in the club. "What do you have to drink?"

"Vodka?" I asked.

Her smile, like everything else she did, sold me even more promise.

I opened the minibar and got out the two tiny bottles of Grey Goose, cracked them and poured them together into a glass, seeing her watch me in the reflection off the dead television screen. The act stopped when I wasn't looking at her, the eagerness and accommodation turning dull, but she was very quick, and it was right back as before when I returned to her and put the glass in her hand.

"You're not drinking with me?"

"I don't drink much."

I took the chair nearest where she had been resting her head on the armrest of the couch. She pulled from the glass, half of the alcohol vanishing, then lowered it and ran a finger around its rim, meeting my eyes as she did it. As innuendo, it should have been absurd and ineffective, but she gave it as much commitment as Bacall had ever done for Bogie, and I was surprised at its effectiveness.

"How old are you?" I asked.

"Twenty-two."

It was a lie, but it was to be expected. Every prostitute I'd spoken to had claimed to be twenty-two, even the ones who'd looked forty, the same way every bribe in Georgia and Turkey had been fifty euros. In Kekela's case, though, it didn't appear to be a big one, and I couldn't imagine her much older than twenty-six.

"Where're you from?"

"Mtskheta."

"Where's that?"

An eyebrow rose slightly. "The mountains. North of Tbilisi, on the river."

"Right," I said. "That's right."

"You work in the capital?"

"Used to. Since the war I've been in Batumi most of the time."

She nodded slightly, slowly, then finished the rest of her drink and set it on the coffee table. The glass met the glass without a sound. She straightened up on the couch, ran her hands through her hair, stretching to give me the show as she brought up her arms. The movement caused her blouse to open wide, and her breasts strained against her bra. Even at two in the morning it was still almost 35 Celsius outside, and humid, and the air conditioner was running, keeping the room cool, and it was that rather than arousal that had turned her nipples hard.

Kekela held the pose for a beat longer than she needed to if she had been merely stretching, once more boldly meeting my eyes. Her mouth opened slightly, the start of a naughty smile.

Then she froze, and her arms came down, palms planting on either side of her on the cushions, as if preparing to spring. The performance mask disappeared, too, and her jaw set. The warmth in her eyes died.

"All right," she said, and the husky tone had gone the same way of the warmth, her voice turning hard and climbing half an octave higher. "What is this?"

"What do you mean?"

"What the fuck is this?"

"I don't know what you mean, Kekela," I said.

"I mean you keep looking in my fucking eyes. You don't look at my legs. You don't look at my tits. You don't look at my ass. You look me in the goddamn eyes."

"Well," I said, "you've got very pretty eyes."

She snorted. "Are you going to fuck me or not?"

"I'd rather talk."

"I don't do talk." Kekela pushed off the couch and onto her feet. She began buttoning her blouse. "I do oral. For extra, I let you cum in my mouth. I do anal, I do threesome, I do ass-to-mouth and I do ass-to-cunt, I do just about anything you can think of."

Her blouse was closed. I hadn't moved. She scooped her two hair clips from the coffee table with one hand, then fixed a glare on me.

"But I don't. Do. Talk."

I stayed exactly as before, not moving, presenting no threat, unless she took the slight smile I had on my face as one. She turned from the hips, locating her shoes, then snapped her attention back to me, as if expecting that I'd have tried something in the second she'd looked away.

When she saw that I hadn't, she added, as if I was an idiot, "And you're not from Tbilisi."

"No, I'm not. If you want to leave, you should. I won't keep you here against your will."

"I *am* going to leave."

"It's just that you're from Georgia," I said. "And I was hoping that would give us a connection, no matter how small. Hoping that the language would give us a foundation of trust."

Suspicion danced on her face. "Why?"

"I need help."

"You need help?" She snorted at me again, much the same way Alena did when she felt I was being unreasonably dim-witted. "Fucking obvious, you need help."

I shrugged.

"You're paying me nine hundred dirham because you need help?"

"I can pay more."

I expected greed, but what I saw on her face then was curiosity, instead. She looked me over, this time much more thoroughly than she had at the nightclub, then gave the room another survey. It was a very nice room. Considering how much I was being charged for it, it damn well better have been.

"What kind of help?" Kekela asked.

I indicated the couch. Her mouth drew tight, nearing a scowl, and she snorted yet again. Then she sat back down, this time at the opposite end. Her feet stayed on the floor.

"What kind of help?" she asked again.

"I'm trying to find a girl," I said, and I told her the story of Tiasa Lagidze.

"The ratio of men to women in Dubai, right now, at this moment, is three to one," Kekela told me over a late breakfast at the pool bar. "That's a lot of men looking to get laid."

She was feasting on a plate of fresh fruit and yogurt, washing down bites with her second mimosa. We were speaking in English and Georgian alternately. Her English was very good and barely accented, and when I'd asked her about it, she'd explained that it was the *lingua franca* of Dubai. It was almost eleven in the morning, and hot, already nearing 40 degrees Celsius. June marked the beginning of the off-season, the weather cruel enough to send even the most die-hard hedonists running for milder climes. Only a dozen guests moved around in the pool, and beyond it I could see perhaps half that number playing along the shore. The water of the Gulf and the water in the pool were almost the exact same shade of impossible blue. Almost everyone I saw was Caucasian—European or CIS—though two were Chinese. The service staff at the hotel, on the other hand, was almost universally Southeast Asian or Filipino. Of the few guests I was seeing, the majority were female, uniformly young and beautiful. There were no kids.

Kekela followed my gaze, then forked another piece of mango. "You're wondering if the women are all prostitutes."

"Are they?"

"The Marina isn't so good for that, at least, not during the daytime. Other hotels are better. But maybe all of them, they are whores of one kind or another."

"What does that mean?"

"They're here the same reason I'm here, Danil. They're looking for money."

I moved my attention back to her. She was wearing a black one-piece bathing suit she'd picked out and that I'd bought for her from one of the multiple hotel shops this morning, after she'd finally awoken. I'd slept on the couch, despite her offer to share the bed, a freebie bonus to the "consulting service" deal we'd negotiated the night before. Bathing suits and breakfast, it seemed, were part of the package, as well. Compared to what the other women were wearing, her suit was practically modest. Outside of the hotel, it would get her fined; on the road to Abu Dhabi, it could get her killed.

"That's why you're here?" I asked. "For the money?"

"Not at first." She finished chewing, swallowed, smiling ruefully. "No, you wouldn't believe me."

"Try me."

"Maybe I'm looking for Mr. Right."

"Your search has taken you far from home."

"I sure as hell wasn't finding him in Tbilisi."

"And how's it going?"

She sipped again at her mimosa. "I've been here for three years, and I'm still single. The money is good, but it's not enough, not for what I want."

"Nine hundred dirham a night, that's—"

"About a hundred and fifty euro," Kekela said. "Most of the time it's not for the night with me. Three hundred for two hours. If it's a good night, I can make six hundred euro. At home that's good money; here, it's enough to get by. I have to pay the government, I have to pay rent, buy clothes, food, medical, everything. Then there are bribes—you have to pay the places you work out of, the clubs and the bars. I try to send money back home, too, you know. And because everyone here has so much money, everything costs so much money."

"You pay the government?"

"For my work visa, as an entertainer. Sixteen hundred

dirham, every couple of months. Prostitution isn't legal, but it isn't so illegal they want to stop it. Three to one, like I said, and of those three, many are like you, traveling alone on business of one sort or another. Dubai wants their money, so they make it easy for them to spend it on the things they like."

"Maybe you should raise your rates."

"I'd price myself out of the market," she said, without a hint of irony. "I already charge the most I can get away with for what I am. The Chinese and Asian girls, they're the cheapest. Then you get the Africans, then girls like me, the CIS girls they call us, all the Confederation of Independent States that used to be the Soviet Union. Russians, Uzbeks, Georgians, Ukrainians, Kazaks, you know. We're mid-range. The really high-end, expensive ones, those are the regional girls. Except for the Iraqis, they used to be more expensive, but there are so many now, the price for them has dropped."

I drank some orange juice, thinking that Kekela talked about her work with the same disconnect that Alena and I talked about ours.

"Still doesn't tell me how you got here."

Kekela brushed stray hair out of her face. "A friend from my village, she had been abroad. She came home, said that there was a lot of work for girls in Dubai, that I could get a job in a restaurant, or maybe even singing in a club."

"You believed her?"

"I didn't have a reason not to. And rich Arabs had to be better than where I was." She turned her champagne flute in her fingers, looking at her reflection in the glass. "It's not like with your Tiasa, Danil. I came on my own, I paid my own way, I had my own papers, so I was in a better position, I could make a choice."

"Is that what this is for you? A choice?"

"You are asking me a lot of questions."

"That's the arrangement, isn't it? I ask questions, you answer them."

"The deal didn't cover questions about me."

"I'm curious."

She put the glass down, removing her sunglasses. I'd bought them for her at the same time I'd bought the bathing suit. At her request, of course.

"Worry about saving one girl at a time," Kekela told me. "I'm going swimming. Would you like to join me?"

I shook my head.

"Then I'll see you back in your room. Say, three hours."

She headed into the water, diving from the edge of the pool, breaking the rippling sheet of blue. I watched as she swam the length, reached the opposite end. She took hold of the ledge, looking back toward me, and there was enough distance between us that I couldn't make out her expression. She was probably laughing.

I charged the meal to my room, then went to find the health club, hoping for an outlet for my impatience and my doubt. Two hours managed most of the impatience, but the doubt still lingered as I made my way back to the room and into the shower. Kekela's game was obvious, and we both understood it. She would take me for everything she could, but in the end, she would have to balance that with a result, something to square the account. The money didn't matter to me. What mattered was the time.

But until the sun went down and the expats flooded the clubs, there wasn't much either of us could do but wait.

I was out of the shower and going through Bakhar's address book for the eleventh time when there was a knock on my door.

When I checked the spyhole, I saw Kekela, in her swimsuit, towel wrapped around her hips and another around her hair. Beside her, with a hand on her upper arm, stood a grim-looking Filipino man, short and burly, in the plainclothes uniform of hotel security.

"He needs my passport," Kekela told me when I opened the door. She spoke in Georgian, her tone flat as a board.

"Mr. Joshi," the man said, using English. "This woman says she's your guest?"

"I hope that's not a problem," I said.

He released her, and I could see the color on Kekela's skin from where he'd held her arm tighter than he'd needed to. I moved out of her way, letting her into the room.

"We need to make a photocopy of her passport," the man said. "It's hotel policy."

"Sure," I said. "Just a second."

I left him holding the door open, stepped around into the bedroom, where Kekela had left her clothes from the night before. She'd already opened her purse, had her passport in hand. I took it from her.

"It's not a problem," Kekela said, in Georgian. "It happens, it's happened to me before."

"Did he hurt you?" I asked.

She looked surprised, needed half a moment to recover. Then she shook her head. "No. No, I'm fine."

From my wallet, I took out three five-hundred-dirham bills, folding them together once and then once again. I tucked the money inside the front flap of her passport. The document looked legit, dog-eared and well thumbed, and according to the vitals, Kekela's name was Kekela Alkhazovi, and she was twenty-seven years old.

"Get dressed," I told Kekela, then went back to the door,

where the man from hotel security was waiting patiently, just as I'd left him. I handed him her passport.

"I trust you'll bring it back promptly," I said.

The man ran a stubby thumb along the edge of the document, feeling the bulge made by my bribe. "Right away."

"And I trust this won't happen again."

He frowned slightly. "Will you be bringing any other female guests to the hotel, Mr. Joshi?"

"Not planning on it."

"Then this will certainly be the last of the matter. You have my apologies for any inconvenience."

I thought about saying that I wasn't the one he should be apologizing to, then thought it would be an absurd thing to say. Prostitution was clearly such an open secret the hotel felt obliged to keep their own records of the transactions, the same way they kept records of their guests. Everyone, it seemed, knew the part they were to play, except for me.

He departed, and I shut and locked the door. The shower had started in the bathroom. I returned to the desk where I'd been working, pulling out Bakhar's little black book once more, again checking it against the files I'd pulled off the BlackBerry. Neither had any numbers for Dubai, and I wasn't finding anything new.

Eight minutes after hotel security departed, there was another knock on the door, this time a bellboy returning the passport. He'd brought a complimentary bottle of champagne up, as well. I sent him away with a tip, thinking that it bordered on farce, that I was giving money in return for a gift that had come from a bribe as a result of the prostitute in my room.

I locked the door yet again, turned back to see Kekela emerging from the suite's bedroom. She was naked. She also, it turned out, shaved her pubic hair.

"You're not looking in my eyes," she remarked.

I corrected myself. "Put on some clothes."

"We're not going to be able to start looking for your girl until tonight." She started coming toward me, grinning. "Ten at the earliest. That gives us seven hours."

"Plenty of time," I said. "Get dressed, I'll take you to the Deira Souq, we can go shopping."

"It's too hot to go out."

She stopped in front of me, took the champagne and the passport out of my hands, then dropped them on the floor. The champagne hit the carpet with a solid thump.

"Kekela," I said. "Put on some clothes. Now."

"If you're afraid that you'll catch something, Danil, please, don't be. I get checked every two weeks, and I have an AIDS test every month."

"Yes, you're very clean, I can see that."

I stepped around her, heading toward the bedroom. She followed me quickly, rushing past at the last minute and throwing herself across the bed. Then she rolled onto her side, flipping wet hair back over one shoulder. She held open her arms for me. I didn't break stride. There were two complimentary terrycloth robes in the closet, and I yanked one free from its hanger and tossed it onto her on the bed.

She sat up, and from her expression I could see she still didn't get it, that she was trying to puzzle my behavior into something that made sense to her. She pulled the robe onto her lap, but didn't open it, made no further move toward covering herself up.

"Is it a kink? Do you need me to play with myself first? Do you want to watch?"

"No," I said, and the exasperation started to creep into my voice. "I want you to get dressed, Kekela."

"You don't like my body? I don't turn you on?"

"Don't be stupid."

"Then why not? What are you so worried about? You have a wife? A girlfriend? She'll never know."

"*I'll* know," I said.

She stared at me, and I couldn't tell if it was simple incomprehension or pure disbelief I was seeing. Then she snorted, began pulling on the bathrobe as she slid off the bed. When she had tied it closed, she spun around once, in place, then threw up her hands.

"Happy now?"

"No," I said. "But I can work with what I've got."

"You are fucked up. Are you gay, is that it? I mean, seriously, it's fucking sex, that's all it is."

"I know what it is."

"Everyone cheats. Every single one cheats. Your girl, she cheats, too. Right now, I'll bet she's cheating on you. But you won't touch me."

"Not everyone."

"Yes. Everyone."

"No wonder I feel so lonely," I said.

CHAPTER
Twelve

At ten minutes past eleven on my third night in Dubai, with Kekela on my arm, I came off the stairs into the UV lights of a nightclub called Rattlesnake, full of cigarette smoke, bad music, and working girls. Given the state of Dubai aboveground, the nature of the off-season, I'd expected the place to be nearly empty. I could hardly have been more mistaken. Kekela kept a hand on me, just above the elbow, much the same way that hotel security had escorted her to my door, and with much the same grip, I imagined. It wasn't because she was afraid I'd run off.

I counted twenty-eight women looking to do business before I gave up trying to keep track. They were as Kekela had described. Perhaps a third of the women hailed from China. The rest looked either CIS or African, with a smattering of Southeast Asia thrown in to round them out. Ages ran from late twenties to early fifties, the different ethnic groups self-segregating into discrete pockets.

"The Chinese girls wait for you to come to them," Kekela shouted in my ear as we edged our way to the bar. "The others, they'll look for a cue, maybe you meet their eyes, maybe they think you look like a good prospect. Be prepared."

I nodded, sparing my voice, trying to take in the room without inadvertently soliciting a come-on. I was having a hard time finding alternate exits, mostly due to the lighting, but also in part to the crowd. In addition to the night butterflies, as they were called in Russia, there were easily another fifty or sixty men, most of them appearing my age or older. Most wore the wearied, desperate energy of business travelers, and these comprised as international a group as the women. Unlike with the women, however, I was seeing a Middle Eastern clientele, as well, though how many were local, I had no idea.

"Are they all like this?" I asked Kekela, shouting in Georgian.

"You mean the clubs? The bars?"

I nodded.

"There was this place, Cyclone, the government had to shut it down a couple years back, just after I'd come here. The mongers called it the United Nations of Whores."

"Mongers?"

"Whoremongers," Kekela said. "Punters, the British call them."

"What are we doing here?"

Her smile was sly. "Buy me a drink, vodka and tonic. I'll be right back. Don't go anywhere."

The last sounded as much like a warning as a request. She detached from my side, waded into the darkness. The black light made her glow like a ghost, the cigarette smoke as if she was disappearing into a mist. I got the attention of the nearest bartender, bought a drink for Kekela and a club soda for myself. Before they came, the space she had vacated on my right was filled by a blonde. At my left appeared a companion brunette.

"Have you been in Dubai long?" The blonde used English, and her accent was German.

"A couple of days."

She watched as the bartender delivered my drinks. "Those both for you?"

"I'm waiting for my friend to get back."

"We are very friendly," the brunette told me. Her accent was closer to Russian, but it was hard to make out over the music. "Or very nasty. Six hundred, you can have us both for two hours."

"No, thanks. I've already made arrangements for the night."

The blonde looked in the direction Kekela had disappeared. "She's not coming back."

"Did you pay her already?" the brunette asked. "How much did you pay her?"

"We're still negotiating," I lied.

The brunette laughed. "You never pay in advance," she advised. "Half, at most."

"We can beat her price." The blonde returned her attention to me. "Two-for-one offer. Where are you staying?"

I picked up my drinks and stepped away from the bar. "Nice talking to you."

They let it go, or at least I didn't hear it if either of them offered a comment as I left. The band fell silent, breaking between sets, and the noise level dropped appreciably, enough that I could make out voices. Most were in English, all were loud. I saw a youngish-looking Chinese woman dancing in the middle of a wolf pack, all of them ogling her, passed a tall African woman negotiating with an Indian, telling him that seven hundred would cover the night. He asked if she meant dirham or euros.

I found a table, set down my drinks, and felt myself being sized up by almost every set of female eyes that fell upon me. The appraisals felt clinical and made me feel like a piece of meat. The way people lurked and lunged in the black light made us all look like zombies.

Kekela emerged from the smoke. She picked up her drink and drained it in two gulps, then reached for my hand, to pull me to my feet.

"I want you to meet someone," she said.

"Who?"

"An old friend. Come on."

She dragged me after her, along the floor. A club mix had begun playing on the sound system, and more people were dancing to that than had done for the band. We skirted their edge, pushed through a clump of laughing men and women, reaching another table wedged near the back wall, by one of the stacks of speakers. Two women sat at the table, speaking to a Caucasian man. The women were both Chinese, one of them perhaps in her thirties, the other one younger, but it was hard to tell by how much. The man I put in his forties.

"She's new," the older one was telling the man. "She needs someone who can teach her."

"You're asking me to do you a favor," the man said. His English was American, the sound of it jarring. I hadn't heard an American accent outside of my own, it seemed, for a long time.

"Six hundred."

"For the night?" He shook his head. "Xia, you're asking me for a favor. Four hundred."

"Five hundred."

"Dirham?"

The older woman, Xia, nodded. Seated beside her, the younger one didn't move, didn't speak. The smile on her face looked like it had been injection-molded in a factory, and about as sincere.

"All right, done," the man decided.

Xia turned to the woman beside her, speaking quickly in Mandarin, or Cantonese, I couldn't tell. The younger woman perked up immediately at whatever was said, however, and the plastic smile turned to something approaching genuine. She rose, moving around the table, and the man got to his feet, and they headed off together.

"This is your friend?" Xia asked Kekela.

"Danil," Kekela said. "He's from Georgia, too."

Xia turned the palm of her right hand, sweeping it at the empty seats.

"Xia was the first girl I met when I got here," Kekela told me. "She's been here for ten years. She knows everything."

"She's being generous."

Kekela shook her head. "No, no. If it wasn't for you, I'd have been in a lot of trouble."

"You're very sweet, Kekela."

Kekela smiled at the other woman fondly. Now that we were closer, I could see the beginnings of lines on Xia's face, found myself revising my estimate of her age upward, into the mid-forties. Unlike the other women I'd been seeing, even Kekela, Xia's outfit was more subdued, speaking less of sex than experience.

"Kekela is my friend," Xia said to me. "And if you are hers, then I would be happy to help you."

I glanced at Kekela, and she nodded. From inside my jacket, I took the photo of Tiasa I'd printed from the security system back in Kobuleti. I unfolded it, then handed it to Xia, checking to see if anyone was watching. Nobody was paying us the slightest attention.

Xia studied the picture for several seconds. "Who is she?"

"The daughter of someone I know," I answered. "She'd have arrived a week, maybe five days ago, from Turkey."

"She looks young."

"She's fourteen."

Carefully, she folded the paper closed and set it on the table, between us. "You say 'arrived.'"

"'Shipped' might be better."

"I understand."

"Can you help me?"

Xia lifted her gaze from where she'd been watching the paper, looking first to Kekela, then to me. "I don't know."

"Xia," Kekela said, "please, he's a friend."

"I didn't say I wouldn't. I don't know if I can."

"I don't understand," I said.

"If she came here like you say, she could have been sold as a domestic anywhere in the Emirates. She could be in someone's house in Abu Dhabi, working as their servant."

"Working as their slave," I corrected. "Servants get paid."

Xia stared at me for a moment. Then she nodded. "It would make her impossible to find."

What Alena had said when I'd called her from the airport in Istanbul came back to me, the questions. It might take never, she'd said. And Xia was telling me the same thing, but this time without the qualification.

"There's another possibility," Xia said. "She could have been sold to a brothel. There are many here in Dubai, places that service the skilled laborers and other clients."

"How many specialty places?"

"Very many."

"You know who to ask," Kekela said. "You could help us."

Xia frowned, then reached out for the paper, unfolding it once more. She studied the face, small crow's-feet visible at her eyes. Then, with a sigh, she looked up at me. "May I keep this?"

I nodded. As it was, I had a second picture of Tiasa, taken off Vladek's BlackBerry. It wasn't my favorite, but I had it.

"I will ask around," Xia said. "It may take a few days."

"I'll pay for your time," I said.

"Then I will keep track of it. Kekela has my number, and I have hers. I will call if I learn anything."

"Thank you, Xia," Kekela said.

Xia gave her a small, almost maternal smile. Then she wished us both a good night.

"I have to get back to work," Xia told us.

CHAPTER
Thirteen

The UAE and Georgia share the same time zone, each of them at GMT +4. It made the math easy for me when the time came to call Alena the next day. According to our rolling schedule, she would be expecting her phone to start ringing at seventeen minutes to nine.

I'd been up for a couple hours already, having found it difficult to sleep. Rattlesnake had left a bitter taste in my mouth, and I couldn't put my finger on why, exactly. I was in no position to pass judgment on the men and women I'd seen. Any battle fought for the moral high ground I was guaranteed to lose, anyway; in the pantheon of sins one could commit, I was confident I had prostitution beat hands down.

The women I'd seen had appeared to be doing what they were doing of their own volition, but I had to wonder at the circumstances that made such a choice a viable one for them. It wasn't, as Kekela suspected, that I had an aversion to sex. I was quite fond of sex, though admittedly not as desperate for it as I'd been when I was younger. I was also a big fan of allowing consenting adults to do whatever they damn well pleased with other consenting adults. It wasn't the sex, per se.

Poverty was the engine, and against the backdrop of Dubai, with its man-made islands formed to look like a map of the Earth or giant palm fronds or even, as was currently under development, the entire galaxy, it seemed all the more obscene. Like Kekela, most of the working girls sent whatever money they could afford home, back to Bangladesh and Beijing, Moscow and Moldova. I knew from Kekela that the money was, in many cases, the only thing allowing their families back home to survive.

"Xia is married, has two kids," Kekela had told me. "They're back in China. She's supporting them."

"When was the last time she saw them?"

"I don't know. Years." She'd paused, then added, "I don't think she'll ever go home."

We'd returned to the room, and I'd taken a shower, trying to wash the layer of smoke and sweat from my skin. I had purchased new clothes the day before, and I changed into a pair of shorts, then made up my bed on the couch. Kekela watched me from the edge of the bedroom, leaning against the doorframe, but she didn't comment.

"Sleep well," I told her.

"Yes," she said. "You too."

She'd left the door open when she'd gone to bed, and I'd climbed onto the couch and stared at the ceiling, managed to doze off only to come awake an hour or so later, feeling that I hadn't slept at all. After that, it'd been impossible for me to settle. I'd spent the rest of the night looking out at the Gulf, the lights of the dhows and the yachts, listening to the air conditioner and Kekela's occasional rustle beneath the sheets. When dawn began to show itself, I stowed my blankets and pillows back in the closet and got dressed in fresh clothes. I looked in on Kekela, and she was sound asleep, curled small in the middle of the very big bed. She was sleeping naked. I carefully closed the door.

The BlackBerry had been recharged off the USB cable to the computer. I swapped out the SIM, switched it on. There were no messages, no voicemails, which meant that Alena hadn't tried to reach me, not on that number, at least. I checked the alternate SIM, and it was the same thing. I checked the clock on the BlackBerry, and dialed.

There was no answer.

After six rings, I was shunted to voicemail.

I hung up and rechecked my math. I found no flaw in it. I dialed again.

There was obstinately no answer.

After six rings, I was again shunted to voicemail.

"This is Yeva. Leave a message."

"It's me," I said. "Checking in. Call me when you get this."

I hung up, looked at the smartphone in my hand, then tossed it onto the desk and went back to staring out the window. The sunlight was already rising bright, even behind the tint of the glass.

Alena knew when to expect my call. That she'd missed it wasn't, by itself, a cause for alarm. We had fallback protocols in place, alternates we were to use if the initial contact failed. In this case, the rule was to wait two hours after the primary attempt, and then to call again. If that, too, failed, there was a secondary number either of us could call to leave a message for the other, similar to the way I'd contacted Sargenti. Each of our go-bags had a prepaid mobile phone, as well, never used, entirely clean. If all else failed, that was the phone of last resort.

I marked the time, began counting down the initial two-hour window, trying not to worry. It wasn't easy. Alena didn't make mistakes, not about things like this. If she hadn't been able to answer the phone at a quarter to nine in the morning, it was because she couldn't, either due to circumstance or misfortune.

I was really hoping it was because of circumstance.

Kekela woke at twenty past ten, and I heard her thumping around in the bedroom. When she came out, she was wearing one of the complimentary bathrobes, her hair a wild tangle. She yawned at me before asking if it was all right to order up some breakfast.

"Go ahead," I said.

My tone earned a somewhat confused look, and then she went back into the bedroom. I listened to her pick up the phone, order breakfast for two, which was polite of her, but then again, she wasn't paying for it. She hung up, and a few seconds later I heard the shower start. By the time she was out and dressed, the food had arrived. She'd ordered light, the continental breakfast, and when the knock came at the door I answered and signed for the meal, then went back to where I'd been sitting at the desk. Kekela poured coffee for herself, orange juice for me, offering me the glass. I took it and set it down untouched, still watching the clock.

When it hit seventeen to eleven, I used the BlackBerry, dialed Alena's mobile again.

Same result as before.

I killed the connection, waited thirty seconds, hit redial. Six rings, and then to voicemail. I hung up and this time dialed into the service, cutting through the menus as fast as I could and punching up the mailbox to check for messages. There weren't any. I backed out of the box, reentered the code, waited for the tone.

"Call me," I said.

I hung up, tossed the phone back onto the desk.

"Something's wrong?" Kekela asked.

"No."

The question was apparent in her expression, but she didn't cave to it immediately, instead sipping at more of her coffee. She took it sweet and light, with so much cream it looked more like milk than coffee. She'd found a croissant that she liked the looks of in the basket, was dipping one end into her cup. She munched, walking to the windows, looking out at the water.

"She's your girlfriend?" Kekela asked.

"No."

"But you have a girlfriend? A wife? Someone?"

"Someone."

"I think you must love her very much." She sighed. "She's very lucky."

"You don't know me," I said.

It came out colder than I'd intended, and it caught her by surprise. She put her back to the window, her brow creasing, wondering what it was she could have done to offend me.

"I've seen enough," Kekela said.

"No, you haven't. I know what you want. I know what you're thinking, Kekela, I know what you've been hoping for. And I hope you find it, I really do, because I think you deserve it, I think you deserve better than hooking in Dubai. I hope the guy comes along someday with all the money, and that he falls in love with you because of who you are and not what you do, and he gives you your escape route."

She didn't move, staring at me, barely breathing. If I was hurting her with my words, I couldn't tell, but with my usual grace and style, I most likely was. I didn't want to, but I didn't want either of us deluding the other any longer.

"I'm not that guy," I told her. "I'm not Mr. Right. Not for you. Not for anyone."

There was a tremble starting in her chin. She fought to control it. When she spoke, it came out as a whisper.

"You could be," Kekela said.

"Maybe once," I said. "Not anymore."

She might've had a counter, might've tried again to convince me otherwise. I'll never know.

In the bedroom, her mobile phone began to ring, and she went to answer it, seizing the escape. I turned to the BlackBerry once more and confirmed that I hadn't missed a call, a text, or a voicemail. I swapped to my alternate SIM, had just started to check that, too, when Kekela called out to me.

"It's Xia," she said. "She thinks she's found your girl."

CHAPTER
Fourteen

The reason the ratio of men to women in Dubai was three to one was precisely the same reason I could walk into Rattlesnake and twenty minutes later walk out with a woman on each arm willing to do whatever I wanted. The reason was money, Dubai's *raison d'être*.

Most of the men in the equation are what the expat community refers to euphemistically as "skilled laborers," when, in truth, they are almost exactly the opposite. Like the women, they've come to work, they've come seeking respite from the desperate poverty of their homes. Like the women, many of these men have been tricked, either through willing self-delusion or honest ignorance. They have been recruited by construction suppliers, transported by traffickers, led under false pretense. Like many of the women, many of the men arrive to find their passports confiscated by their "employer." Like the women, they are told about the enormous debt they have incurred, the cost required to bring them to this new land of opportunity. Like the women, they are told they must now work to pay that debt off.

The similarities end there, and not only because the men work on their feet and not on their backs. As a group, they lack the broad diversity of the women, most hailing from India, Bangladesh, Pakistan, and the Philippines, with a few from Egypt, Jordan, and the like. They live in worker camps, which sounds marginally better than "labor camps," but it's a syntactic distinction. Hundreds of them are packed into tents or prefab structures or nine-room homes. They sleep six, ten, twenty to a room. If they're lucky, they get an air conditioner or a window, but they never get both. A single bathroom serves thirty. There's room enough for only one or two meals to be prepared at a time. If they're industrious, they sometimes pool money together to buy a television. There are no phones allowed, but sometimes a supervised call is permitted once a week or a month, just to tell the folks back home that everything is fine.

They rise at five, arrive on the work site by six. While the rest of Dubai hides in climate-controlled shopping malls, restaurants, and hotels, the men labor nonstop in the heat. During the summer, the mercury effortlessly breaks 40 Celsius. The humidity is oppressive. They get an hour for lunch, eaten out of doors, in whatever shade can be found in the middle of the day. Then work resumes until six, seven, eight at night. Back to the camps. Do it again. That many, if not most, of these laborers are Muslims in an Islamic country mitigates nothing; the hammers fall, the drills whine, the machines clank, the sounds of construction drowning out each and every one of the muezzin's calls.

That's the day shift. Work goes on twenty-four hours. It's been estimated that work-site fatalities occur at the rate of two a day.

The men earn, on average, the equivalent of a dollar an hour. In many cases, they go months without seeing a penny of it, their wages withheld to keep them from running away. As it is, it's against the law for a worker in Dubai to change his job without his employer's permission. When they do get paid, almost every man sends his wages back home, retaining only enough to survive. Some are never paid at all.

By some estimates, there are over two million of these men.

And they get lonely.

We were in a cab, speeding south along Sheikh Zayed Road, which was more of a highway than a road. Outside our air-conditioned bubble the sun was high and merciless, glare flashing off the rising towers of glass and metal. The driver was a local, wearing wraparound sunglasses. He drove like he was trying to qualify for Le Mans, which was possibly my own fault. I should never have told him we were in a hurry.

"She's going to meet us?" I asked Kekela.

Her nod was curt, staring straight ahead. Since leaving the hotel, she'd refused to meet my eyes, and her body language now was all about anger, though she was doing her best to conceal it. I'd hurt her, and she didn't like that. Perhaps of all the things I could've done to her, that had been the worst.

"What more did she say?" I asked.

"Nothing. Just that she thought she'd found the girl."

"Do you trust her?"

Her jaw worked, lips compressing tightly. First I hurt her, then I insulted her friends.

"I trust Xia with my life," Kekela said.

I didn't press. I wasn't going to get anything more even if I did. Instead, I went back to watching Dubai zip past, then pulled out the BlackBerry and checked it again for any messages I might've missed. I hadn't. I tucked the phone back in my pocket. Aside from it, I had my Danil Joshi passport and my wallet. My wallet held almost three thousand euros, twice that much in dirhams. I hoped it would be enough to purchase Tiasa's freedom, but if it wasn't, it didn't matter.

If she was at our destination, she was leaving with me.

The skyscrapers and fields of construction cranes fell away abruptly, and for another ten minutes we sped through the desert. The terrain was harsh, browns and yellows, packed earth and then sand, clichéd as a movie set. Traffic that had been light and constant thinned out even more. Our driver slowed enough to keep from rolling the car when we turned inland along a freshly paved road that seemed to lead to the middle of nowhere. After another two minutes, an apartment block came into view, as if it had been dropped from above onto the landscape.

The cab pulled into the makeshift dirt lot, amidst a battery of other vehicles, most in considerably worse condition than our own, pickups and vans, even a couple heavy-class construction vehicles. Two caught my eye, a new BMW sedan and a Toyota SUV. Both lacked the thick layer of desert dust that seemed to coat everything else. I paid the driver, and Kekela and I got out. Heat collapsed on us like a curtain, drier than it had been in the city, yet more severe. The car pulled away, wheels crunching gravel, then sped off the way we'd come. For a moment after it left, there was the illusion of silence, and then noise began filtering to us from the building.

Now that we were out of the cab, I could see the structure was actually multiple buildings, all of the same design, as if modeled on some old Soviet-style housing plan. They'd been built so close together it looked like there was barely room enough to walk abreast between them. This was further complicated by the fact that a chain-link fence ran around the perimeter, topped with concertina wire. Piles of trash, some of it in bags, most of it not, sat heaped along the fence.

There was noise coming from within the buildings, the voices of too many men in too small a space, barely heard behind the din of two dozen air conditioners. I could smell overflowing sewage.

"Now what?" I asked Kekela.

"I don't know. She said she would meet us." She looked confused.

"There's a brothel here?"

"At least one, yes."

"Why here? Why not in the city?"

"Your girl, Tiasa, she's young." Kekela glanced around, perhaps searching for Xia, perhaps afraid we'd be overheard. There was no one in sight. "A lot of men like them young, but the young ones, they can't work the bars. So they put them in houses, they hide them in places like this."

I pointed to the BMW and the SUV. "Either of those Xia's?"

"I don't think so. I don't know what she drives, though. Customers, probably." She shifted, uncomfortable with the subject. "Like I said, a lot of men like them young."

I looked the buildings over again. The heat was intense enough that my sweat evaporated the moment it reached my skin, made my flesh tighten. When I looked back in the direction of the city, I could just make out the tops of the high towers, the upper floors floating in the heat haze.

There was a clank from the fence, and Xia was opening the gate, motioning us to her. Kekela moved first. I followed. The gate had a padlock, and Xia replaced it once we were through, but she didn't lock it.

"This way," Xia said. "Quickly."

She started immediately along the narrow alley between the blocks. Laundry lines made from scavenged work-site cable were strung between support posts, draped with clothing and bedding, obstructing vision everywhere I turned. Xia hurried, Kekela close after her. Every door we passed was closed, every window set high and made small, impossible to see or escape through.

"Over here, this way," Xia said.

We turned, came around the corner of one of the buildings into a courtyard, this one devoid of laundry or refuse. In the meager shade provided by the balcony above him, a man sat opposite us, beside a closed door. He looked in his twenties, wearing the traditional shirt-dress *dishdasha* that Emirati men favored, but this one was teal instead of the old-fashioned white. His head was bare, no *gutra,* his hair cut fashionably, just a little long. A cigarette burned in one hand.

"Here he is," Xia said, indicating me.

The man let a mouthful of smoke leak free as he looked me over. Then he showed me an anemic smile.

"*Mar haba,*" he said.

"*Al-salaam alaykum,*" I answered. *Peace be upon you.*

"*Wa alaykum e-salaam,*" he answered. *And upon you peace.*

The insincerity was palpable to all of us.

He rose from his seat, dropping the cigarette and grinding it out with his toe, his attention, for the moment, on its destruction. He was wearing Nikes. They looked new. When he was certain he'd ground the butt to shreds, he looked up again, this time at Xia.

"You can go," he told her.

Xia took hold of Kekela's forearm, started trying to move her back in the direction we had come. "Come on."

"No," Kekela said. "No, I'm staying with him."

"Keke, please," Xia said, trying to move her again. "We should go."

I'd been keeping my eyes on the man, the same way he'd been watching me. There was no question, now, that Xia had set me up, and from her behavior, I was willing to give her the benefit of the doubt, that she'd done so against her will. There had always been the chance this was how things would play out; the moment I'd handed over the picture of Tiasa, it pretty much guaranteed that the wrong people would take notice. But the wrong people for Xia were the right people for me, and I'd played the gamble willingly, and I'd settle it now, no matter the cost.

At least, no matter the cost to me.

"It's okay," I told Kekela. "You should go."

"No! What's going on?" She jerked herself free from Xia's grip, turning on her. "What did you do? What have you done, Xia?"

Xia didn't answer.

"I told him he could trust you! I told him because I trust you!"

"If she won't leave," the man said to me, "she's welcome to come inside with you. I have friends who would be happy to keep her company."

"I'm sure you do," I answered. "That's why she's going to leave."

"No, no I won't, I won't go. I'm staying with you, Danil!"

I broke from the staring contest, faced Kekela. She looked miserable, guilty and afraid. I put my hands on her shoulders, spoke in Georgian.

"Either they have Tiasa, or they know where I can find her, and that's why I'm here. You got me this far. You did everything I asked you to. But now you have to go."

"Oh God, oh my God." Her voice had gone tight. "This is my fault. It's all my fault."

"It's not."

"They're going to kill you. That's what's going to happen, isn't it?"

"First they'll have some questions for me."

"Oh God, oh God. No, no, I can't leave you."

"If you go in there, Kekela, they'll use you against me. It's like you said by the pool. I need to concentrate on saving one woman at a time."

It took her a second to parse, to remember, and then she half laughed, half sobbed.

"You *are* fucked up," she told me.

"Without question," I agreed. "Go. Please."

This time, when Xia took her arm, she didn't resist. I watched them round the corner, going out of sight. Kekela didn't look back.

When I turned again to face him, the man's smile was exactly as it had been before. He indicated the door he'd been seated beside. "Shall we go inside?"

"After you."

"No." The smile died, turned to ice in the middle of the desert. "After you."

CHAPTER
Fifteen

Before I went through the door, I thought that I'd play it their way, at least for a while. They had questions, I was sure. At the very least, they wanted to know my interest in this fourteen-year-old girl they'd seen in the picture Xia had shown them. They wanted to know who I was, why I cared. If I was some crusading law enforcement officer, or someone in the business, someone trafficking, though the last seemed highly unlikely.

So I thought that I would let that run, let them intimidate and threaten and even hurt me, if that's what it took. Just to get them talking, just to see if Tiasa really was here, and if not, to find out if they knew her, knew where she was. It was risky as hell, but it seemed the best idea.

Then I stepped inside, into a spare and ugly makeshift waiting room with a couple of rundown chairs, some pillows in the corner surrounding a large *sheesha* pipe. Digital photos, printed on plain paper, were tacked to the wall opposite me, the menu of the day, the girls available. A single door, closed, led out of the room opposite me.

I took it all in as I entered, the man in the *dishdasha* closing the door after us even as another man stepped out from where he'd been against the entry wall. Maybe another Emirati, I couldn't be sure, this one dressed in loose linen pants and an overlarge white linen shirt. He had a shotgun in his hands, a stubby little pump-action Serbu model with an after-market gold finish. As soon as the door closed, the man in the *dishdasha* said something in Arabic, and the man with the shotgun stepped toward me, the barrel of the gun not quite in-line, and I could tell he was going to use it as a prod.

At which point I thought, *Fuck it.*

I swept my forearm up to clear the barrel of the shotgun, pivoting into him, catching hold of the weapon in my right hand. At the same time, with my left, I punched my fingers into his throat, just beneath his Adam's apple, then again, into his left eye. He lost the shotgun to me, choking as he staggered back.

I spun back to the entrance, saw that the best reaction the man in the *dishdasha* had managed as yet was to be stunned, which suited me fine, and frankly was kind of the point. He was still looking stunned as I kicked him in the knee with my left. Adrenaline turned the kick more vicious than I'd intended, and something in the joint buckled and broke, and he toppled, screaming in Arabic. Then he was on the floor, and I kicked him in the face, hard, and he cut to silence.

I flipped the shotgun around in my grip, turning again to the man I'd taken it from. He had fallen back against the wall, struggling to keep his feet, blood running from his eye, his face swollen with the need for air. His right hand was going behind his back, and I knew he was drawing on me, forcing an escalation that didn't leave me any option. I shot him point-blank, and whoever had loaded the Serbu had chosen birdshot for it, and it was as devastatingly messy as it was effective.

There was a half beat of silence as I went to the body, searching it. By the time I'd pulled the pistol from the dead man's hand, the first scream had come, childish and high-pitched. Footsteps pounded on the ceiling above me, at least two sets. The pistol was a semi-auto, a Beretta, and I tucked it into my jeans, then glanced back at the man in the *dishdasha*. He was semiconscious, bleeding and groaning.

The room I was in had only the two doors, the one leading out, the other leading deeper within. I needed to go deeper, because if Tiasa was here, that's where she'd be. But deeper meant more men with guns. Going outside would give up the initiative and lose me time, and I'd get neither back. Staying where I was wouldn't work, either; unless whoever was coming in response was either dense or mental, he'd pause outside to assess, rather than charging into the room headlong, because he couldn't know who had shot whom. Once he realized his friends weren't answering, he'd then as likely spray the room with bullets as not.

I jacked the next shell up on the shotgun, moving to the inner door, and opening it without hesitating. It wasn't that I was sure of myself; it was that I didn't have time to be cautious. The hallway was short, maybe fifteen feet, turned ninety degrees left at its end, rooms on either side. I closed the door behind me silently, listening to movement above, the sounds of whimpering, the hush of men's voices. The rapid movement had turned to caution.

I took the door on the left, as fast and as quiet as I could. It was a bathroom, broken tile and one shit-stained seat, the bowl half-filled with excrement and urine. The light was on, and I left it that way, shutting the door silently after me. I swung the front grip down on the Serbu and forced myself to breathe, trying to replenish and stockpile oxygen, listening hard for movement in the hall.

It didn't take long, cautious footfalls passing my door by within a handful of seconds, then a voice calling out, "Murab? Zafar?"

I took my hand off the front grip long enough to open the bathroom door, kicked it clear, and stepped out, facing the way I'd come. There were two of them, Western dress, each with an AK, each showing me their backs. They heard me coming. I fired, jacked, fired again, and the birdshot and the close range guaranteed I didn't need to do it a third time. Both of them fell, one hit in the back before he'd managed to turn, the other in the side, as he'd been coming to bear.

There was more screaming, and I realized some of it was coming from the room opposite me.

I dropped the shotgun, took one of the AKs. It, too, had a gold finish, and showed pride of ownership, complete with a hand-tooled leather carry strap. I slung the weapon, took out the Beretta, checked the chamber-loaded indicator, and verified there was a round waiting, then dropped the magazine into my hand. It was full. I replaced the mag.

The screams had stopped.

I could hear the whine of an air conditioner above me, but no more movement. With the Beretta ready, I moved to the first door in the hall that I'd passed, tried the knob slowly. It gave without resistance, and I went low, pushed it gently open. No one shot at me in response. I peered in, discovered it was a small kitchen, as filthy and potentially unsanitary as the bathroom had been.

I moved to the room from which I'd heard screaming, repeated the procedure, taking the soft entry, slow on the knob, gentle with the door. There was no noise from inside as it swung open. A mattress was on the floor, thin and naked with an old bloodstain at its center, no other furniture, not even a pillow.

There was a girl inside, Pakistani perhaps, not older than thirteen. She huddled in the corner opposite the mattress, in a T-shirt and panties, and when she saw me she wrapped her head in her arms, buried her face against her knees, attempting to disappear.

"It's okay," I whispered. "It's okay."

And because I was a liar and it absolutely wasn't, I moved on.

There was another "bedroom" on the ground floor, this one occupied by two girls. As in the previous room, they were huddled together in fear, the arms of the elder around the shoulders of the younger. The younger appeared about the same age as the Pakistani girl I'd seen, though this one I thought was from India. The older girl looked CIS, maybe Russian or Ukrainian.

She was also visibly pregnant.

"Tiasa," I said. "Tiasa Lagidze."

Nothing in response. Their fear was palpable, it was something I could smell, something I could taste in the stuffy air. I checked the hallway again, looking toward the stairs, straining to hear the sound of any movement from above, then glanced back at the two girls. They were too afraid to even look at me.

"How many?" I asked, then repeated it in Russian. "How many men here? How many keeping you here?"

The pregnant girl raised her eyes. They were big and brown and maybe just a little bit hopeful. She held up her right hand, five fingers splayed.

One left, I thought.

"You're going to hear more shooting." I kept my voice soft, sticking with Russian. "Stay still. I'll come back when it's over."

I shut the door silently, checked the hall again. Above me, a floorboard creaked. The close air and the heat had me perspiring heavily, and I could feel sweat running down my neck, making my glasses slip on my nose. The stairs loomed at the end of the hall, narrow and dangerous and offering me no other choice. Stairs were a trap, one of the few tactical situations where nothing was on your side. They offered no mobility, no scope, no eyelines. The last man was on the floor above me, and he knew, like I knew, that the only way to reach him was the stairs, straight up the mother of all fatal funnels and into a blind turn.

I backed down the hall the direction I had come, watching the stairs until the corner. I turned, stepped over the bodies blocking the door to the front room, entered low. The man in the *dishdasha* was where I'd left him. I sidestepped over to the *sheesha,* lifted it in one hand and dumped the contents of the water pipe on him. He spluttered, gagging.

I put the Beretta to his neck and forced him to his feet. He nearly fell when he tried to put weight on his broken knee, his face creasing with pain.

"Stay silent, you might live through this," I told him.

He bit down on his suffering, nostrils flaring as he fought to control his breathing, jaw clenched so tight I could see the muscles working. As much fear as the girls carried, he doubled it in hatred, and every ounce of that hatred was directed at me.

"We're going upstairs," I whispered to him. "You first."

Carefully, keeping the Beretta on him, we moved back into the inner hall. At the corner, I pulled him around, put him in front of me. He needed a hand on the wall to steady himself.

"Go," I told him. "Keep it slow. Not a word, not a sound."

He looked back at me with my gun, decided that was enough persuasion to do as I said, and began hobbling slowly toward the stairs. I followed a few feet before stopping, keeping distance, letting him lead me.

The stairs were hard for him, and his progress slowed even further. One step at a time, careful, painful, measured. It wasn't that different from how I'd have climbed the stairs, knowing what was waiting for me at the top.

Whoever was up there thought so, too.

The shots came at an angle, blowing through the drywall on the right-hand side, angled down, a long chatter from another assault rifle. Only a few hit the man in the *dishdasha*, and he slammed against the left wall, then tumbled back down the stairs in a heap, head over heels until he was sprawled on the floor, broken and dead.

I brought up the Beretta and waited. I didn't have to wait more than a minute, but it felt longer. Sweat slipped down my back and into my eyes, making them sting. Then I heard the floorboards creaking again, the rustle of movement, and I saw the feet on the stairs, black sneakers. Then the legs, the barrel of an AK, and that was enough for me. I put one from the Beretta into the left sneaker, heard the scream, watched the last man fall face-first down the stairs, onto the body of the man in the *dishdasha*. He'd managed to keep hold of the AK when he fell.

I shot him twice more, and made sure he'd never be able to use it again.

CHAPTER
Sixteen

There were eight girls in all. The eldest of them was around seventeen. The youngest, I think, was eleven. I don't know. I didn't have the heart to ask.

Tiasa wasn't among them.

I went room to room, telling them to get dressed as quickly as they could, trying to get them mobilized. Aside from the pregnant girl, there was another who understood my Russian, and a third girl who could manage in pidgin English. I asked if any of them knew how to drive, and the pregnant girl did.

"Where are you from?" I asked her.

"Volgograd."

I gave her the keys to the Toyota SUV that I'd found on the man in the *dishdasha*.

"Go to the Al Maidan Tower on Al-Maktoum Road," I told her. "It's easy to find, just follow the signs. Go straight there, straight to the Russian Federation Consulate, it's on the third floor. Take all of the girls with you. Tell them where you were, what they did to you. Leave me out of it."

"I understand."

Together, we hustled the girls out of the building, to the Toyota. The camp had begun to stir, and a couple of the men there watched us pass without expression or comment or apparent interest. The girls shuffled, some of them crying. Mostly, they seemed numb, very much in shock.

Before they were all loaded, I stopped one of the girls, the other one who'd understood my Russian. I'd seen her before, on Vladek's BlackBerry, the picture of her smiling as she believed his lies. It hadn't been more than ten days since he'd shipped her to Turkey, but all the same, I had to check the smartphone to be sure.

"Wait," I told her.

She looked at me with alarm, the fear that had begun dissipating instantly in evidence again.

I brought up Tiasa's picture on the BlackBerry. She cringed at the sight of the smartphone in my hand, perhaps recognizing it as Vladek's, perhaps simply because of the association it held. She started to bring a hand to her face, to hide it from the camera, before she realized that I was trying to show her something on the screen.

"This girl," I said. "Do you know her? Have you seen her?"

She shook her head, anxious.

"The man in Georgia," I said. "The man who sold you, he sold her, too. That man can't hurt you. He'll never hurt you again. It's all right, you can tell me the truth."

She bit her lip, then nodded.

"You remember her?"

"I remember her. Tiasa. She was ... she cried all the time."

"I was told she was here, that she came with you and some others to Dubai. Do you know where she is? Do you know where I can find her?"

The girl shook her head.

"You don't know?"

The girl looked to the SUV, where the others were waiting for her to join them. The engine started up. She looked back to me, afraid of telling me something I didn't want to hear.

"She didn't come to Dubai," the girl said.

"You're sure?"

"She didn't come to Dubai."

"Do you know where she went? Do you know what happened to her?"

"Please, mister ..."

"Do you know where they took her?"

"No!" The girl was nearing tears. "No, I don't know, I swear. Please, please can I go? Please can I go now?"

I saw then that she was shivering despite the heat.

I helped her into the SUV. I closed the door. The vehicle pulled out almost immediately.

I looked at the picture of Tiasa Lagidze on the BlackBerry for a few seconds. Then I switched to check for messages. Like my search for Tiasa, the result was identical.

I had nothing.

Absolutely nothing.

CHAPTER
Seventeen

They'd burned my home to the ground.

I sat behind the wheel of the Škoda Danil Joshi had rented all of fifty minutes earlier at the airport in Batumi, listening to the engine idle and the rain beat against the roof, to the whine of the wiper blades swiping at the beads of water trickling down the windshield. It was after midnight, and the only illumination came from the headlights on the car, and while the picture was incomplete, it was enough, and I could feel my pulse beating in my temples.

The fire had burned hot. Blackened concrete broke through the rubble of charred wood and glass, the fractured pieces of the house's foundation. If anyone had come to fight the blaze, they'd come too late. It had been left to burn itself out. The only structure still resembling a structure at all was our little studio. Two of its walls and the roof had gone entirely. One mirror, cracked and charred, still hung within, reflecting light back at me.

The Benz, parked where we always parked it, was a burnt-out husk.

I got out of the car, into air bitter with smoke and the after-taste of gasoline, the stench mixing with the new moisture falling from the sky. The rain was cold, but I didn't much feel it, because I'd seen something on the ground, glittering in head-lights.

Shell casings.

Then I saw the discolored earth, and I knelt and touched it, brought my hand back so I could see my fingers in the light, a thin film of bloody mud on them now. I wiped my hand on my pants leg, standing up again.

Now that I knew what to look for, I was seeing a lot of shell casings, and at least one other patch of ground that might've been a blood spill. This one was much closer to what had once been our front door, and maybe it had come from someone try-ing to get inside.

And maybe it had come from someone trying to get out.

The Benz was a diesel, after all, and that wasn't what I was smelling. I was smelling petrol. I was smelling Molotov cock-tails.

Gasoline burns exceptionally fast, and it burns incredibly hot. Fast enough that two or three or four thrown in the right places would create an instant inferno. Hot enough to bring a building to its foundation. If Miata and Alena had been inside, they wouldn't have had time to do anything much more than flee.

And then shell casings.

It was the Benz that scared me most of all, because it was still here. Whoever had burned our home had lit the car, too, stealing that avenue of escape. Probably had lit it at the same time they'd set fire to the house. So Alena had been here when they came.

It was now almost forty hours since we'd been meant to check in with each other, and still Vladek Karataev's BlackBerry gave me nothing but silence.

I was going to have to look through the ruins, I realized.

I was going to have to look for Alena's body.

After seeing the SUV on its way, I'd headed back inside and, as quickly as I could manage, gone through the rest of the building, looking for anything that might point to Tiasa's whereabouts. It was a fool's errand, and I was rewarded like a fool for it, coming away with nothing. One of the beds in one of the rooms actually had a sheet on it, and I used that to fashion a makeshift sack, loading it with every weapon I'd touched.

The keys to the new BMW sedan had been in the pocket of the last man I checked, the last man I'd killed. No more than ten minutes after seeing the SUV depart, I pulled out, cramming as much distance between myself and the work camp as quickly as I could, speeding back toward Dubai. Given the way most of the drivers handled the road, you couldn't tell I was in a hurry.

Back in the city, I continued past the hotel, turning off Sheikh Zayed and taking Umm Hurair to the Al-Maktoum Bridge, across the Dubai Creek. I turned off again, parking near the Dhow Wharfage. Despite its name, the Dubai Creek is not, in fact, a creek, but rather a major inlet from the Arabian Gulf, deep and wide enough that it effectively cuts the city in half. Traversing it requires the use of one of two bridges, a tunnel, or a ride on an *abra,* one the local water taxis.

I left the keys in the BMW, but took my sack with me, then found a waiting *abra,* piloted by a long, thin, and sandblasted old man. None of my languages worked on him, but he understood both my gestures and the sixty dirham I gave him well enough. We started out, angling more northward, toward the mouth to the Gulf. Once we were about midway across, I dropped the sack overboard. The old pilot watched me without a change of expression or a word. When we made the other side, I gave him another hundred dirham. He said something in Arabic, laughed, and pulled away.

I caught a cab back to the Marina, stopped at the concierge desk on the way through the lobby, and told the impeccably coiffed man working there that I needed the soonest flight I could get back home to Georgia, which was hardly a lie. Then I told him I'd be down within twenty minutes to check out, and he promised me he'd have something by then.

The room was as I'd left it, except that the maid service had come, and all of Kekela's things were gone. None of my belongings looked to have been disturbed, and it surprised me a little bit. It wasn't that I'd expected Kekela to rob me; but given how we'd parted company, and how bad the situation had looked for me, at least to her eyes, I wouldn't have blamed her if she had. Dead men don't need laptops, after all.

Whether she'd left my things alone out of respect for the departed or in the hope that I'd come to collect them, I had no way of knowing. It was unlikely I ever would. I wouldn't be seeing her again.

While I was settling the bill, the concierge presented me with the reservations he'd been able to find, apologizing profusely. The best he'd come up with was a flight from Dubai to

Tbilisi, via Istanbul. That was workable, though not ideal. What was even less ideal was that the flight departed Dubai at a quarter of three in the morning. I thanked him, headed to the airport, where I confirmed that the earliest I'd be leaving the UAE for Turkey was at two forty-five. I booked a new connection from Istanbul, this time directly to Batumi. I spent the next eight hours checking my phone for messages and worrying, which had turned into the same thing.

I managed about an hour of sleep on the flight to Turkey. I didn't manage any on the flight to Georgia.

The journey from Dubai to what had once been my home took nineteen hours. It wouldn't have mattered if it had taken nineteen minutes.

I had arrived too late.

For a long time, I don't know how long, I stood in the rain, trying to get myself to move, to do what had to be done.

I just couldn't do it.

At some point, I found myself standing in what remained of the studio, looking at myself in the blurry and broken mirror. The heat had made fractures in the glass, including a major one that bisected my reflection, splitting my head into two broken pieces, out of alignment, out of proportion. The fissure ran down, tearing off a portion of my neck before jinking again, cutting neatly across my chest. As a visual metaphor, I thought it was spot-on.

Vladek Karataev's phone was ringing.

I took it from my pocket, stared at the display telling me that some Unknown Caller wanted me to answer. One of Vladek's business associates, maybe, calling to gloat. A wrong number.

I keyed the phone to answer, put it to my ear.

Her voice came soft and anxious, her strange mutt accent of all the languages the Soviets had made her learn. She was speaking English.

"Are you all right?" I had no voice to answer, and she asked it again. "Atticus? Are you all right?"

"I am now," I told Alena.

CHAPTER
Eighteen

Kobuleti's chief of police, Mgelika Iashvili, lived by himself in a sweet-looking cottage off the town's main street, facing the beach and the Black Sea. In daylight, it was a brightly painted, almost garish, domicile, in baby blue and pine green with bright orange trim, colors meant, I presumed, to foster a sense of joyful beach festivities. At night, in the rain, it was monochrome and ugly, a gingerbread house that had been robbed of its treats.

I parked my rental across the street, killed the engine, and eyeballed the block. Most of the houses along the beach were rented to tourists during the summer season, now at its height. Lights burned in a few of them, including at least one in Mgelika

Iashvili's home. By the clock in the car, it was three minutes to one in the morning, and the rain had finally stopped.

I got out, made my way across the street. There was nobody about, and the only thing I was hearing was the rustle of the Black Sea. A weak dome of light rose up from the south, where the clubs and cafés kept their doors open all hours. When I strained for it, I could catch an occasional thread of music through the noise of the tide coming in. With the departure of the rain, the summer warmth tried to return. If I hadn't been soaked to the skin, I might've been comfortable.

His car was parked out front of the house, rainwater dripping slowly off the fenders. I squatted down and took a look beneath, and the ground below seemed as wet as everywhere else. I put a hand to the hood, felt it cool, though it might've been the rain as much as time that was responsible for that.

I went to the door and raised my hand to knock, then saw it was already slightly ajar. I checked the street again, and nothing had changed, and I didn't see any vehicles parked nearby other than my own, and I didn't know what to make of it. Paranoia and common sense began to wrestle around in my skull.

Paranoia won, and I prodded the door open further with my foot, then slipped through as quietly as I could. The entrance dumped straight into a small living room, the layout not dissimilar to what my house had been. Nothing looked to be out of place, and it was clear that Iashvili had a taste for both the modern and the expensive.

I moved forward, passing the open door to the bedroom. Music was playing softly inside, some jazz fusion. When I looked I saw that the bed was unmade and empty. I held there for a second, listening for movement that wasn't my own, anything that would tell me if there was another body present, and nothing came back. He'd been here, had been here recently, but there was no sign of the man.

At the far end of the kitchen was the back door, ajar the way the front had been. An empty bottle of wine stood in the sink, along with a set of dirty dishes. Nothing was broken, nothing was stained with blood.

I went out the back, down a short run of stairs and onto the rocky beach, wondering if the chief of police had been expecting me to come calling.

"Where are you?" Alena had asked.

"Kobuleti."

Her inhale was sharp in my ear. "It's not safe. Get out of there."

I tried not to laugh, but the relief at simply hearing her voice made it impossible. I'm sure I sounded just shy of hysterical. "No kidding. Where are you?"

"Sochi."

"Russia."

"I had to take the ferry from Poti. I'm heading west tomorrow, I have a room booked at the Londonskaya, in Odessa, name Angelika Radkova." She paused for breath, and I realized that tension was releasing for her much as it had for me. "Meet me there."

"I will," I said.

For a few seconds, we listened to the sound of each other breathing, the proof of life.

"What happened?" I asked.

"Men came. Three of them, just after sunrise yesterday. Iashvili called to warn me. He woke me up. Miata and I would have died in the fire if he hadn't."

"He warned you?"

"Yes."

"They weren't looking for you," I said.

"Whether for me or for you, it doesn't matter. They came to kill whoever they found."

"Either I owe Mgelika thanks, or he owes me an explanation."

"Or both."

I had stepped out of the ruined studio as we'd been speaking, now took another look around the place that had been our home for almost six years. I'd liked Georgia; I'd liked Kobuleti; I'd liked it enough that I'd been willing to spend the rest of my life here with Alena.

We'd never come back, I realized.

"I'll want an explanation before I consider gratitude," I said. "He knew they were coming. He just as likely pointed them at you."

"The Londonskaya," Alena said. "In Odessa."

"Tomorrow night."

"Did you find her? Was she in Dubai?"

"No."

"I'm sorry."

"I'll see you tomorrow night," I said.

"Yes," she said. "Please."

He was on the beach, maybe twenty meters from his home, and when I first saw him I thought he was dead, facedown near the edge of the tide.

Then I saw he was moving.

Then I saw the woman he was moving with.

She saw me first, but that was mostly because she was on her back, and by the time she noticed me, I was practically standing on top of them. When she saw me, she screamed.

Iashvili stopped mid-stroke, looking down at her, confused,

then up to see me. It was hard to make out his expression, but I was pretty sure alarmed was a good place to start. He scrambled backward, onto his haunches and then onto his backside. He still had the muscles of a weight lifter, the solid core, barrel chest, and girder-thick arms. The woman rolled, gathering the blanket she'd been lying on around her.

"Hi, Chief." I spoke in Georgian. "We need to talk."

"David! Jesus Christ!"

I turned to the woman, who'd succeeded in concealing most of herself with the blanket. It was hard to tell, but I put her in her forties, attractively so.

"Mgelika and I have some things to discuss," I told her. "Why don't you go wait for him in the house?"

She looked at Iashvili, still sitting on his ass on the rocky beach. He hadn't taken his eyes off me. " 'Lika?"

The chief and I stared at each other, and then he reached for his shorts, discarded nearby, saying, "Yeah, go back inside, Vicca. Open another bottle of wine, okay? I won't be long."

Vicca looked at me doubtfully, then back to Iashvili. "You're sure?"

He was standing now, shorts firmly in place. He held out his hand to her, and she took it, allowed him to help her to her feet.

"I'm sure," he said, and he kissed her cheek for good measure. "Won't be long," he promised.

We watched as she worked her way back to the house, saw her silhouette pass through the doorway. She looked back at us once more before going inside, and Iashvili gave her a reassuring wave.

Only when she was out of sight did he turn his attention back to me.

"You going to kill me now?" Mgelika Iashvili asked me.

"You going to give me a reason to?"

He considered, then shook his head. After a half second, he gestured along the edge of the water, and I nodded, and we began walking, side by side.

"Before you went down to Batumi, I never had reason to fear you," the chief said.

"And now you do?"

"I know what you did there. I know it was you. I can't prove it, I wouldn't even if I could. But I know you killed that fuck Karataev."

"It was Karataev who bought you off?" I asked. "Paid you to say that Bakhar had killed himself and his family?"

"He gave me a choice." Iashvili stooped, scooping up one of the wave-worn rocks from the beach without breaking stride. He threw it overhand out at the water. "I could take their money. Or they could kill me and make it look like I did it."

"You're the police."

"And who the fuck are you?" He glared at me. "Who the fuck are you telling me that? You killed four men in Batumi and fuck knows how many more wherever you've been. And you killed that other one, too, right? That one of Karataev's we found at Bakhar Lagidze's home when we found his family."

I shrugged.

"So don't fucking condescend to me, David-Mercer-whoever-the-fuck-you-really-are. You're not from this place; you think you know, but you don't. People who do the right thing, you've seen what happens to them. People like Bakhar."

The logic seemed circular to me, but I kept myself from saying so. We resumed walking.

"I did you a *favor*," Iashvili told me. "They showed up, fucking put a gun in my mouth, asked where the fuck you lived, where David Mercer fucking lived. You don't lie to people like that. You lie to people like that, they come back and make sure you take a long time dying."

"I know."

"As soon as they left me, I called your wife, I called Yeva, to warn her. You know why I did that?"

"So you could sleep at night?"

"So this wouldn't happen, this thing right here, right now! You understand what I'm telling you? I did you a fucking favor!"

"For all the wrong reasons."

"Jesus on the cross, you judge me? She's still alive, right? Yeva's still alive!"

"Who were they?"

"The ones your wife fucking killed?" He shook his head, morbidly amused. "Is that what you two do? Between teaching ballet and jogging through town, I mean, is that it? You go around killing people?"

"Sometimes I try to get in a little light reading. I like the works of Stephen Crane and Tim O'Brien."

He didn't laugh.

"Were they friends of his?" I asked. "Of Karataev's?"

"Man like that didn't have friends. He had partners, he had colleagues, people he made business with. That's who they were. I told you when you left for Batumi that day, I told you that you had no idea who Lagidze was, what he was into. Now you know, but I think you still don't, not at all."

"Which is it?"

He stopped again, turned to face me. We'd covered a fair stretch of the beach, his house lost behind us. The clouds had blown through enough to allow pieces of the night sky to sneak through. There was no moon.

"This isn't some American gangster movie bullshit," Iashvili said. "There isn't some Don Corleone like that, someone sitting at the top, someone giving the orders. This is only about money, about business, that's all it ever is about.

Nothing else matters. Russian mob works with Albanians, Italian Mafia works with the fucking Roma. South Ossetians work with Georgians like Bakhar Lagidze, and Georgians like Bakhar work with Russians like Karataev. Doesn't matter who hates who, who wants to kill who, Muslims, Christians, new capitalists or old communists, doesn't matter. Everyone's involved if there's money, and the money is the thing keeping them together.

"You want me to give you a name or several names, it doesn't matter. You fucked their business, you've cost them their money. They don't allow that. So they come looking for you, to kill you, and while they're at it, they'll kill your wife and your dog and anyone you talked to if they can, they *don't care*. You cost them money, and now you're marked, David fucking Mercer. It doesn't matter how long it takes, how many times it takes, they will remember. And eventually, they will find you, and they will kill your Yeva, and they will kill you, too. You're walking dead."

He went silent, shaking his head and turning away, as if I was incapable of grasping the concepts he'd just laid out. Everything he'd just said, the prophecy he'd issued of my and Alena's eventual fate, had been delivered without rancor. It was the world the way he saw it, and, unfortunately, the way he saw it was a lot like the way I was beginning to see it, too.

"They will do to you what they did to Bakhar and his family," Mgelika Iashvili told me.

"Not if I do it to them first," I said.

CHAPTER
Nineteen

She had been sleeping, Alena told me, when Mgelika Iashvili called to warn her that there were three men driving out to the house. It had been poor slumber, the way she described it, the kind where you're aware that you're sleeping badly, but not awake enough to do anything about it. It had taken four rings before she'd managed to pull herself to the phone, groggy and cotton-mouthed. The clock on my nightstand said it was seven minutes past six in the morning.

"I was certain it was you," Alena told me as we sat together on the bed in her room at the Londonskaya. She was leaning back against my chest, warm and strong, my arms around her. I was having trouble letting her go. "Calling early again."

"Good that it wasn't," I said, thinking that a busy signal then would have cost her her life.

She'd been surprised to hear the chief's voice, enough so that it took her precious seconds to realize who was speaking.

"Do you hear me, Yeva?" Iashvili was telling her. "They're on their way to your home now, they will kill you if they find you there. You have to get out. You have to get out now."

Groggy or not, that had been all it took.

Alena dropped the phone, not bothering to hang up, and rolled out of bed, reaching for the nightstand and the Walther P99 she kept there. It was her favorite pistol, at least for the time being, and the one she felt most innately comfortable with, and that was why she kept it close. She was on her feet and readying a round when Miata and the security system both went off at the same time. For Miata, that meant a frantic scrabbling at the bedroom door. For the security system, that meant a smoke detector–like shrieking that filled the house.

With the gun in her hand, she moved into the hall, stopping long enough at the linen cabinet to yank the power cords from each laptop and silence the alarm. The sound of it was loud enough to be heard outside, and now, working only from Iashvili's warning, she was desperate to maintain some element of surprise.

"They'd come early in the morning," Alena said. "I had thought that meant they would try to breach, to take me in the house. If that was the case, I thought it best to remain inside and let them come to me. I thought my knowing the floor plan and them not knowing it, that would be an advantage."

With the silence restored, she'd held in the hallway, putting one hand on Miata's back, to keep him beside her. She could feel the Doberman trembling anxiously, eager to move forward, but heard nothing from outside. She spared a moment to curse herself for disconnecting both computers from power, because in doing so, she'd cut off her own access to the external cameras, and had no way to visualize what was happening.

Then she heard the breaking glass and the rush of air being sucked into sudden flame, and she smelled the gasoline and the smoke. She realized she'd been wrong; they weren't coming inside.

They were going to burn her out.

The house had been constructed out of wood when first erected, and all our efforts to restore the place in the past years had been in keeping with that. It was summer in Kobuleti, and while sea damp could chill us to the bone during the winter, things had begun drying out since the late spring. The fire had everything it needed, and it took it all greedily. By the time Alena had realized what had happened, the temperature was already rocketing, and smoke was beginning to lead the flames inside.

Her mistake having been made, she moved immediately to correct it, releasing her hold on Miata and sprinting for the back door of the house as quickly as her weakened left leg would allow. It was a calculated risk; the fire had come so quickly upon the arrival of the car, Alena was gambling that no one had circled around the back yet. She cut through the living room, Miata at her heels, threw open the door, then held long enough to check her sight lines and assure herself she wouldn't be running into any bullets. She didn't see anything. Behind and above her, she could feel the flames, and the smoke was already making her eyes tear, her lungs labor and burn.

Again leading Miata, Alena started out, planning another sprint for the concealment of the treeline. She'd just begun out the door when she caught movement in her periphery, coming around the left side of the house, managed to arrest herself and veer off for the woodpile. A chatter of submachine-gun fire chased after her, and she slid as much as tumbled into cover, listening as bullets buried themselves in the logs and earth.

For a moment, then, she was certain she'd been trapped. The pile of wood had been stacked a meter away from the side of the house, perhaps even less, an attempt to give it shelter from inclement weather beneath the eaves. There was no immediate cover to either side, and, at her back, the house was rapidly becoming engulfed in flames, fire now racing up the walls, close enough that the heat had gone from uncomfortable to painful. Things had moved quickly enough she'd had no time to dress, still in the tank top and underpants she'd worn to bed, and she could feel her bare skin beginning to burn.

Another burst from the submachine gun chewed up the logs, and she heard shouting from the other side of the house, and then from the man gunning for her in response. They were speaking Russian, and the one who had her pinned down was shouting for one of his friends to come around the side, that he had her cornered. There was a percussive bang from the front side of the house, almost an explosion, and Alena realized that the Benz had been set alight, too, that one of the tires had burst from the heat.

She also realized that Miata wasn't with her, and when she looked, she could see the Doberman still holding in the back door, looking at her. She gave him a hand sign, ordering him to come to her, and the dog started to do as commanded and then, to her horror, broke off into a run, and she realized what he was doing and shouted at him to stop. She heard the submachine gun rattle off another burst as she spun out of the cover of the woodpile and fired two double-taps at the man trying to kill her. All four bullets hit, and the man collapsed.

Fast as she'd been, she hadn't been fast enough. She got to her feet, racing to where Miata lay in the open ground between the burning house and the treeline, where the dog had fallen halfway to target. The pool of blood spreading beneath him was enough to make her certain he was dead, but as she reached him, Miata managed to lift his head, tongue lolling, chest heaving, finding her.

Knowing it would get her killed, she stopped long enough to pick him up anyway, then ran for the trees beyond the man she'd just dropped.

"At least one of them was coming from the other direction," Alena told me. "Coming to try and flank me, as his friend had told him to. I couldn't leave Miata lying there. I couldn't do it. What if he'd decided to finish him?"

I nodded my understanding, thinking but not saying that she'd been luckier than she'd ever had a right to be, something she already knew, anyway. I also didn't say that carrying eighty-seven pounds of Doberman in her arms while being shot at was possibly the most stupid, foolish, and noble thing she'd ever done in her life.

She and Miata were almost to the trees when the second man, the one who'd come around the right side of the house to flank her, opened fire at her exposed back. He, too, had come with a submachine gun, and the burst he laid down was long, which cost him accuracy. Two rounds scored, one creasing her right thigh an inch and a half below the hip, the other cutting a trough out of her upper arm, also on the right side, across the tricep. Between her perpetually weakened left leg and that, she went down, dog and mistress tumbling together through branches and brush. She scrambled herself behind the thickest tree she could find, pulling Miata after her by his paws. She had no idea how bad off Miata was, and wasn't even sure how wounded she was, herself, but she was seeing a lot of blood. More bullets cut through the woods, snapping branches and showering pine needles around them.

The house was engulfed entirely in flames now, and the roar of the fire was tremendous, creating its own breeze. She could hear glass shattering inside, but no more shouting, and she risked a low peek past a tree, trying to spot the new shooter. He'd retreated, backing off from the inferno he'd created with his friends, and Alena tried to capitalize on that, firing twice at him and missing both times.

I was staring at her, and Alena grew indignant.

"I'd been hit in the arm," she reminded me. "I was doing the best I could."

The man lay down a return burst to cover his retreat, but it was suppressing more than targeting, and only succeeded in hurting more trees.

For a second, then, Alena had a moment to consider her options, and not one of them was to her liking. She spared a moment to assure herself that her wounds were minor, or at least relatively so, then put her hands to Miata. The dog was not do-ing well, his breathing rapid and ragged, his eyes half-closed. She tried to stop the bleeding, but realized she had nothing to stop it with, and if she didn't do something soon, Miata would hemorrhage out. Taking him up again and making a run through the woods wouldn't work; even if she could make it through to the road on the far side, near the Lagidze house, the men remaining had a car, and they had automatic weapons. Trying to evade them now would only make sure she died winded and tired. And the Benz, she was now positive, was a to-tal loss.

Which meant she had to take their vehicle, and that meant she had to take them.

She gave Miata a kiss on the muzzle, promising him she'd return, then made her way back to the treeline, dripping blood from the wounds on her arm and leg. The man she'd killed was only a meter or so away, but she passed him by without stop-ping, staying in the trees as she made for the right side of the house as fast as she dared, as fast as her weakened leg would al-low, following the direction the last shooter had retreated. She took the corner wide, still in the woods, and saw no one.

Here, she decided that she needed to rely on speed more than stealth next, and to do that, she required open ground. She had just come out of the woods, preparing to make a run for the corner, when she heard a spasmodic crack and then, im-mediately, an even more tremendous bang as, inside the house, the major support beams gave way, one after another. The roof collapsed in a shower of sparks, splinters, and embers. Burning debris pelted her even as more heat blossomed, somehow more intense than before. She recoiled involuntarily, bringing her right arm up to shield her eyes.

When Alena brought it down again, she saw that the walls

had collapsed along with the roof, and she was looking across the ruins and the flames at an angle, to the front of the house. Through the rippling air she could see two men, the one who'd fired at her last and another, each of them likewise reacting to the destruction of the building.

And they could see her.

She brought the Walther up, moving to her left as she did so, firing on the man nearest to her, the one she'd dogged around the side of the building. She shot him twice, adjusted while still in motion, and fired off another double-tap at the last man standing. Once again she missed, or thought she did, because he returned fire with a submachine gun of his own, and somehow managed to miss her completely.

Then he sagged to his knees, and pitched forward, and she realized that she had succeeded in hitting him after all.

Skirting the ruins of the burning house, she moved to each of the two men in turn, dumping an additional round into their heads. The car they'd arrived in was an Audi sedan, a new one, parked close to the mouth of the road, perhaps ten meters back, most likely to spare it from the fire they'd known they were going to start. She searched each of the men, finding no keys. She emptied each of their wallets of all the bills she could find, stuffing them down the front of her underpants, then ran back to the first man she'd dropped. He had the keys, and more cash, and she took both, as well as the denim jacket he wore and his belt, for good measure.

Miata was unconscious but breathing when she got back to him. With the jacket and the belt, she fashioned a pressure dressing as best as she could around the Doberman, then lifted him and carefully brought him to the Audi. She laid him across the backseat, then climbed behind the wheel and spun the car around, chewing dirt and gravel with the tires, leaving our still-burning home behind.

■ ■ ■

She headed north, pushing the Audi as fast as she dared given the road, covering the almost fifty kilometers to Poti in thirteen minutes. She couldn't stay in Kobuleti, she knew, and heading south to Batumi had instinctively seemed like a bad idea; I had left bodies in Batumi, and she was certain the men who had come to Kobuleti and what had happened there ten days earlier were connected. Batumi was out.

She needed a doctor or a vet, and she needed one fast, and that left Poti as the only option. So she raced along the coast road, swerving around the sparse early morning traffic and flooring it whenever there was opportunity, all the while talking to Miata, all the while telling him that she would take care of him, the way she had before.

For Alena, the situation had kindled a disturbing sense of déjà vu. Miata had become her dog in very similar circumstances, when she had taken money from one man who dealt and packaged large amounts of cocaine to kill another who did the exact same thing. The target in question had guarded his workplace with a variety of booby traps and dogs. The booby traps were one thing, but the dogs had posed a problem entirely of their own. Each had been treated in the same way, abused and beaten, their vocal cords severed. Dogs need their voices, and denying them it can drive them mad, which, of course, was just what the dealer in question had desired.

When Alena had come for his reckoning, she'd had to deal with the dogs first, and most of them she'd been forced to kill. After all had been said and done, only Miata was still alive, though wounded. Then, like now, she had loaded him into a car—a Mazda Miata—and rushed him to a doctor.

■ ■ ■

It was twenty minutes to seven in the morning when she arrived in Poti, and she lost another ten minutes driving the city's confusing streets, desperately trying to find someone to help her. The first two civilians she saw fled from her when she stopped, and it wasn't until after the second that she realized why, how she must've looked to them, stained with blood and smoke and sweat, in her underwear, the wheezing Doberman across the backseat of the car.

The third time she asked for help, she held out a fistful of the bills she'd taken off the dead men, and that helped overcome fear long enough for her to acquire directions to a veterinarian. By the time she actually reached the doctor's home-slash-office it was three minutes to seven, and Miata's breathing had gone from labored and rapid to shallow and dangerously slow.

She parked the car literally in front of the house, less than a meter from the door, leaning repeatedly and hard on the horn before getting out of the vehicle. The man who emerged from the house was bleary with sleep, silver-haired and stocky.

"My dog's been shot," Alena told him, already opening the back door.

The doctor balked, not unreasonably, given what he was seeing. Alena lifted Miata out of the car, brushed past him, heading inside. There was an examination room just through the door to her left. The man followed her, watched as she lay Miata gingerly on the table.

"Help him," she told the doctor. "Please."

Then she went back outside to the car. She was gone less than thirty seconds, and when she came back, she saw that the vet had unfastened the belt around the makeshift bandage, had begun examining the wound. Then he noticed she'd returned and said, "It's not good. I don't know if I can save him."

"You can."

The vet saw the Walther that Alena had just retrieved

from the Audi. Whether it was the sight of the gun, or her tone of voice, or both, or neither, the man hesitated for only a second before setting to work, quickly trying to save the Doberman's life.

"I didn't point it at him," Alena hastened to clarify. "I never pointed the gun at him."

I told her that given how she must've looked at the time, she damn well knew that showing the gun to him was more than enough. She shrugged, then continued.

For the first couple of minutes while the vet struggled to get Miata stabilized, Alena did nothing but stand there, watching. The adrenaline was dropping away like a wave retreating from the shore, uncovering all the aches and sores it had been concealing, the searing pain from the wounds on her arm and leg. She was afraid to sit down, afraid to leave the room to tend to her own needs, suspicious that the vet would capitalize on her absence.

After several minutes, the vet said, "I have to operate on your dog."

"Go ahead."

"I'll need you to help me."

"Tell me."

The man looked at her. She thought he was in his fifties, perhaps. The gun in her hand made her feel guilty, the lack of clothing made her feel ashamed.

"You have to get clean first," the vet told her. "There's a bathroom in the back, and some clothes in my daughter's room. Wash up, then come back."

She didn't move.

"Did you do this to him?" the vet asked, sharply.

"No." The question confused her at first, and then she remembered the gun again. "No! He was trying to protect me."

"Then you have no reason to fear me." The vet indicated a roll of gauze on one of the nearby tables, a pile of bandages. "Take these, get clean. Hurry."

She did as instructed, using the bathroom first to hastily wash herself off. The bleeding on her arm and leg resumed when she went to clean the wounds, and she bandaged herself as best as she was able. The daughter's room, she thought, hadn't seen use in quite some time, and the clothing she found there seemed to bear that out. She pulled on a pair of pants that were both too short and too wide for her, secured them in place with a beaded belt. She stuck the Walther in her waistband, at the front.

When she returned, the vet was still attending Miata, now delivering plasma to the dog through an IV he'd set up. He acknowledged Alena's return, then told her to come and stand beside him.

"Do what I tell you, when I tell you."

With Alena assisting him, he began to operate.

As I was walking into a brothel in the desert outside Dubai, Alena was changing Miata's IV in Poti. While I was showing a frightened young woman Tiasa Lagidze's picture, she was holding a clamp while the vet pulled bullet fragments from Miata's liver. While I was checking out of the Marina, she was watching the vet stitch our dog closed once more.

"He'll live," the vet told her. He pulled his bloodstained gloves from his hands and threw them into the trash beneath the sink. "But he'll be weeks, if not months, to recover from this. How old is he?"

"I don't know," Alena told him. "Ten? Maybe older."

"He's an old dog."

She nodded, then said, "I have money. I will pay you."

"If you like."

Alena fumbled cash from where she'd moved it to the pockets of her borrowed pants. She hadn't taken time to count it, to really examine it at all. She guessed she was holding somewhere in the neighborhood of several hundred euros. She gave him two hundred of them, and the vet took the money without comment.

"We have to go," she told him.

"I would caution against moving him. You both can stay here awhile longer."

The offer was a tempting one, Alena told me, an extremely tempting one. The vet clearly lived alone, and no one had come calling during the course of the operation, which led her to conclude that he didn't get much in the way of clients or visitors. Having trusted him this far, trusting him further would have been easy.

The problem was that she had no way of knowing who else might be hunting for her, if anyone else would be coming at all. Given how she'd departed Kobuleti, given that it had been the chief of police who had warned her, if there were more hunters on the trail, it wouldn't take them long to expand their search to Poti. The last thing she wanted was another fight. The second to last thing, at that moment, was to bring such a fight to the doorstep of the man who'd helped her.

"You're very kind," Alena told the vet. "But we can't."

He sighed, then turned to one of his cabinets and began

assembling gauze and bandages, putting them into an empty cardboard box. When he was finished, he handed it to her, everything Alena needed to make replacement dressings for Miata's—and her own—wounds.

"Simple food for him for a while," he said. "Lots of water. Watch for infection. He won't want to move about, which is good. You must let him rest."

"I will. Thank you."

The vet sighed again, looked at the dog sleeping on the table in front of them.

"I will help you carry him to your car."

There was an overnight ferry from Poti to Sochi scheduled to leave at six that evening, and for extra you could get your own room. Alena bought a ticket for herself and then bribed the clerk to allow Miata on board. She bought herself a jacket, a backpack, and several bottles of water, and at five she carried Miata, still drugged and sleeping, to their tiny, run-down little cabin. She set him on the fold-down bed, changed his dressings, and waited for the ferry to depart. Six o'clock came and went, and then seven, and then eight, and just as Alena was beginning to think that this wasn't simply engine trouble but maybe something more, perhaps the occupying Russians flexing their muscles, the ferry went into motion, and they set sail across the Black Sea.

She lay down beside Miata, feeling his heart beating, listening to him breathing, and for the first time since the phone had rung that morning, she allowed herself to relax. That was when she remembered that she'd missed our check-in, and realizing that put the rest of her problems into sharp focus.

Of the money she'd taken off the dead men, two hundred

and sixteen euros remained. She had no phone and no immediate access to one. She had no credit cards and no documentation. Of the cash she carried, she knew most of it would be required simply to bribe her way into Sochi.

In Sochi, she would find a phone. She would call Sargenti, and he would wire money, and she would find a place for her and Miata to hide.

Then she would call me.

And realizing there was nothing else she could do for the time being, she forced herself to fall asleep, one hand on the Walther she'd snuck on board in the crotch of her too short and too wide pants, the other on Miata's flank.

CHAPTER
Twenty

Miata licked my hand, then, exhausted from the effort, dropped his muzzle back to the blanket he lay upon and shut his eyes once more. I stroked his neck, scratched behind his ears, then rose and crossed the expansive room back to where Alena sat on the bed, knees drawn to her chest, watching me. She'd purchased clothes that fit, Levi's and a black T-shirt, her feet bare. The bandage on her upper arm peeked out from beneath the sleeve, fresh white gauze that still smelled sterile.

"Did you speak to Iashvili?" she asked.

"Oh yeah." I moved to the window, parting the curtains enough to look out. It was after midnight, and the traffic on Primorksy Boulevard was light. Somewhere nearby, I had been informed, were the famous Potemkin Steps, but if they were visible from where I was standing, I didn't see them. I let the curtains fall back.

"Did he know who they were?"

"Business associates of the men who took Tiasa."

"The men you killed in Batumi."

"That would be them, yeah."

"He had no names?"

"He told me the names didn't matter." I moved to the bed, sat down beside her and began unlacing my boots. "He says they'll try again."

"That seems possible."

I pulled my boots free, set them together on the floor, then flopped back on the bed and stared up at the ceiling. The ceilings in the Londonskaya were high, easily fourteen feet, painted yellow-gold. The hotel was Old World, built in the late 1860s, one of the finest in all of Odessa. I was pretty sure the chandelier hanging in the center of the room was real crystal and not simply cut glass.

After a moment, Alena lay down, as well. "You haven't told me about Dubai."

"It wasn't good."

"I would like to hear it."

I told her, and she listened, and when I was done she didn't speak for a long time.

Then she asked, "Did you sleep with her? Kekela?"

I turned enough to look at her. She didn't move, her face in profile.

"You really have to ask?"

She closed her eyes, then shook her head once, slightly.

"But you asked anyway."

"I apologize," she said.

I sat up, angry, knowing I should let it go but not wanting to. "Why would you ask me that? Why the hell would you ask me that?"

Her eyes remained closed, and her mouth went tight. "I apologize."

"I don't want you to apologize, I want to know why you would even think that."

She didn't say anything.

I got up again, agitated. "You're the one lying to me, I'm not lying to you."

That brought her back, and she pushed herself up enough to rest on her elbows. "I haven't lied to you."

"I know you didn't go to Tbilisi to meet Nicholas," I said. "So, yeah, you did lie to me."

Her expression washed out, turning neutral. She moved slowly to sit fully upright, her feet on the floor, her hands at her side. She was watching Miata, once again asleep.

"Yes, I did." She moved her gaze to me. "I went to see a doctor."

I stared at her. "And you couldn't tell me that? If you wanted to look into another surgery on your leg, you could have told me that. We could go back to Switzerland, or Germany; there are better places for that than Tbilisi."

"It's not my leg. I'm at thirteen weeks."

"You're at thirteen weeks of what?" I asked.

She stared at me like I was an idiot. Since I honest to God had no idea what she was talking about, I stared right back at her, waiting for an explanation.

"I'm thirteen weeks pregnant, Atticus," she said.

I kept staring at her, still waiting for an explanation, because I was sure I hadn't heard *that* right. "What?"

"I'm pregnant."

The words rolled around my head for a few seconds.

"Say something."

"I . . ."

"You what?"

". . . thirteen weeks?"

"Fourteen now, I think."

I went back to her side. The way I was feeling, oddly enough, reminded me of how I'd felt in the shower when I'd returned from Batumi after Vladek Karataev had died, but without the dry heaves. I took off my glasses, rubbed my eyes. I put my glasses on again.

"Why didn't you tell me?" I asked her.

"Fears." She was looking at Miata again, not at me.

"More than one?"

She almost laughed. "Too many to count."

"I'm listening."

"We never even talked about it, not once. It was never something we'd even discussed, it had never seemed a possibility." Alena took a deep breath, let it out slowly. "I lived my life from the moment the Soviets took me out of the orphanage in Magadan until the moment I met you believing I would live a life alone. That was simply the way it was. Twenty-five years, I was alone, and that was fine, because they made me someone who was supposed to be that way. I was supposed to be alone, always, until I was dead."

She turned to meet my eyes, then, and she hadn't been lying at all. She was scared, and I could see it.

"Then I met you, and you loved me, and I will never, ever know why. And I am not alone with you, even when we are apart. I could not have allowed myself to imagine it, you see? More than I would have dreamed, if I had been allowed to dream. And to have a child with you, to be a mother?"

She laughed, not because it was funny, but because, I think, the irony was so strong it actually hurt her.

"Me? A mother?"

I thought about her with Tiasa, the care she'd shown her, the time she'd given her. The way they had talked when they thought I couldn't hear them. The way Alena had taught her, the tenderness she'd failed to hide behind not-quite-stern-enough rebukes. The way they had played.

"I think," I said, "that you could be a very good mother."

She blinked at me, her face smoothing. "I didn't think you would want it. I didn't think you would want me to have a baby."

"I don't want you to have *a* baby," I told her. "I want you to have *our* baby."

Then I put my arms around her, and I laid her down on the bed, and tried to show her just how much I meant it.

She was still sleeping when I awoke the next morning, and I let her be. Miata was awake, and up, though he seemed unsteady on his feet, and I dressed and took him out of the hotel for a very short walk, just long enough for him to relieve himself. He was slower on the way back, and when we returned to the room he went straight to his blanket and curled up on it once again. I put some water in one of the bowls Alena had secured for him, and put some kibble in the other. He didn't seem to have much appetite, but he drank the water readily enough.

I got cleaned up and prepared for the day ahead, thinking that I didn't know what the day ahead would bring. I knew enough about human trafficking to know that Ukraine wasn't exactly the safest place for us to be hiding at the moment, but then again, fleeing to Canada didn't seem to be an immediate option, either.

I went to the desk, took out my laptop, and opened up the files I'd taken from Vladek's BlackBerry. He had contacts in Ukraine, it seemed, but whether or not any were in Odessa, I couldn't tell. Flipping through the address book on my screen, I saw Arzu Kaya's name again.

It had to have been he who'd pointed Vladek Karataev's friends at Alena, perhaps hoping he'd been pointing them at me. It had to have been he and not, as I'd begun to speculate, Zviadi. Zviadi had never known my name. But Arzu had dealt with David Mercer, and David Mercer had been known to live in Kobuleti.

Arzu was the only person I could think of who knew where Tiasa Lagidze had been sent. Hell, he could've held her back in Turkey, I could've been within a meter of her when I'd visited Trabzon, and I would never have even known it. But whether Tiasa was still in Trabzon or had been sold somewhere else, I was sure of one thing: Arzu was my only lead, the only chance I had left to find Tiasa Lagidze.

This morning marked two weeks, exactly, since Bakhar Lagidze's family had been slaughtered in their home. Fourteen days exactly, since Tiasa had been pulled from her bed and sold into slavery, a child bought and sold to pay for the sins of her father. I thought about Kekela and the girls she had led me to in Dubai, the abuse they had to have suffered in that foul, over-heated brothel. It didn't matter who they were, who they had been, not any of them. No one deserved that.

No one.

I shut the top on the laptop, stared at the little light on the front of the machine as it began to pulse softly. Behind me, I heard Alena shifting in the bed. She was still asleep, her lips slightly parted, one arm drawn across her belly. For the moment, there was no worry on her face, just the peace of her slumber. When I'd first come to know her, her sleep had been plagued with nightmares, the subconscious upthrust of every pain she buried while awake. Over the last years they had come with less and less frequency, until, now, it seemed they were lost to history.

I was, in so many ways, a bad man. I had killed people, and I knew I was going to do it again. Sometimes, even oftentimes, it was in self-defense, or at least in situations where I could rationalize it as such after the fact. But once already in my life I had committed a murder, plain and simple, as calculatedly cold-blooded a killing as any Alena herself had performed while under the Soviet yoke or after, when she'd sold the only skills she had. I was not, by any stretch of my imagination, a good person.

Tiasa Lagidze hadn't known that the day in our little studio when she asked me to dance. She'd thought I was nice, and safe, and kind, and when she gave me a kiss on the cheek after we were done and then turned away from me, she'd forgotten one wall was all mirrors, and that I could see she was blushing.

She was alive, I was sure of it. Her worth as a commodity required it, and that was how whoever saw her now imagined her, the same way Arzu had done. Merchandise. She'd been turned into a consumer good, a color television, a stereo, a car.

From behind me, in the bed, Alena said, "Where will you look next?"

I turned. She lay exactly as she had before, only now her eyes were open. I left the desk and went to her side, sitting on the edge of the bed. Hair had fallen across her cheek, and I brushed it back behind her ear.

"I was thinking I'd go back to Trabzon," I said.

"That is logical. It is the last place you know, for certain, that she was."

"There's more than that. The man I dealt with there, I think he's the one who pointed Karataev's friends at Kobuleti."

"All the more reason to speak to him."

I brushed more of her hair back, let my fingers trail along the side of her neck. Like my own, her body had more than its share of scars, but her neck was smooth and I liked the feel of her skin. The bandage on her right tricep had come loose while she slept, falling away enough to reveal the top of the wound there. The bullet track looked like a burn.

"I don't want to leave you alone," I said.

"Pregnant does not mean incapacitated. I can take care of myself."

"You can, but I don't want you to have to, not alone. Not with Miata the way he is."

"And."

"And yes, the bun in the oven changes things, I think you'll agree."

"Yes." She rolled onto her back, looking up at me. Her expression was frank. "We could hire someone, perhaps. Someone who did what you used to do."

"I'm not leaving you with some bodyguard I don't know the first thing about."

"The problem," Alena said softly, "is that everyone you ever trusted is dead."

"No," I said. "Not everyone."

CHAPTER
Twenty-one

It took her less than a step into the apartment to realize something was wrong, and I heard it in the way she moved, even though the front door was out of sight from where I was seated. Then I heard the door shut again, and I listened to the deadbolt snap back in place, the jingle of keys as they were dropped onto the butler's table by the coatrack.

"Erika?" Bridgett Logan said, coming around the corner.

Then she saw me sitting in the easy chair beside the couch, and stopped cold.

"No," I said. "Me."

She stared, the surprise on her face quickly retreating, her features going neutral. Bridgett's poker face was good, always had been. One of the many things she hated was people knowing what she was feeling.

She looked the same as the last time I'd seen her, could well have been wearing exactly what she'd worn seven years earlier. Black motorcycle jacket over white T-shirt, never mind that early July humidity in New York made it an exercise in masochism to take on such a heavy layer. Black jeans that had seen enough of a washing machine to start turning them gray. Black biker boots, scuffed at the toes. A couple of bracelets wrapped tightly around her right wrist. Even the little gold hoop that pierced the side of her left nostril was the same.

But maybe an extra line or four to her face, the etching just a touch deeper at the corner of the arctic blue eyes. If gray had started trying to find its way into her black hair, she'd either dyed it into submission or eliminated it altogether, strand by strand.

"Atticus," Bridgett Logan said, and the poker face went away, and she smiled at me, her teeth very white against her oxblood lipstick.

"Hello, Bridgett."

"Wait right there, okay?" Her smile broadened, and she showed me her right index finger, indicating just one moment, then pivoted on her toe and headed past the counter that marked the edge of her kitchen, down the hall. I watched her go. At the end of the hall, she ducked right, into her bedroom, out of sight. For a couple of seconds there was silence, and then I heard her fumbling around.

"It's right here," I said.

She stuck her head out of her bedroom, saw me holding up the Sig Sauer in one hand, slide locked back. With my other hand, I held up the magazine for the pistol.

Her smile, if anything, got larger.

"You motherfucker," she said cheerfully, coming back down the hall.

"I didn't want you shooting me before we had a chance to talk."

"That's all right, that's fine." She had reached the kitchen, turning into it. I heard the sound of a drawer being opened, the clatter of cutlery.

"Bridgett." I set the pistol and mag down on the coffee table in front of me.

"Shut the fuck up." She found what she was looking for, turned, showing me a large carving knife, the blade maybe six inches long. "This'll do."

"Bridgett," I said again.

The smile was as bright as ever as she came around the edge of the counter. She was holding the knife all wrong, her right fist tight around the handle, blade pointing down, but I thought telling her that probably wouldn't help things much.

"You really going to stab me in your living room?"

"Yeah," she said, bending her elbow and bringing the knife up to her shoulder. She was still far enough away that I wasn't sure she was going to do it. "I think I am, actually."

There was a knock at the door.

Bridgett stopped her advance, the knife still up.

"You should get that," I said.

She looked in the direction of the door, then back to me, and the smile was no longer anywhere to be seen, most likely no longer in the borough of Manhattan, I suspected.

"Why?" she demanded.

"Because I think it's your sister, and I'm hoping you're marginally less inclined to murder me if there's a nun in the room."

"I could keep her waiting in the hall, let her in after I'm finished."

"That's true. Hard to explain, though."

"I hate you," Bridgett Logan informed me, tossing the knife onto her couch, and moving out of sight again, this time to answer the door. I heard her greeting her sister, a mock cry of "Cashel! What a surprise! Come in, come in!" and took the time to get up enough to move the knife from the couch to the coffee table, setting it beside the pistol.

Cashel came into sight first, Bridgett following her. Together, there was no mistaking the family resemblance, though Cashel was an inch or two shorter than her older sister's six feet, her eyes more gray than blue. She was wearing a tan blazer over a white blouse and black slacks, removing the coat as she entered. I could see the lapel pin on the blazer, the tall and thin rectangle with the engraving of a rolling hillside, a cross at its summit, the symbol of her order.

She smiled when she saw me, and unlike Bridgett's, it was genuine. "Atticus."

"Hello, Sister."

Her eyes caught the implements of death and pain on the coffee table, and the smile shrank, turned wry.

"Looks like you were correct," Cashel said.

I shrugged.

Bridgett, nostrils flaring, glared at her sister, then at me, then back to her sister.

"You knew he was here? You knew he was in New York?"

"We met for coffee this morning," Cashel said. "He said it might be best if I stopped by."

Bridgett rounded on her sister, eyes blazing. "You know who he is? What he's become? This isn't the Boy Scout I told you about all those years ago."

"I'm not sure he ever was," Cashel replied, moving to the couch.

"You set me up." Bridgett bounced her look between her sister and me once more, then decided she was angrier at me, which I thought was more than fair. "You fucking set me up."

"Yeah," I confirmed. "But I have a reason."

"It had better be a damn good one."

"It is to me," I said. "I need your help."

"You have no right to *ask* for my help, Atticus! It's been, what, seven years? You made your choice back then. You made your decision, you walked away from everyone you knew, everything you were. You chose the bad guy over us. You have no *right*."

"Not everything is black and white," I said.

"Oh, forgive me, I thought murder was wrong, I thought it was, what's the word?" Bridgett turned to her sister. "What is it again, Sister? Oh, right! It's a *sin*! It's a *fucking sin*!"

Cashel made a slight face. I suspected Bridgett was being liberal with her profanity simply to annoy her younger sibling.

"God detests the sin," Cashel pointed out. "Not the sinner."

"Do you know what he's become?" Bridgett demanded. "Do you know what he *does*?"

"You don't know what I do," I pointed out.

"You're a fucking assassin, Atticus," Bridgett said. "Spin it however you like, you kill people for money, that makes you a fucking goddamn *assassin*."

Cashel looked at me.

"I'm not," I said. "Despite what your sister may have convinced herself of, I do not sell what I can do. Have I killed people? Yes. Will I do it again? If I have to, yes. I'm not proud of it. I'm not eager for it. But that's how it is."

Bridgett ran a hand up the side of her face, into her hair, taking a fistful of it to tug. She let it go, shaking her head.

"I think you should listen to what he has to say," Cashel told her sister.

"You don't know what he did." Bridgett let her hair go, shoulders slumping. All of her seemed tired, suddenly, and her voice went soft. "You don't know how many of our friends died because of what he did, because of the choice he made."

Cashel reached out for her sister's hand, gave her fingers a squeeze. "Listen to him."

Bridgett snorted wearily, then nodded.

"Alena's in a hotel in Odessa," I said. "She won't be there much longer, she's looking for a place to move to, to hole up. She's alone, and I need someone I can trust to be with her, to help keep her safe."

Bridgett's expression turned to incredulity, the fatigue dissipating in a new wave of outrage.

"Fuck you."

"She needs help."

"Fuck you!" Bridgett appealed to her sister. "You know who he's talking about? You know who this woman he's talking about is? Even if you believe what he's telling us about himself, he can't say the same about her—"

"She's pregnant," I interrupted.

Over coffee, when I'd told Cashel that Alena was pregnant, her response had been one of genuine pleasure.

Bridgett, not so much. I might as well have punched her, the reaction was so immediate and so physical. Her head snapped back, came around to stare at me. Her mouth opened, lower lip working, and then she closed it again. She backed up, bumping into the kitchen counter, put a hand on one of the barstools there. After a second, she took the seat.

"Yours?" she asked, finally.

"Yeah."

"She's having your baby?"

"Yeah."

She shook her head once more, muttering, before she said,

"You don't need my help. That woman, pregnant? Anyone fucks with her they'd be dead twice before they hit the ground."

"I need someone with her I can trust. Someone who can back her up if it comes to that."

"And is it going to come to that?"

"I don't know. There's a chance. I've made some people very angry lately."

"Not including myself."

"More recently."

"Why can't it be you?" There was the edge of new suspicion in the question. "She's having your baby, after all."

"Because I have to find someone first," I said.

Most of what I told Bridgett about Tiasa Lagidze I'd already told her sister when we'd met for coffee in the Bronx that morning. After arriving at Kennedy the night before, I'd checked into a hotel near the airport, traveling under the Anthony Shephard ID. Jet lag had me up before five, and I'd used my laptop to find a phone number for Cashel Logan, a Sister of Incarnate Love. It hadn't taken long, but I'd waited until after seven before putting in the call, asking to meet her.

Bridgett listened without comment, but with visible emotion. When I described the women I'd seen in Turkey, the girls I'd found in the brothel in Dubai, the fury writ itself large on her face.

"I've done some counseling with victims of trafficking," Cashel said. "It's increased substantially in the last couple of years, as more and more cases have come to light, as law enforcement has become more aware of the crime."

"There was that case in New Jersey," Bridgett said. "Last year, it made the *Times*."

"Yes. And the arrests in Kansas and Florida."

"This girl could be anywhere in the world," Bridgett told me.

"Maybe. Some places more likely than others. I've got a lead I need to chase down."

"The experience is uniformly brutal, but it is survivable," Cashel said. "You can recover from it, make a life again. But the longer the slavery, the harder the recovery. And the younger the victim, the more damage that has to be undone."

"So you're going to rescue the girl, and you want me to protect the little lady?" Bridgett asked. "That's why you're here?"

"If you want to put it like that," I said.

"Once upon a time, you knew a lot of bodyguards," Bridgett said. "I'm not a bodyguard, I'm a private investigator. Why haven't you asked them? Or did you do that already and they all told you what I'm inclined to tell you?"

"I thought about it," I answered. "But I can't trust them the way I can trust you."

"You son of a bitch."

"I've got nobody else."

"And whose fault is that, Atticus?"

"No one's but my own."

"You would say that." She glared at me for a long time, then slid off the barstool. "Fuck it. I've always wanted to visit Ukraine. I'll go pack."

We watched her disappear back into her bedroom.

"This girl, Tiasa," Cashel said. "I may be able to help her, or at least put you in contact with people who can, wherever you find her. If you find her."

"I'm going to find her, Sister."

Sister Cashel Logan gave me a small smile.

"I'll pray that you do, Atticus."

CHAPTER
Twenty-two

When we were waiting in the security line at Kennedy for our flight the next morning, Bridgett leaned in over my shoulder, whispering, "So what happens if I tell them Anthony Shephard is a guy named Atticus Kodiak?"

I gave it a second's thought. "I don't know. Want to try it?"

She snorted the exact same way Alena would've done had I said the same thing to her.

We cleared security without a problem.

In keeping with my newly established tradition, I used Vladek's BlackBerry, with a new SIM I'd purchased the previous day, to call the Londonskaya as we were waiting at the gate to board.

Bridgett had gone off in search of a Starbucks, leaving me alone for the time being; at least, she'd claimed to be searching for a Starbucks. She might've been serious about ratting me out to the TSA, but that didn't seem very likely.

Alena answered before the second ring, and I told her where I was, and what the plan was, and who I was sending to back her up. When I gave the name, Alena swore in Russian.

"She hates me."

"She talks a good game."

"Logan hates me, Atticus. How can I trust her?"

"So maybe she hates you. At least you know where you stand with her. I trust her. She'd never have agreed if she wasn't willing to see this through."

"Perhaps." She went silent. It stretched long enough I began to wonder if the call had dropped. Then Alena said, "Did you tell her?"

"Yeah. She was overjoyed for us."

"You are lying."

"Yeah, I am," I said, catching sight of Bridgett returning to the gate, a frighteningly large paper cup in one hand. "I'm gonna go. I'll call you from London, give you her ETA."

"You're not coming with her?"

"No. Trabzon."

"Of course. I will wait to hear from you."

She hung up, and I stowed the phone back in my pocket as Bridgett resumed the seat next to me. She popped the top off the cup, releasing a cloud of steam, took a sip, then sighed.

"Black bean of life," Bridgett said. "Never used to like coffee, now I drink it all the time."

"You're off the Altoids?" I asked. When I'd known her, she was always popping one sort of candy or another, always carrying a roll of Life Savers or a tin of some flavor of mint in a pocket. She took them the way smokers took cigarettes, but instead of feeding an addiction, it had been her way of fighting one.

"Couple years ago."

"No kidding?"

"I went to the dentist, he took one look at my molars and started pricing new cars. I had fractures in three of them, had to get crowns made. That pretty much put an end to that."

"Ah," I said.

"Was that her? On the phone?"

"Yeah."

"She knows I'm coming."

"She does now."

"And?"

"She was overjoyed," I said.

"You're a fucking liar."

I grinned.

"What's so fucking funny?"

"Nothing. Never mind."

She glared at me, but I wasn't going to add anything more. After a couple seconds, she gave it up, and went back to savoring her coffee.

Somewhere about halfway across the Atlantic, Bridgett woke me with a not-so-gentle punch to my shoulder. The cabin lights had been dimmed, and everyone else in business class was either dozing or hiding behind their sleep masks and noise-canceling headsets. I fumbled my glasses into place, focused on Bridgett, staring at me.

"What?" I asked.

"Nothing," she said. "I just wanted to hit you."

I took my glasses off, readjusted the inadequate pillow beneath my cheek. "Fine."

"Dick."

I nodded, pretended to go back to sleep. She let me maintain the charade for about a minute.

"You know what pisses me off most?" she asked.

"That I'm still breathing," I said.

"That I missed you."

I rolled my head to look at her, blurry without my corrective lenses. She had the aisle seat, taken for the slight advantage in leg room she could eke out of it.

"I missed you, too," I said.

"I don't love you."

"I didn't say you did."

"No, I'm saying I don't love you, not anymore. I think I did, once. I thought I did. I tried."

"I know you did."

"Maybe you do, but it took *me* a while to get there." She shifted in her seat, trying to adjust her hips, wincing. "For a long time—I mean a long fucking time—I thought you'd chosen her over me."

"I did."

"Wow," Bridgett said. "That was cold."

"You want me to lie to you?"

"No, actually. That's the last thing I want you to do. Seriously."

I put my glasses on once more, straightened up, remembering. Bridgett and I had tried to be lovers, before I'd ever met Alena. We'd tried very hard at it, in fact. But it hadn't worked, even when it looked like it had, and when Alena entered my life, that had become abundantly clear. Who Alena was had simply provided a convenient, if reasonable, excuse.

"You seeing anyone?" I asked Bridgett.

"Yeah, actually. That surprise you?"

"Not if it's on your terms."

That got a grin. "He's like me. Doesn't want to settle down. We call each other, email, video chat on the computer. Comes into town for two, three weeks at a time, and we have a good time together, and then he goes off and I go back to my life. I don't have to change anything for him."

"I'm happy for you."

She heard the sincerity, and accepted it, and we started talking then, in a way we never had back when we'd pretended we were sharing everything with each other. She had questions, a lot of them, and I discovered that I did, as well. We talked until England rolled out beneath us, our voices low. We remembered friends who had died, and she told me what she knew about the ones who were still living, but of all but one of them, she knew very little, having long since lost touch. Over the one we still shared, a young woman named Erika Wyatt, she scolded me, telling me that I owed her contact.

As the plane began its descent in earnest, we came around to where we started.

"You say you picked her over me."

"No, you said I picked her over you. I just agreed."

"It's the same thing, asshole."

"If you say so."

"There never really was a choice to make, though, was there?" Bridgett asked.

"I don't think you get to pick who you fall in love with," I said. "Just what you do once you've fallen."

"Oh, wow, that's deep." She reached for the pouch on the seatback by her knees. "I need an airsick bag, I'm going to puke."

"Let me know when you're done."

"You believe that?"

"Maybe. Sure sounds good," I said.

Bridgett Logan shook her head, bemused. "Seven fucking years to turn you all hardcore. And beneath it all, you're still the same."

"Am I?" I asked, because I sure as hell didn't feel it.

"Yeah," Bridgett Logan said. "You're still a hopeless fucking romantic."

CHAPTER
Twenty-three

There's an old cop saw, goes like this.

Question: How do you catch a drug dealer for the fiftieth time after he's walked free the other forty-nine?

Answer: You buy drugs from him.

Habits don't change, and even if I'd managed to give Arzu's business a bloody nose two and a half weeks earlier—something I had every reason to doubt—there was no way he'd quit and turned over a new leaf. If he had been rousted when I'd called the police on him, he certainly would have been released quickly enough, once the appropriate palms had been greased. Back on the street, he wasn't going to stop pimping, and he wasn't going to stop trafficking. The way I saw it, in fact, there were only two options. Either Arzu would return to what he'd been doing with a vengeance, eager to make up lost money and lost time, or he would return to what he'd been doing with more caution, for fear of getting burned.

I had no doubt that he knew he'd been burned, and that it'd been I who'd burned him. The attack on the house in Kobuleti guaranteed that. But when my initial searches for him in Trabzon turned up nothing, I assumed—incorrectly—that was because he had gone to ground. Maybe Arzu had heard that Kobuleti hadn't gone as well as he would've liked. Maybe he knew that three more of his and Vladek Karataev's associates were dead. He'd been greedy when I'd met him, but that wasn't the same thing as stupid. Knowing his efforts to punish me had failed, he would have concluded that the trail from Kobuleti would lead straight back to him.

It made sense that he would keep his head down, at least for a while. At least until he felt it was safe enough to raise it again.

My problem was the same as it had been all along. Tiasa didn't have the time to wait, and for that reason, neither did I.

I lost most of two days trying to locate him. I hit the hotels that weren't hotels, and the brothels that didn't even try to pretend. I went back to the apartment block where Arzu had shown me the three young women, spent twelve hours on a surveillance that turned up nothing. If the location was being used for anything at all, I couldn't tell from the outside.

When I broke in at three in the morning, I found the place abandoned, and nothing that told me where I should look next.

■ ■ ■

My third morning back, walking past the tiny shops and stalls crammed onto Uzun Sokak, I saw the *natasha* Arzu had ordered to keep me company the night I'd first met him. I wasn't certain it was the same woman and kept my distance for a few minutes. She was even paler in the sunlight, sickly-looking and visibly shaky. Her shorts and T-shirt, both too tight, were filthy, and I watched while she was verbally abused by one stall owner, then another, each of them shouting her away from their bustling stands on the busy street.

At the third stand she approached she made her move, her hand darting out to snare a plastic sack filled with *kuruyemis,* dried fruits. Desperation made her foolish, and she timed it badly, and the owner caught her by the wrist before she could draw her arm back. He wasn't a big man, but there was more to him than there was to her, and he yanked her toward him hard enough to nearly take her off her feet, screaming at her in Turkish. She slammed into the side of the stand, and he twisted her arm until she cried in pain.

There were a lot of people around, shoppers and pedestrians, and those who noticed stopped to watch and listen, and seemed mightily amused. They seemed even more amused when, still holding her by her wrist in one hand, still berating her, the owner punched her in the face.

I was there by then. In Russian, I said, "Stop that."

He looked at me in some surprise. He was clearly a Turk, a local, clean-shaven and middle-aged, and I imagined he worked very hard for his living, to support his family. I could even understand why he would be tired of people stealing from him. But there was more to it, as well. The ultranationalist sentiment in Trabzon is strong, has led to violence against foreigners in the past. I didn't speak Turkish, but I'd picked up enough words here and there to know that, of all the things the man had called her, "whore" and "foreigner" had figured repeatedly and prominently.

The girl stared at me, her arm still trapped. Blood was streaming from her nose.

I took a ten-euro bill from my pocket, then picked up the same bag of *kuruyemis* the *natasha* had been trying to steal. I held the bill up for him to see, then dropped it in front of him. I handed the bag of dried fruit to the girl.

"Let her go," I said.

He let her go.

The second he released her, she ran.

The stall owner's laughter followed us both.

She gave it her best effort, three blocks, cutting through alleys and dodging people. She lost one of her cheap plastic shoes at the square off Atatürk Alani, but kept going anyway, the bag of dried fruit in her hand. I grabbed the shoe without stopping, stuffing it into my windbreaker as I tried to stay with her.

Then she ran into traffic, looking back at me as she did so, and that meant she didn't see the white minibus heading straight for her. The screech of its brakes and the howl of its horn snapped her attention around, and she panicked and stopped dead. The bus came to a halt with perhaps an inch between her and its front fender, and I'd caught up by then. I put a hand on her shoulder and another on her arm, and led her back off the street as more horns called furiously after us for disrupting traffic.

The shock of the near miss let me get her off the road, but the moment we were clear, she tried to yank free from me again. I kept my grip on her, aware that by doing so I was only making matters worse, only scaring her more. I couldn't imagine the number of unwanted hands that had been on her body, and now I was just one more pair of them.

"I'm not going to hurt you!" I told her in Russian. "You have to calm down!"

"Fuck you! Fuck you fuck you fuck you fuck you let me go!"

I turned her to look at me. The run had made the bloody nose worse, a flow of crimson that ran off her chin and into her shirt. The T-shirt, I saw now, was pink, with a faded silver star on it, and the word *porn* printed above it in English. She struggled like a bird against my grip, and maybe weighed as much.

"I'm not going to hurt you," I said again. "You need money? I have money, I can give you money. Please, calm down."

She stared at me, furious and hateful, but went still. Then she tried to break my grip again, hoping that I'd bought the change. I hadn't, and I didn't let her go.

"I have money," I told her. "And you don't have to give me your body to get it. Please. Believe me."

Then I released my hold on her, stepping back, showing her my palms before dropping my hands to my sides.

She looked horribly unsure then. On either side of us, pedestrian traffic hustled past, barely giving us a glance.

"You'll give me money?"

"Yeah."

"What do I have to do?"

"Answer a question or two, that's all."

She tasted the blood running over her lips, wiped at her nose and saw the result on her hand.

"Oh God," she breathed. "I'm bleeding."

"Let me take you somewhere. You tell me where."

The suggestion confused her. "Where?"

"You pick," I said. "Someplace you'll feel safe."

"I don't know where that is."

I looked around, saw a restaurant, a sign in Turkish and English telling me its name was Petek. I pointed to it. "In there? You can use the bathroom. I'll buy you lunch."

I handed her back her missing shoe.

"Okay?" I asked.

She nodded miserably, still trapped.

Petek wasn't much of a restaurant, but they had a bathroom, and they let her use it. I bought two kebabs and a couple of cans of Fanta, waited for her at a table, trying not to be impatient. I hadn't followed her for obvious reasons, and if there was a rear exit to the restaurant and she wanted to hoof it, I wasn't going to try and stop her.

She was gone for nearly half an hour, but eventually she joined me at my table. She'd cleaned herself as best as she could, dried blood clinging to the inside of her nostrils. Her shirt was still a mess. There was no sign of the bag of dried fruits, and I realized that she must have eaten them all before returning, before someone could take them from her.

"How much will you pay me?"

"How much do you need to get home?" I asked her.

She looked at me incredulously.

"A thousand?" I asked. "Will a thousand be enough?"

"I can't go home."

"You don't remember me, do you?"

She shook her head.

"We met a couple weeks ago. Arzu told you to keep me company."

His name made her mouth tighten, her eyes narrow, and she gave me another appraisal. Then she nodded. "The man who didn't answer his phone."

"That was me."

"You said . . . your name is David?"

"Right. And you said your name is Natasha. I couldn't tell if that was a joke."

"Vasylyna." She took one of the cans of Fanta, the grape, and cracked the top. "You will give me the money to go back to Kiev?"

"I can't control what you do with it. But I'll give you the money."

"Just for my help?" Vasylyna asked, then gulped at her soda.

"I'm trying to find Arzu," I said, deflecting the question. "I need to talk to him. Do you know where he is?"

She set the can down, eyeing the kebabs. I nudged them closer to her.

"The money first," she bargained, quietly. "You give me the money first."

"You think I won't give it to you after?"

"What if you don't like what I tell you?"

I brought out my wallet, emptied it of cash into my hand, then folded over the bills and slid them to her. "You have your passport?"

"Arzu took it. I don't know where it is."

"I can take care of that, too. We can get you a new one. Tell me where I can find him."

"You can't." She choked on a sob, caught herself, staring at the money on the table. "You can't find him."

"He's dead?"

"In jail. He got arrested a couple of weeks ago, but they let him go, he paid the police. But then he got into a fight last week, with another pimp, and he was arrested again." She pushed the money back at me, tears shining in her eyes. "You won't let me have it."

I pushed the money right back.

"Vasylyna," I said, "you're going home."

CHAPTER
Twenty-four

The man who ran Trabzon's jail was a Turk named Besim Çelik, in his early forties, average in height and maybe twenty pounds overweight. He carried it well enough, and when we met at the Trabzonspor Club two days after I'd promised Vasylyna a way home, he moved himself with the certainty of a man used to pushing around others. The bar was the clubhouse of Trabzon's football team, and despite the fact that there was no match in the offing, the place was bustling when I arrived, and I was afraid I'd have trouble spotting him, but I needn't have worried. He was the only person in the place wearing a police officer's uniform.

"Anthony Shephard?" He spoke in heavily accented English.

"Captain Çelik?"

He picked up his glass of beer and motioned to the back doors of the clubhouse that opened onto the patio. I nodded and followed him, and we took seats at one of the corners. It was quieter outside, but almost as crowded, patrons enjoying the pleasant July weather.

"I appreciate you coming to meet with me, Captain."

"The message—yes, message?—my assistant gave me made me curious. You want to talk about a prisoner?"

I nodded. It had taken the rest of the previous day and another five hundred euros to simply get this far, and I was having a hard time controlling my mounting impatience. Every hour that passed seemed to take Tiasa further away from me, not closer.

"What is it I can do for you, Mr. Shephard?"

"You're holding a friend of a friend of mine. His name is Arzu Kaya."

Çelik pursed his lips, then took a sip of his beer. "We have this man."

"My friend is very worried about Arzu. I hate seeing him like this, I really do, and I was hoping I could discuss with you some means of getting them together, if only for a few hours. Maybe by making a donation to a charity you support, something along those lines."

With absolute seriousness, he remarked, "It would need to be a large donation."

"I was thinking around ten thousand euros," I said.

"That would be an acceptable amount."

"The thing is," I said, "I want to surprise them both, Arzu and my friend. I want it to be a gift."

"A gift?"

"Yeah. Maybe I could even get it wrapped."

Çelik didn't blink. "Gift-wrapping is extra."

"I'd expect it would be." I took out the piece of paper I'd been carrying folded in my pocket, handing it over. "If I could get him delivered to this address."

He took the paper, opening it one-handed. "Not a very busy location."

"I want the reunion to be private."

Captain Çelik nodded sagely, drank some more of his beer, looking past me, at the clientele. "He couldn't be away for more than two or three hours."

"I think that'll be more than enough time for them to discuss what they need to," I said.

He checked the address on the paper I'd given him again, then folded it and tucked it into his breast pocket, beneath his badge. "Also it would need to be at the right time."

"Of course. Wouldn't be a surprise otherwise. I was thinking around two in the morning."

"Then he will be dropped off at two, and picked up no later than five." He looked at me impassively. "Half of the donation will be expected when he arrives. The rest of it when he is picked up."

"That'll be fine. There's one other thing."

He fixed me with his dead brown eyes, bored.

"I'm wondering if someone could provide me with some information about his family," I said. "My friend wanted me to speak to his wife, and I don't know where I can find her."

"I'm sure we have that information," Çelik said. "In fact, I'm sure I could get that for you now. But I would have to see some sort of gesture on your part, that my charity will actually be rewarded."

"Would five hundred euros be enough?"

"No. A thousand." He finished his beer, then rose. "I will make a call, see if I can find out about his family for you."

He walked back into the clubhouse, and I took out my

wallet. I'd restocked it since meeting Vasylyna, but was going to have to restock it again. I put ten one-hundred-euro bills in a stack, and then slipped the stack into a paper napkin. I moved the napkin over to where Çelik had been seated.

After six minutes, he returned, sat, and put the napkin on his lap. He kept his head down for a few seconds, counting the money, then shifted in such a way I knew he was pocketing the bills. From the same pocket that he'd stowed my little piece of paper with the delivery address on it, he produced a new one, handing it to me.

Then, with no other word, he rose and left me with the address of Arzu Kaya's family.

Two in the morning meant I had ten hours before I'd be seeing Arzu, and there was a fair amount I needed to do between now and then. First, I found a bank and withdrew the cash I was going to need. Next, I did some shopping. Finally, with the aid of a map, I found the address Çelik had given me. That took the most time, and I was there for nearly three hours before I had what I needed and could depart.

It was already dark when I returned to the hotel I was staying at on Gençoglu Street, a place called the Otel Horon. One of the two women manning the front desk called out to me as I came through the lobby, saying that a package had arrived for Anthony Shephard. I thanked her and took the UPS pack back to my room, then dumped the new papers Nicholas Sargenti had sent out on the bed.

There were two sets of documents, a fresh set for me, in the name of Matthew Twigg, a citizen of the United States who lived in Tukwila, Washington, just south of Seattle. Along with the passport and the Washington State driver's license was an Amex and a Visa. The second set of documents were all Ukrainian, two passports—one for domestic travel, the other for international. I checked these carefully, using the lamp at the desk to verify the laser imprinting on the photographs, and was impressed that everything looked perfectly in order. Then I flipped through the two documents, noting the stamps.

Nicholas had outdone himself.

I moved my new set of papers to my bag, then took the Ukrainian ones with me down the hall, to the room where Vasylyna had spent much of the last two days. I knocked on the door twice, identifying myself, and after a few seconds she let me inside, cautiously backing away as I shut the door behind me. I showed her the documents, each of them in her full name, Vasylyna Pavlina Kozyar. She took them with wide eyes, opening each in turn, gazing at the photographs of herself. I'd taken the pictures of her with the camera on the BlackBerry, using the shower curtain in the bathroom as a backdrop. Then I'd emailed the pictures to Sargenti.

"The stamps say you came to Turkey two weeks ago," I told her. "This room is paid for until tomorrow morning. You could be in Kiev by tomorrow afternoon, if that's what you want."

She looked up from the documents in her hand, bewildered. Bathed, wearing garments that she had picked herself, clothes that fit, with two safe nights of sleep behind her, she looked better, but, sadly, younger.

"I didn't believe you," Vasylyna said.

"I know."

She was holding the passports as if afraid they might sprout wings and fly away from her. I headed to the door.

"Good luck," I told her.

■ ■ ■

At 10:43 that night I did a SIM shuffle on the BlackBerry and called Alena for the second time since leaving New York. We were back onto our convoluted schedule, and she was expecting me.

"Still in Trabzon?" she asked.

"All goes well I should be leaving early tomorrow."

"You received what you were waiting for?"

"Got it this afternoon. Had to make a large withdrawal, too."

"There's enough money. Don't worry about that."

"How are you?"

"Miata is doing better."

"Good," I said, aware that she hadn't answered my question. Then I heard Bridgett in the background, saying that she wanted to talk to me. "Put her on."

"I know what she's going to say to you," Alena said. "She wants you to agree with her."

"About what?"

"I'll let her explain."

There was a rustle over the speaker as the telephone changed hands on their end, and then Bridgett came on the line, saying, "She's being stubborn."

"I'm pretty sure that's not how she sees it. Stubborn about what?"

"About the fact that I want us to leave Odessa."

"That's always been the plan."

"Yes, I know that's the fucking plan. But she wants to stay in Eastern Europe and I don't."

"Where do you want to go?"

"Someplace I speak the fucking language. Ireland. All I am right now is a warm body to draw fire if things go to hell. At least there I've got some connection with the people, I know something about the country, and I speak the goddamn common tongue."

"I agree," I said.

"It's stupid to stay here and you what?"

"No, you're right, it makes sense. Let me talk to her about it."

The phone exchanged hands again. This time, Alena spoke in Georgian.

"I knew you would agree with her."

"Because she's right," I said, using English.

"It's too long a trip for Miata."

"Then take it slow. And do me a favor?"

"What?"

"Switch back to English. Speaking in Georgian just proves her right."

"Fuck her," Alena said, then switched to English, petulantly asking, "Better?"

"Much."

There was a pause, then she said, "We've been in Odessa too long already."

"I was thinking the same thing."

"We'll move tomorrow. Check the box, I'll leave the new contact there."

"I will."

There was another pause, and I knew what she wanted to say, and why she wasn't saying it.

"I know," I told her.

The address I'd given Çelik was for a truck depot near the Trabzon harbor, on the east side of town, close to the water. Like Batumi, Trabzon was another port city, built upon the trade that came over the Black Sea, trade that the residents traced back to Ancient Greece and beyond. I'd driven by the location the previous day, then returned to it this morning, parking and taking a walk around on foot. The depot was a warehouse farm, and it was busy with forklifts and lorries, but near the southwestern side was a section that clearly suffered from disuse. I pried the door open at the side of one of the warehouses, and within discovered a space that looked like it would give me the peace and quiet to do what I needed.

I wasn't going to leave Trabzon without Tiasa's location. One way or another, Arzu was going to give it to me.

From eleven until one in the morning, I staked out the location from my rental car, twice leaving it to scope the area on foot. Just as in Batumi, the depot rolled twenty-four/seven, creating plenty of ambient noise. For the entirety of my surveillance, no one even came close to the warehouse I'd chosen.

Just past one I took my gear and headed inside. There were fractures in the ceiling, missing pieces of roof, and through the gaps small packets of city light managed to reach inside. It wasn't a lot of illumination, but it was enough to work by. I unfolded the metal chair I'd purchased, set it smack in the center of the space. Then I opened the carry-all I'd bought, checking its contents once more. It was exactly the same as it had been the last time I'd looked. I took out my laptop, set up everything I was going to use on it, then closed the top and put it to the side until it would be needed. Next I took out the knife I'd purchased, moving it to a pocket, and then finally removed the first of the two envelopes with Çelik's payment. Finished, I took a slow walk around the interior once more, giving my eyes time to adjust, waiting for the arrival of my guest.

They were prompt. By my clock it was two precisely when the same door I'd used was pushed roughly open and two uniformed police officers entered, dragging a hooded and bound third man with them. Çelik followed after them, saw me, saw the chair, and spoke in Turkish to the officers. Then he crossed to me, and we watched together as his officers maneuvered their struggling cargo into the seat. Metal rang on metal as they handcuffed him to the chair.

"Complimentary," Çelik said.

One of the officers, finished, came over and handed him the key to the cuffs. Çelik held it out to me with one hand, his other open and waiting. We exchanged items, the envelope for the key. I tucked the key into a pocket while Çelik counted the money, checking the stack of euros in the weak light, taking his time to be certain he wasn't being ripped off. When he was satisfied, he replaced the bills, then stowed the envelope inside his jacket.

"We will be back at four."

"You said three hours," I told him.

Çelik shrugged. "I meant two."

Then he and his two men left the warehouse.

I waited for a minute after they were gone, not moving, just listening. In the chair, Arzu had stopped struggling, but his head beneath the hood was swiveling around, searching desperately for some sort of noise. I watched him, and after another thirty seconds or so, he began pulling at the cuffs, making the chair beneath him hop and scrape on the concrete. The third time he pulled at his restraints, he twisted and went off balance, toppling over and slamming his left shoulder into the floor. The sound he made was muffled by his hood and gag.

I moved around behind him, not saying anything, not making a noise, then took hold of his shoulders and righted him in the chair. His reaction to the contact was instant, more muffled words, pleas. I couldn't understand what he was saying, realized he was using Turkish.

Still standing behind him, I pulled the hood from his head and cast it aside. He strained to find me, but I'd positioned myself well, and he couldn't get an angle. I opened the blade on the pocketknife and used it to cut the gag from behind. He spat it out immediately, began speaking quickly again in Turkish.

I closed the knife and replaced it, then brought out the BlackBerry and put the picture of Tiasa Lagidze up on its little screen. The illumination from the device was like using a small, weak-celled flashlight, but any light in that place was enough, and Arzu's Turkish came faster.

With my free hand, I took a handful of his hair and yanked his head back so he could look up at me. Then I put the BlackBerry in his face, so he could see the screen.

"This girl," I said in Russian. "Vladek Karataev sent her to you just over three weeks ago. You sold her. You're going to tell me to who and where."

He blinked rapidly, looking past the BlackBerry's screen up at me. The recognition was not happy.

"Go fuck yourself," Arzu said.

"You want to rethink that answer." I turned the BlackBerry off, put it away again as I moved around in front of him. "I mean, you *really* want to rethink that answer."

He spat on me. "What's she to you, David? Huh? Why you so fucking desperate for that skinny ass?"

"Tell me where she is."

"You wanted that virgin cunt for yourself, is that what you wanted? You wanted to bite her little tits? You wanted to be her first fuck, to have her cherry? You're too fucking late. We opened her like a fucking garage, we fucking split her in—"

I punched him, shattering his nose, sending the chair over backward. His head smacked into the concrete hard enough that he went abruptly, dangerously silent. For a second, I thought I'd hit him too hard in my anger, that I'd knocked him out, or worse.

Then he croaked out a laugh.

"Yeah, you wanted her little cunt. Something small enough to make you feel big."

I took a breath, trying to calm myself, then moved to him and righted the chair once more. Blood from his broken nose flowed in a black stream over his lips, reminding me of Vasylyna.

"It's one girl," I told him. "I'm not after your network, I'm not after your business. I'm after just one girl. Tell me where she is."

He spat again at me, this time ejecting blood. This time I was expecting it, and he missed.

"Fuck yourself."

"You're going to tell me."

"Fuck yourself. You might kill me, David. But I give up my contact, he *will* kill me. And if not him, the ones he works with, the ones who work with me." He shook his head, spat out more blood, this time directing it at the floor.

"This is the second time you've been in lockup in three, four weeks," I said. "You think the people up the line don't already think you've turned rat? You think the people who supply you, the people who work for you, don't already think you're compromised? You think they still believe they can trust you?"

"I'm getting out. They'll buy me out."

"You're going to tell me," I said.

"No, David. I'm not."

"Have it your way," I said, and went back to where the carry-all waited on the floor. From inside I removed a hammer, a hacksaw, a pair of pliers, and a bottle of lighter fluid. I showed Arzu each item as I brought it out, then set them, in a line, on the ground so he could see them.

"You're going to fucking torture me?" There was bravado in his voice, so obvious that I knew he was scared. "You're going to fucking cut me? Beat me?"

"Oh, no," I said, opening the laptop. "These aren't for you, Arzu. They're for them."

I turned the computer, showed him the pictures I'd put up on the screen. The glow on the monitor illuminated his face, showed me the recognition and then the horror.

"You never should have told me you were married," I said.

"You cocksucker," he whispered.

"Your wife is very pretty. And the kids are good-looking, too. Your youngest, how old is he? I'm thinking he can't be much older than ten."

Arzu pulled his stare from the monitor to me, his expression warring between hate and fear.

"You fucker, you cocksucking motherfucker, you stay away from my family!"

"Well," I said. "That's really up to you now, isn't it, Arzu? You can tell me where I can find the girl, who you sold her to, or you can keep it to yourself. But you do that, you better pray to God that you can buy your way out of jail quick. Because if I don't get what I want by the time Çelik comes back to collect you, you better believe the first stop I make after leaving here is your home."

I snapped the lid of the laptop down, letting the gesture serve as emphasis, then set it aside and met his eyes. He stared back at me, brimming with hate, believing every one of my words.

That I would never—could never—bring myself to follow

through on my threat didn't matter. Arzu could imagine the
horrors I threatened to visit upon his family, because Arzu
could imagine himself doing the exact same things. What was
beyond the pale to me was simply the way you did business to
him. He believed me, because he still thought that we were
alike.

"Theunis Mesick," Arzu muttered.

"Where do I find him?"

"Amsterdam." Arzu shook his head, angry. "I don't know
where."

"You have a way to contact him," I said. It wasn't a question.
"Tell me the procedure."

"You motherfucker."

"I can head over to your home right now. That what you
want?"

"Fuck you! I have a number, all right? A phone number, it's
for a landline somewhere, I don't know where. I leave a message
for him, tell him I have a friend who'll be coming to town, give
him a number. He calls me back, we set it up!"

I pulled out the BlackBerry again. "Give it to me. Now."

"I can't remember!"

"Try harder, Arzu Bey."

He closed his eyes, struggling to recall the number, then
slowly recited a string of digits. I punched them in, dialed, then
put the phone to my ear, waiting for it to connect. It rang twice,
and then a man's voice answered me in Dutch.

"Hallo?"

"I'm looking for Theunis," I said, in English. "Theunis
Mesick."

"He is not here now," the man said. "You leave a message, a
number, I will tell to call you back."

"I'll try again later."

I hung up, began replacing all of my things in the carry-all, all the tools, the laptop. I removed the remaining envelope of money, put the handcuff key inside it, then dropped it on the ground. All the while, Arzu was shouting at me.

"You got what you want? You fucking have what you want, you happy, you fucker? You motherfucker! You fucking stay away from my family! You stay away, you stay away from my boys, I will kill you! I will kill you myself, I will fuck your corpse you touch them, you go near them again!"

I zipped the carry-all closed, hoisted it onto my shoulder, and turned to face him. He was breathless, going hoarse in his outrage.

"You fucking stay away from my fucking family!"

There was nothing that I knew about the man in front of me that I liked. Nothing about him that I could think of worth preserving. He kept, bought, and sold slaves. He had sent men to my home to murder me, and in so doing, had nearly cost me Miata, Alena, and a child I hadn't known existed.

What I needed to do now, I knew, was kill him.

"Arzu," I told him, "if I have it my way, you'll never see me again."

I left him there to shout in the darkness, screaming threats and promises that I hoped he'd never be able to keep.

CHAPTER
Twenty-five

The number Arzu had given me was for a fuck factory off Marnixstraat. It took two phone calls and almost exactly twenty-four hours to arrange a meeting with Theunis Mesick there. I was in a hurry to make up for the time I'd lost in Trabzon, and went directly from the airport in Amsterdam to meet him.

Mesick was another of the thug brigade, big the way Vladek Karataev had been big, but blond and younger, maybe in his early to mid-twenties. He wore leather pants and a muscle shirt that showed off full-sleeve tattoos on both arms, elaborate skin art that had been thrown together without rhyme or reason, with naked women and death's-head skulls and bleeding roses.

I dropped Arzu's name along with two hundred euros, saying that I'd been told he could help me find "the right girl." The combination was enough to buy a trip across town in his company, to a houseboat moored just off the Nieuwe Herengracht canal.

Things were going well, or at least I thought they were, right up to the moment we stepped into the living room of the boat. Then Theunis Mesick turned on me with a knife in his hand.

I was jet-lagged and feeling ragged already, and I paid for it in reaction time. His first cut caught me high on my right forearm, going deep as I tried to get out of the way. The arm went numb with shock for a second as I backpedaled. I was still carrying the small duffel full of my belongings on my shoulder, and I swung it around with my left to block the next stab, and it worked, but he batted the bag away and then I had nothing left.

Knives suck, and fighting someone who has one sucks even worse, because there's no way to survive without getting cut, and I already had one to show for it. For some reason, people think of knives as somehow less dangerous, less lethal than firearms, and it's a bullshit and very dangerous assumption, because, like guns, knives are lethal weapons. Knife fights are something that happen between the Sharks and the Jets, that's it.

Everywhere else, it's not a fight, it's just someone trying to goddamn kill you.

I stumbled backward, trying to backpedal to the door, the way I'd entered. He didn't give me the time, slashing repeatedly for my throat with sharp, quick cuts. It wasn't a particularly long blade, maybe two inches at the most, but two inches of steel will kill just as easily as six. I knocked over furniture, scrambling to the side. There was a vase of tulips on the coffee table, and I kicked that at him as I went past, and it missed, and he drove forward at me again, jabbing repeatedly. He knew enough about using the knife to keep it moving. I managed to grab one of the cushions off the couch, put it between us as a shield. The cushion was purple.

"What the fuck?" It came out of me as a gasp.

"Arzu doesn't give out my name," Mesick answered, and he came at me again.

I used the cushion, tried to catch the knife with it, but again he kept the blade moving, refusing to let it sink. He punched with it repeatedly, and I put a kick out, hit one of his legs, but I missed the knee, and the most I got out of him was a readjustment to the side. I moved right, trying to get away from the blade, losing the cushion as he swiped the knife beneath its edge. The tip caught me on the left side of my abdomen, and I felt the pain of my skin peeling and separating.

It had been maybe six seconds, and already I was bleeding from two separate wounds. He was going to cut me to pieces.

This is why I fucking hate knives.

There was a table, maybe for dining, the only thing on it an ashtray. I threw it at him, and it missed, but I followed the ashtray with the table itself, and he had to move to avoid it. Then I followed the table, trying to keep my arms in to protect my vitals, leading with my left hand extended. The knife came around again, split my palm, but before he could bring it back I was inside his guard, my right hand gripping the wrist holding the knife, pinning it against him as I slammed my body against his. We crashed back into a bulkhead, and I smashed my forehead into his face twice, and the second time felt my glasses snap at the bridge. I followed with a knee between his legs, and he still wouldn't let go of the fucking knife. He brought his free hand up to my throat, driving a thumb into my Adam's apple, and I got my bleeding left to his face, hooked my thumb in his nostril, pushing a finger into his eye. He howled, moved off my throat, trying to break my grip where I was threatening to tear his nose from his face, and that put his hand in front of me.

I bit him, hard, breaking the skin at the back of his hand, feeling my teeth meet.

He screamed.

He also dropped the knife.

I let him go, stepped back, hoping that would be enough. It wasn't. He was going for the knife again, bending to reach it, and I let him try, then kicked him in the face. He rocked back, dazed, and I kicked him again, and then once more for good measure.

He slumped and stopped moving.

I kicked the knife clear, then thought that wasn't going to be enough and picked it up myself. My hand was shaking, and I fumbled the grip the first time, had to steady myself before I could actually do it. Oddly, I wasn't feeling too much pain at the moment. Once the adrenaline ran itself out, that would change.

Before that happened, I needed to take care of Mesick.

The houseboat, it turned out, belonged to him. The way I figured it, he'd planned to kill me and then maybe take a little journey by boat to someplace nice and dark and secluded where he would be able to dump my body. I'm not sure he thought he'd get away with it or not, but then again, the way he'd come at me with the knife, he hadn't seemed the type to really think these kinds of things through.

I went through the boat as quickly as I could, starting with the room furthest from us and working back toward the living room we'd entered. The furthest room was the bedroom, and I got lucky in there, finding a roll of duct tape in a bureau drawer, along with some other heavy bondage equipment, including manacles for the wrists and ankles. I bled my way back to Mesick, still lying on the carpeted floor of the living room, and secured him with them, setting his wrists behind his back.

I gathered the two halves of my eyeglasses, took them and the duct tape to the bathroom. It was off the single hallway, to the left, and I stumbled into it, dropped them on the counter, and began yanking out the drawers and opening the cabinets, searching for a first aid kit. The best I managed was a bottle of rubbing alcohol, and it popped out of my grip when I tried to take it, my hands now thoroughly coated with my own blood. I sat myself on the closed toilet and tried to stop the bleeding.

The cut on my right forearm, his initial cut, seemed the worst of the ones I'd received, had split skin and fat and muscle, almost to bone. I could still move my fingers, and I figured that counted for something, that I'd been spared major nerve and tendon damage. The cut across my left palm was messy, but I'd gotten very lucky, and it looked like all that hit was the tip of the blade, and that just barely. A fraction deeper and I could've lost the use of the hand. The abdominal slash I couldn't be sure about, and didn't want to risk the required twisting for a further examination. Nothing seemed to be spilling out of my guts other than blood.

I used the rubbing alcohol first, pouring it straight over my wounds to wash and, maybe, hopefully, sterilize them, at least somewhat. Then I tore strips of duct tape and tried to put myself back together. I had pretty good luck on my arm, able to use my left hand to pinch the wound closed as I lay the strip down, then drawing it tight. It was harder going with my palm and side.

When I was finished, I just sat there, leaning against the

wall. The delayed pain had begun creeping in, and for several minutes it felt as if I was doing nothing but sinking in it. Spots of light danced about in my vision, and I knew I was close to passing out, realized I was hyperventilating. With effort, I got my breathing back under control.

There was noise coming from the living room, the sound of Mesick, conscious again, thrashing against his restraints.

With effort and the aid of the bathroom counter, I pulled myself back to my feet. The dancing lights returned as soon as I was upright, and I froze, drawing controlled breaths. They passed faster than they had before, but I took the warning seriously, and when I started moving again, I kept it slow and deliberate.

He was worming his way toward the kitchenette, using his bound feet to push himself along on his back. When he saw me, he froze, shocked, and I knew he'd thought I'd gone, that he was alone.

I stepped over Mesick without a comment, to where I'd set the knife on the countertop of the kitchenette. Then I turned to him and, knowing it would hurt, bent and took hold of the restraints at his ankles, using them to haul him back to the middle of the living room floor. I did everything I could to keep the pain I was causing myself from my face.

I looked down at Theunis Mesick with his knife in my hand and said, "You were wrong about Arzu."

It was a complete non sequitur as far as he was concerned. His mouth worked for a moment, trying to process my English, perhaps. "What?"

"You were wrong about Arzu. You said he didn't give out your name. Remember?"

He nodded, just the barest tilting of his chin. I had him confused, and worried, which was exactly what I was hoping for.

"He gave it to me," I said, running my thumb lightly along the edge of the knife for added effect. It was theatrical to the point of farce, but if I was going to play the part, I figured I'd best play it to the hilt, as it were. "He gave it to me just before I killed him."

Theatrical it may have been, but it sure as hell worked. Theunis Mesick's eyes snapped open enough to give me a generous view of their whites, my blurred vision making them appear to have no iris at all. His mouth worked even more frantically, and he tried the worm-crawl again, pushing himself backward. I smiled while I watched him do it. After a few seconds, I began to follow him, taking my time.

It didn't take long for him to realize there was nowhere for him to go.

"What?" he shrieked at me. "What do you want?"

"I want to kill you," I told him. "I'll settle for information."

"Anything! Anything, don't kill me!"

"Arzu sent you a girl, almost a month ago. A Georgian girl. Black hair, skinny. Young. Fourteen."

"*Ja*, her, *ja*! I remember!"

I looked at the knife, made a point of studying its curve in the light. I asked the question softly, loading it with menace. "Where is she?"

"I don't have her anymore! I don't have her!" He looked at me hopefully. "I give you another girl, fine, *ja*? I give you another girl, a younger girl!"

Still with the blade as before, I stared him into silence.

"I don't want *another* girl," I told him. "I want *that* girl."

"She's gone! I don't have her!"

"You know where she went."

"America! I take her there, give her to a man there!"

"Someone you've dealt with before?"

"*Ja,* for Arzu I have done it before, two, three times! Same man!"

"Then you'll know where I can find him," I said.

Misery crossed the fear in his face. "I don't know where he is! I call a number, get a message where to be meeting, when to do it!"

"You know where you took the girl. You're going to tell me that."

"I can't," Theunis Mesick said. "I can't."

"You can," I told him. "If you want to live."

CHAPTER
Twenty-six

It was still dark when I reached Schiphol Airport. The darkness had served me well on the way, hiding me in the back of the too-expensive cab I'd hired to take me out of Amsterdam, but once inside the airport, there was no such luxury. I zipped my windbreaker closed before subjecting myself to the lights, and my jeans were dark enough that the blood on them maybe wouldn't look too much like blood.

As a connoisseur of airports—by necessity, if not by choice—Schiphol was one of the best I'd ever encountered, at least where amenities were concerned. The problem was the hour; nothing would open until seven in the morning, which meant a wait before I could resume further repair work on myself. The duct tape was doing a reasonable job holding my forearm closed, but I was still leaking from my side and hand. Of the two, my palm was faring better, but the cut in my side was beginning to really worry me.

I made my way to a very clean and frighteningly well-lit bathroom, locked myself into one of the stalls, and once more found myself seated on a toilet. Using what was left of the duct tape, I tried to repair my eyeglasses, and ended up with something that looked like a nerd cliché. When I put them on, they sat at an angle, and threatened an immediate headache.

With the BlackBerry, I called into the mailbox of the singles' service in London. There was a message from Alena, left in Georgian. They were safely in Ireland, she said, and left a contact number. I did my best to commit it to memory, then hung up and switched to the laptop. Schiphol had wireless available, and the signal, though weak, penetrated the bathroom. I searched up a flight, booked Anthony Shephard on Aer Lingus to Dublin, departing in four hours.

Then I put everything away and struggled to keep from falling asleep until the shops opened.

At seven, I was waiting outside of a store called Etos in the Schiphol Plaza. Mostly Etos seemed to sell perfumes and other beauty supplies, but they had a selection of first aid items, and I pretty much bought one of everything that I thought might be useful, and a small pack of what passed for superglue in the Netherlands. There were several stores selling clothes on the plaza, as well, including an H&M that catered only to women, and a Nike store. Nike wasn't going to work for me; the way I was feeling, and, no doubt, the way I was looking, I'd need more help than that.

I went with a shop specializing in menswear, called Paolo Salotto, used Anthony Shephard's American Express card to get myself a complete makeover—suit, slacks, penny loafers, two ties, and two dress shirts. Then I took everything I'd bought back to the bathroom, hanging the new clothes on a stall door. I stripped off my shirt and worked at the sink with the mirror there, and it was still early enough that I had a fair amount of privacy. The abdominal cut had split further apart, and I used some of the sterile gauze I'd bought to examine the site. Mesick had gone deeper than I'd realized; I only hoped he hadn't broken the muscle wall. I bathed the wound again, this time with some of the Betadine I'd purchased, packed fresh sterile gauze into the wound, then taped everything down.

I cleaned the incision on my palm much the same way, but this time used the superglue to close the incision.

While I was working on my forearm, a fellow traveler came in to use the facilities. There had been a few before him, but this time, while he was washing his hands off to my right, he made a comment to me in Dutch, clearly as concerned as he was curious.

"It was a rough night," I told him with a big smile.

He laughed, shook his head.

I'm pretty sure he called me a tourist.

I packed my bloodstained clothes in the plastic bag that had held my Etos purchases, then dumped it in a trash can in the plaza, on my way to the gate. Well before hitting the security checkpoint, I removed and stowed my broken glasses. Between that and my expensive new suit, no one stopped me.

Waiting to board, I called the number Alena had left, got Bridgett before the first ring was out.

"I'm arriving Dublin, Aer Lingus, flight 603," I told her. "Flight gets in at a quarter past eleven."

"Bully for you," she said. "We'll see you when you get here."

"I'm not good to drive," I told her. "I need someone to pick me up."

"Oh Jesus."

"It's not that bad," I lied. "I'll see you when I get there."

I managed to stay awake through boarding, even into my seat.

I was asleep before the plane left the gate.

CHAPTER
Twenty-seven

Most of the Logans, I had been told, came from the North of Ireland, County Antrim, but at some point before Bridgett's great-great-grandfather had voyaged across the water to New York, a handful had made their way to the South, to County Galway. That was where Bridgett had taken Alena, to a farmhouse still owned by a distant cousin, south of Ballygar, some 130 kilometers west of Dublin.

"He rents it out," Bridgett told me in the car. She drove the way she'd always done, far too fast, even though the rented Ford clearly hadn't been built for it. At least she was staying on the correct side of the road. "We've got it for as long as we need."

"You left Alena there alone?" I asked. I was feeling light-headed, and it took me a couple of seconds to formulate the question.

"You say it like I had a fucking choice in the matter, Atticus. That bitch doesn't give choices, she makes up her mind and that's pretty much it. I swear to God, I tell her left, she says right just to be contrary."

"Miata."

"Yeah, she didn't want to leave the dog. The dog's company, by the way, I enjoy considerably more than hers."

I couldn't think of anything to say, and so stayed quiet. It was warm and the road vibration was comforting. I could feel myself starting to nod off again.

Bridgett glanced over at me, frowning. "How bad is it?"

"He took her to Nevada," I said. "Gave me the location of the handoff. I'll head there next."

"I'm not sure you're heading anywhere next. You don't look good."

"You don't like my tie?" I asked, and laughed, because I thought I was being very clever.

"You're in shock."

I considered that, or at least tried to. It seemed reasonable. I'd had to use the lavatory on the plane twice in flight to repack the wound on my side. Absorbent though the gauze was, I'd been in danger of soaking through my expensive new shirt. The idea of walking through Dublin customs as a bloodstain spread out from my middle hadn't seemed a very good one.

"I lost a lot of blood," I said, slowly. "Think I'm still leaking."

"You need a doctor."

I shook my head. My mouth was dry, maybe because I was going shocky, maybe from sleep-induced cottonmouth. I was thirsty. "Too many questions."

"Answering questions is better than being dead."

"I'll be all right. Just need a safe place for a day or two. Just to get repaired. Get some sleep."

"'Repaired'? You sound like you're a fucking car."

"Vroom vroom," I said.

The house was an old stone cottage, weathered and small, its front door painted bright red, and the same color had been applied to the shutters fastened open at the windows. A dry stone fence marked the property from the narrow road, a fast-moving stream flowing just beyond, crossed by a metal grate bridge. The actual farmland itself was overgrown and unkept, disused.

"Seamus makes more renting the place to tourists than working the land," Bridgett explained.

"Seamus is your cousin."

"Seamus is my cousin, yes."

"Seamus," I said.

"We're Irish, fuck off," Bridgett said. She parked the Ford with its nose facing the road, yanked the parking brake.

The red door opened, Alena moving into it, concealing her right side behind the frame for a moment before stepping out. She had a shotgun with her, double-barreled, more suited for downing birds than people, but if it worked for Dick Cheney, it would sure as hell work for her. I got out of the car carefully. Bridgett had already grabbed my bag.

"He was stabbed," Bridgett told Alena.

"Cut, not stabbed," I corrected. "Stabbed would've been worse."

Alena's mouth tightened to a line, her lips losing their color.

"He's in shock. He's going to decompensate."

She held out a hand for me, and I reached for it, but she took me by my elbow instead.

"Nice shotgun," I mumbled.

"It's what was here." Alena guided me through the door. It was considerably darker inside, the windows small, the lights low-wattage. Alena led me to a bedroom, and I started to remove my suit coat, but she stopped me, growling a warning.

"Where?" she asked.

"Left palm, right upper forearm, left oblique," I managed. "Left oblique's still bleeding."

"Stop moving." She came around behind me, carefully began tugging the sleeve off my arm. Bridgett had moved into the doorway, watching, and I heard paws on the dark hardwood, saw Miata peer around her knee at me.

"Hey, buddy," I told him.

Alena helped me with the shirt, and I saw that I'd leaked through it despite all my precautions. She told me to lie down, and I did so for what seemed like the first time in three days, felt my whole body shudder, almost a spasm, as muscles I hadn't known were clenched suddenly relaxed.

"Make yourself useful," Alena told Bridgett, shoving a pillow beneath my legs to elevate them. "Water, towels."

"Bitch," Bridgett said, cheerfully, but left the doorway. Miata hesitated, then came into the bedroom and lay down beside the bed.

"You could make an effort," I told Alena.

"She's just standing there, she shouldn't need to be told to help," Alena said. "This one on your side I don't like. You are tearing it when you move."

"We should probably do something about that."

She knelt down on her haunches, putting the wound at eye level, careful not to touch it. "Only blood?"

"Far as I know."

"So maybe the peritoneum was not perforated." She hissed softly. "I don't want to risk infection, or further infection. We need to sterilize, and we'll need to stitch it."

"Can you do that yourself?" Bridgett had a couple of towels over one arm, was carrying a porcelain bowl with a matching porcelain pitcher resting in it.

"I don't know nothin' about birthin' no babies," I said.

Both women glared at me.

"Nothing," I said. "Never mind."

Bridgett handed Alena a small bottle of antibacterial hand wash. "This help?"

"We need things," Alena said, taking the bottle. She squirted a generous amount onto her hands, began rubbing them vigorously together. "Ringer's solution and a catheter. Betadine or some other sterile wash. Saline, a lot of it. Needle-nose pliers. Thin needle, thin thread, silk is ideal. Antibiotics if we can get them, a Z-Pak would be best."

"I should be able to get all that in Galway. Everything but the Ringer's, at least."

"Then what are you waiting for?"

"Fucking," said Bridgett. "Bitch."

It was dark in the room when Bridgett returned, to find Alena sitting beside me, still holding the towel she was using as a bandage to apply pressure to the wound. I'd either slept or passed out since Bridgett had left, depending on whether one wanted to be charitable.

Bridgett flipped on the lights, then moved to the foot of the bed to dump out the contents of the plastic shopping bag she was carrying. Alena stopped her.

"Show me."

The look Bridgett gave her would've dropped a charging rhino. With a deliberation verging on surliness, she began removing items from the bag, one at a time. Alena told her where she wanted each set down. When she produced two bags of Ringer's solution and a catheter, Alena actually made a noise of approval.

"Did I get everything, ma'am?" Bridgett asked.

"We're going to need more light," Alena replied. "And a candle or lighter."

It took Bridgett a couple of minutes to gather the items and then return, during which time Alena left the bandage at my side to use the antiseptic wash on my arm and hook up the first bag of Ringer's. Bridgett returned as the catheter was going in, and she winced visibly at the sight. She asked Alena where she wanted the lamp she was carrying, placed it as directed.

In my daze, I realized something.

"When was the last time you did this?"

"Long time ago. Afghanistan." She actually smiled at me. "The vet in Poti was a good reminder."

"You are motherfucking kidding me," Bridgett said. "Let's take him to the goddamn hospital!"

"It's the same procedure," said Alena. "We can do this. Come here."

Together, they rolled me onto my right side, propping me up with more pillows. When Alena pulled the towel away from the wound, it pulled the clot that had formed with it, causing fresh pain and bringing fresh blood. She dumped all of one of the bottles of saline on the wound, irrigating it, soaking the bed and the pillows in the process with a mixture of blood and salt water. Then she dumped the antiseptic wash into the basin, scrubbing her hands and forearms. I smelled fire, saw Bridgett prepping the needle. When it was ready, she offered the pliers to Alena.

"No," Alena said, washing the length of thread she'd prepared in the basin. "We might cross-contaminate. You will stitch."

"The fuck you say," Bridgett said.

"I will hold the wound closed, you will do the stitching."

"Not me, sister."

"*Ebi tvoyu boga dush mat'!* Yes, you! Come here!"

"I can't sew him shut! I can't do it!"

I managed to raise my head, focused as best I could on Bridgett. I wasn't sure I was following. "You've got a hoop through your nostril. You have a half pound's worth of earrings in each of your ears."

"That's different! I didn't have to give *myself* the piercings!"

"You used to fucking shoot heroin, Bridgett," I said. "Don't tell me you're afraid of needles."

"Why do you think I'm scared of them, motherfucker?"

Alena swore in Russian again, this time to herself. I thought for certain the next thing she'd say in English would be a threat, and I was still present enough to know that if it was, things would go all the way downhill.

"Please, Bridgett," Alena said. "I need your help."

Bridgett stared at her. "Don't try to play me. Never fucking do that, okay?"

"Okay."

It took another second, then Bridgett moved out of my line of sight, to join Alena behind me. There was more explanation from Alena, what she wanted Bridgett to do, and then I felt the needle pushing through my skin, and it surprised me because it hurt a hell of a lot more than I'd expected. They worked slowly and carefully, and that didn't help, either. It hurt enough that I hadn't realized they were finished until they were moving the pillows, rolling me onto my back.

"Done?" I asked.

"Done," Alena told me.

"Good," I said, and fell asleep then and there, in my blood- and saline-soaked bed.

CHAPTER
Twenty-eight

The day after they closed the wound in my side, Bridgett drove me back to Dublin, this time to drop me off at the airport, rather than to pick me up. I was clean-shaven, wearing my new suit and a clean shirt, with a new pair of glasses that Bridgett had gotten made for me at a one-hour place while I'd been sleeping most of the previous day away. The stitches in my side itched, the skin tight, and again I was suffering cottonmouth, but now it was due to the antibiotics I was taking, and not from the fact that I was in compensated shock. While I'd been unconscious, Alena and Bridgett had also sewn up the cut in my forearm. My palm they'd left to a bandage and more superglue.

"You have any reason to believe this place you're going to in Nevada will get you what you want?"

"None at all," I said. "But I think the information is accurate."

"Why's that?"

"Because the guy who gave it to me believed I would kill him if it wasn't."

"Did you?" She didn't take her eyes off the road.

"No," I said.

Bridgett slowed to pay the toll over the River Liffey. Dublin spread out to the east, hidden in the rain. As she accelerated again, she said, "Guy sells people into slavery."

"Yes, he does."

"Explain this to me."

"Explain what?"

"That fucker didn't deserve to live. But you let him go."

"You think I should have punched his ticket?"

"If anyone was going to do it . . ."

"I thought about it," I admitted. "This other guy, too, Arzu Kaya. Pure piece of human excrement, that one. I thought about killing them both."

"But you didn't."

I shook my head.

"Why didn't you?"

"It's not about them," I said. "It's about me."

I'd booked my flight as Matthew Twigg, flying Continental to Seattle via Newark. Maybe it was because I'd been doing so damn much travel, maybe it was because I'd be flying into the U.S. again, but I took extra precautions this time to reinforce my cover. I abandoned the duffel that had seen me through the last four weeks of globe-trotting, exchanging it for a nice leather two-piece set, one rolling bag, the other a messenger. The rolling bag I loaded with clothes and appropriate toiletries. The messenger carried my laptop and its attendant cables, as well as copies of *The Financial Times* and *The Economist*. I still had Bakhar's little black book and Vladek Karataev's BlackBerry, as well. The little black book I kept in the messenger bag. The BlackBerry I put in a case on my hip, even going so far as to buy a Bluetooth headset for it.

Just your run-of-the-mill globe-trotting financial wizard, that was me.

The problem wasn't with the paper, per se, but with the itineraries. One-way tickets raise eyebrows amongst those who look for such things. While the passport that Nicholas Sargenti had supplied for Matthew Twigg had plenty of international travel attributed to it already, nowhere was there an entry stamp for Ireland. In and of itself, that wasn't extraordinary; most of the EU didn't bother for travel between member nations. But it was another anomaly, along with the one-way itinerary, and it made me nervous.

And sure enough, I was popped coming through customs in Newark.

"How long have you been away, Mr. Twigg?"

"Ten days," I said. "Had a deal to close in Dublin, then took a day to visit the Rock of Cashel."

He nodded slightly, flipping slowly through my passport beneath the purple glow of the blacklight by his terminal. There were plenty of ways he could determine that I was lying, but none of them were quick. Despite whatever efforts governments made to convince people of the contrary, his terminal didn't have a global database of travelers and their itineraries.

"They didn't stamp your entry," the agent said. "Next time you want to make sure they do, all right?"

"They didn't?"

"Nah, I'm not seeing it."

He marked my passport, whacked it with his stamp, and handed it back.

"Welcome home," he told me.

I followed the connecting flight all the way through to SeaTac. It was after ten when I arrived, and I found myself a room at a budget hotel near the airport, booked myself on the earliest flight I could find the next morning to Las Vegas. I took a shower, careful to keep the stitches on my arm and side dry, which actually took some doing, and when I was finished, I felt like I still had a film of soap and sweat clinging to my body. I set the alarm on the BlackBerry to wake me with plenty of time for the flight, then killed the lights and lay on my back on the bed, with the television on low for company.

Theunis Mesick hadn't been able to give me much. He had been, he explained, the middleman. Arzu had handled the money, arranged the sales, as he had arranged the sale of Tiasa. Mesick's job had been to transport her from Trabzon and to take her, via Amsterdam, to the U.S. For doing this, Arzu had paid him almost twenty thousand euros. Mesick had been smart enough not to mention anything else he might have done with Tiasa, which had probably saved his life; if he'd confirmed what I suspected, that he, like all the men before him, had raped her, I'd likely have killed him then and there, and to hell with the rumblings of my conscience.

Mesick had simply been another link in the supply chain, and his information supported that. The only names he knew were Arzu's and Karataev's. He'd been given a phone number to use once he'd reached Las Vegas with Tiasa and told to call it using a prepaid cell phone. When he did, instead of a person, he always reached an answering machine. He would leave a message with the number of his phone, and within an hour of doing so would receive a text message telling him when and where to make the delivery.

It was a clean system, very difficult to trace back, and one that left nothing incriminating in its wake.

Mesick had been sincerely unable to remember the number, despite my threats, but it didn't really matter. The number he was told to call had never been the same one twice. Even had he been able to recall it, I was certain that all it would get me would be an out-of-service message. If the people on this end of the supply line weren't all using prepaid cell phones as well, they were fools. And I knew already that they weren't.

What Mesick had given me instead were directions to the drop site, where he'd brought Tiasa. Why he could recall that and not a phone number I didn't know, and it made me suspicious.

That Arzu had set me up by sending me to Mesick wasn't lost on me. Nor was the fact that I'd left both men alive. But Mesick was convinced Arzu was dead. Unless Arzu managed to buy himself out of lockup, there was no reason for Mesick to believe otherwise. And if I believed Mesick's information—and I didn't see much choice—then Mesick had no way of warning whoever had Tiasa that I was coming.

It wasn't ideal at all, but it was as close to a level playing field as I was likely to get.

It was 101 degrees when I arrived in Las Vegas at eight in the morning. By the time I'd rented a car and checked into a hotel room well away from the Strip, it was ten, the mercury was kissing 108 and still climbing.

My rental had a Magellan GPS unit, and I used it, in conjunction with a newly purchased map, to plot myself a course out of town, heading northeast on Interstate 15. Vegas thinned, then dwindled, giving way to new developments peppering both sides of the highway, some of them left only partially constructed. The housing crash had clearly taken a boot to the nuts of Las Vegas.

Mesick hadn't had an address as much as a location, and with only his directions to go by, the doubt came gleefully creeping back as the Mojave Desert stretched itself out on all sides. After half an hour I passed the turnoff to the Valley of Fire Highway, and that was in keeping with what he'd told me. I stuck to the interstate as he had done, wondering what Tiasa had seen of the landscape, what she had made of this alien world. Wondering if she had been afraid still, or again, or if she'd felt nothing, turned numb by it all.

Some fifty miles out of Vegas, I turned off the highway, making south. Cropped buttes rose to the east and west as I continued away from the interstate. I began to see the first cautious indications of community again, faded road signs pointing me to places called Amber and Glassand. I even saw some green in the distance, where Lake Mead terminated into the Moapa Valley south of me, wresting fertile soil from the desert. Seeing the green would've given Tiasa hope, I thought.

But Mesick hadn't taken her that far.

A dirt road cut off the blacktop, heading east, and I followed it perhaps two hundred yards, the car leaving a cloud of dust in my wake. The road ended as insolently as it had begun, stopping without warning at two cinderblock buildings, each of them easily a sixth the size of the cottage I'd left in Ballygar. I stopped the car, letting the engine run, waiting to see if anyone would emerge from the structures. No one did. Neither of the buildings had windows that I could see. On the one furthest away, perhaps twenty meters, I saw a small satellite dish on the roof, and a compressor for an air conditioner.

I killed the engine and got out. It was furiously hot, as bad as Dubai, but devoid of even the barest humidity, the sunlight bright enough to hurt the eyes. I waited, listening, but there was no sound, nothing. Not wind, not traffic, nothing. I might as well have been standing in a vacuum.

The nearer of the two buildings, the one without the satellite dish, was unlocked. I pushed the door open, then stood in the doorway, waiting for my eyes to adjust. The stench of baked urine and shit washed out at me. I stepped inside, looking around, and quickly learned that there was almost nothing here to see. An empty plastic jerry can lay on its side by the door, and beside it a dented and weathered galvanized bucket. There were no fixtures, no sockets, and I doubted the building ever used power, let alone had been wired for it. I picked up the jerry can, stepped outside with it, trying to get fresh air, then uncapped it and gave it a sniff. There was no scent at all.

I looked back into the building, stomach churning, and no longer from the smell. It wasn't a building; it was a cell. That was probably how it was done. Mesick or someone like him would bring a girl to the location, lock her into the building, then retreat. There were literally hundreds of places in the surrounding terrain where someone could set up overwatch and never be seen. Lying in cover with a pair of binoculars and a bottle of Gatorade, the watcher would confirm the delivery, wait for however long they deemed prudent upon the trafficker's departure, and then move in for the pickup.

Meanwhile, a terrified girl would be trapped in a cinderblock hotbox. *Here's a jerry can of water and a bucket to crap in, little girl, someone'll be back for you later.*

I threw the jerry can back inside, headed for the second building. The door was metal, same as the first had been, but this time was chained shut, the links held fast with a padlock. I pounded hard on it with my right fist, but there was no response. I thought maybe I was hearing a fan running. When I pulled on the padlock, it didn't give.

I hadn't thought it would.

Eight miles south was Glassand. I found a mom-and-pop hardware store and bought myself some bolt cutters, then went around the corner and found a mom-and-pop grocery, where I picked up two liter bottles of water. I finished one bottle driving back the way I'd come, returning to find that nothing had been disturbed. Even the dust had settled once more.

The bolt cutters went through the padlock exactly the way they were designed to. I yanked the chain free and kicked the door open, nervous about what I might find. But there was no stench, no body, nothing like that. Just stale air being pushed around by the whirring air conditioner, and a folding table pressed against the far wall. On the table was a laptop computer, hooked to a power outlet. Another cable ran up the wall, presumably to the sat dish on the roof. Connected to the computer was a cheap cell phone, also on power from the outlet.

I gave the room another looking over before moving inside, thinking that people this careful might well be the kinds of people who set booby traps. Nothing gave me cause for alarm— at least, not more than I'd seen already. I approached the computer, not touching it. A green light glowed at its front, and when I leaned my head down toward it, I could just make out the sound of its internal fans going, struggling to keep the machine cool. The monitor was dark. I looked at the phone next, again not touching anything, and it was on, and while the signal strength I was reading on its screen wasn't terribly strong, it was enough that I knew the phone had reception.

I clicked the button beneath the trackpad on the laptop. The screen flickered to life, an ocean-green background and a password prompt. I considered, then typed in the words "you sons of bitches," running them all together without spaces. I knew it wasn't going to work, and wasn't surprised when the computer told me as much.

What surprised me was the message that followed.

PASSWORD INCORRECT. TWO ATTEMPTS REMAINING.

PLEASE WAIT TEN MINUTES BEFORE NEXT ATTEMPT.

Then the screen went dark again.

That was unusual enough to give me pause, to make me realize that I had, finally, hit a true dead end. The warning and the ten-minute wait said it all; however the computer was protected, it was serious encryption. I wasn't going to get through with blind luck or by trying to reboot the machine.

I looked at the phone again, putting what was before me together with what I'd learned from Mesick. Whoever Arzu and he had dealt with on this end had outdone themselves in the anonymity department. Someone would call into the phone, and the computer would answer, then forward whatever message was left via either text or email. Whoever received the message could then respond with a text or email of their own, sent back to the computer, where it would in turn be routed to the initial caller.

It was elegant and insulated and there was no way that I could see to crack it. All the phones concerned were certainly prepaid cellular, which meant I had no means to trace ownership, especially if whoever had set up the coms system was in the habit of changing the ones they used regularly, which was a given. Getting into the computer would take an expert and time, and while I could think of a few places to find experts in Las Vegas, while I might even be able to spare the time, in the end, I wasn't certain it would be worth the effort. The best I would get would be, perhaps, an archive of messages sent and received, none of which would be incriminating in and of itself. Any phone numbers I found would be useless.

The other option I could think of, at the moment, was to look at the land, dig around in county records, find out who owned the buildings, who was paying the power bills. But like trying to chase down the numbers, I could see how that would end, too. Someone careful enough to have gone to these lengths for their coms wasn't going to drop the ball when it came to leaving a paper trail. Even if I managed to trace owner-ship back through one or two or however many shells and blinds, the odds were I'd end with a farmer who received a cashier's check promptly on the fifteenth of each month for the use of his land, and it was unlikely even then that he'd know who actually was sending him the money.

It felt like Dubai again, and not only because of the heat. For a good five minutes, I stood in that stifling little room, wondering what to do next. I could only think of one thing.

With the bolt cutters, I smashed the computer to pieces. Then I went after the phone. I told myself that I was doing it to put a dent in their finely tuned operation, that, if nothing else, it would slow them down a little while, at least until they found a new place, a new computer, a new phone. They would have to rebuild, set up new protocols. It would take time before they got their system up and running again.

Just not very much time.

■   ■   ■

For most of the drive back to Vegas, I didn't think much of anything. I felt tired, not just in need of sleep, but truly weary. The stitches in my side and forearm hurt, and the skin along my left palm had begun to itch in earnest, now that my hand was starting to heal. When I'd been swinging the bolt cutters, I'd maybe been swinging harder than I should have done.

I stopped for a meal at a diner on the way back to my hotel because I felt I should, rather than because I had any appetite for it. There were multiple racks of free newspapers, nothing more than collections of ads, just inside the entrance, almost all of them telling me that women with names like Juliette and Morgana and Devyne would be happy to take my money to make me happy. A couple of the ads actually used words like "fresh" and "young" and even "barely legal."

It made me think of Kekela, and then I was thinking of Tiasa yet again. When my meal came, I found I couldn't even bring myself to take a bite of it. I paid, left, picked up more water at a convenience store, and finally returned to my room.

I didn't know what to do next.

There were options, of course. Kekela had spoken of the "mongers" when we'd visited Rattlesnake, the men who frequented whores, who made it a game. There were mongers everywhere, certainly here in Las Vegas. With a couple of days, I could probably locate a few. With a couple of weeks, I could maybe earn their trust enough to find the specialists, the ones who knew where to find girls so young that, even in a state with legalized prostitution, they remained hidden.

Or I could head back to Amsterdam. I could chase down Mesick, see if there was something I'd missed, something he had held back. I could go further, to Trabzon, and renew my acquaintance with Captain Çelik, and hope to grab more time alone with Arzu Kaya. I could rewind the clock all the way to

Georgia, and hope that Mgelika Iashvili knew more than he'd said, had one last crumb for me to follow.

Or you could let it all go, I told myself. *You could just walk away.*

But even thinking that, I knew that I couldn't.

One month of chasing after Tiasa Lagidze had led me here. Four weeks that had shattered the life Alena and I had built for ourselves, and in so doing, had also destroyed the walls I had put between the man I had been and the man I had become. Iashvili had said we were the walking dead, Alena and I, and he'd been right, but not in the way he imagined. Like Bakhar Lagidze, I hadn't left my past behind; I'd tried to bury it, alive and kicking, and it had come back on me the same as it had come back on him. Ten men dead by my hand in Batumi and Dubai was the proof.

Everything had brought me here, the same way it had brought Tiasa.

Bakhar. Karataev. Arzu. Mesick.

And one other person, at the end of the line. One person, and I didn't have the first idea where to look.

Bakhar. Karataev. Arzu. Mesick...

It hadn't just been any supply chain, I realized. It had been *their* supply chain. I'd thought that the connection had been between Bakhar and Karataev, that there had been nothing to tie Bakhar to Arzu. Yet there was Arzu connecting to Mesick, and Mesick saying he had brought girls to the U.S., to Nevada, before.

I opened the laptop, brought up Vladek Karataev's files from his BlackBerry, began going through the entries in his address book one at a time. There was nothing that looked like a phone number for somewhere in the States, certainly nothing that looked like one for Nevada. I combed through them a second time, and got the same result.

But there had to be a connection.

Bakhar's little black book was in the messenger bag, where I'd left it, and I dug it out, started going through it again. Same thing, nothing with a U.S. area code, nothing that looked like a number for Nevada. I went back to the listings from the BlackBerry, began comparing each entry, one at a time, alphabetically.

Under the ɜ, Bakhar had an entry, "Pretty." The number, at first glance, was for Ukraine, with a 380 country code prefix. The number ended in 207. When I checked Karataev's, I found an entry under the word *krasívyj*, which also meant "pretty." The numbers weren't identical; Karataev's first four digits were different. But like in Bakhar's book, the number ended in 207.

Reversed, the number began 702.

702 was one of the two area codes in use for the state of Nevada. I knew that, because it was on the goddamn telephone on the desk right before my eyes.

I had two possible phone numbers for "pretty" in Nevada. Whoever the hell that was. If they were still in service. If they were real numbers. If they weren't actually for somebody or some establishment in Ukraine.

Using the BlackBerry seemed like bad luck, like tempting fate, never mind how many times I had changed SIMs on the thing. I used the telephone on the desk instead, hit 9 for an outside line, and dialed the number from Karataev's listing, thinking that one would be the most current.

It rang. Four times.

Then a woman said, "This is Bella."

"Bella," I said. "I understand you're the person to talk to if I'm looking for some company."

CHAPTER
Twenty-nine

A month to the day from when Tiasa had been taken, I was once again on I-15, heading the same direction I had traveled the previous afternoon, but this time when I passed the turnoff to the drop site, I stuck to the freeway for another thirty miles or so. The sun was preparing to set, just beginning to bathe the desert in red and orange, when I drove into the town of New Paradise, following the directions I'd been given along Mesquite Avenue toward the northwest side of town. Lights were coming on, a few people emerging now that the temperature was beginning to descend toward tolerable.

Calling the town New Paradise was potentially a contradiction in terms. A lot that I saw was obviously recent construction, streets of fresh pavement, and everything with a new coat of paint. A small casino, Paradise Rollers, anchored the main street on one end, new-school design with sweeping neon and elegant curves instead of a box with blinking lights. At the other end of the street was a well-watered and vibrant park, grass and trees and bushes and flowers. The water taken to maintain it could probably have irrigated a small third-world nation. It certainly all felt new.

But if Tiasa were here, it sure as hell wasn't Paradise.

There was an Albertson's at the corner of Mesquite and Sawtooth, the supermarket reasonably busy this time of day as people just off work stopped for groceries on their way home. I parked on the south side of the lot as I'd been directed to do, killed the engine. I'd been told no phones would be permitted, and so took the BlackBerry off my belt, stowed it in the glove box, and then waited. I didn't have to wait long.

Less than a minute after I'd parked, a black Town Car pulled into the space next to me, the kind of vehicle normally used by car services. Its windows were tinted. I got out of my car, locked it up, and moved to the new one, climbing into the back.

Inside were two men, one waiting for me in the backseat, the other behind the wheel. As soon as I'd closed my door, there was the thunk of the electronic locks.

The man beside me was in his late twenties, Caucasian, with black hair. He wore blue jeans and a black fitted T-shirt, and from his biceps I could see he liked his barbell set. The watch on his left wrist was bulky and expensive, maybe platinum.

"Mr. Twigg?" he asked, looking me over. I'd made a point, again, of trying to go with the right clothes for the occasion. Today that meant tan khakis and a short-sleeved polo shirt, the kind of thing a businessman closer to forty than to thirty would wear when relaxing. I wore a windbreaker as well, mostly to cover the stitches on my right forearm.

"Yes," I said. "That's right."

"Put your hands on the back of the seat in front of you, please, and lean forward."

I nodded my understanding, did as directed. The pat-down was thorough and immodest, and when it was finished, he had my wallet, an envelope of money, and my hotel key card. He passed the card up to the driver, who immediately pulled out a cell phone and used the number on the key to dial my hotel. I could hear the driver speaking to whoever answered, asking to speak to a guest named Matthew Twigg. While he was doing this, the man beside me was going through my wallet, checking my driver's license and credit cards.

"There's a Matthew Twigg at the Gateway Suites," the driver said, handing the key back. "No answer in his room."

The one beside me replaced everything in my wallet as he'd found it, then opened the envelope. Inside were fifty hundred-dollar bills, and he counted all of them before stuffing them back into the envelope. He handed the money up to the driver, then handed my wallet and room key back to me.

"I guess you're who you say you are, Mr. Twigg," he said.

"I don't know what to say to that," I told him.

The man smiled, friendly. "Nothing you can say. Mike, we're good to go."

Mike put the car in gear, and we started to roll. The man next to me offered his hand with a new smile, said, "Name's Bradley."

I shook his hand. "Matt."

"You can relax, Matt. It's not far."

"I'm trying not to be nervous."

"First time?"

"Kind of. I, uh...I did something similar last time I was in Eastern Europe."

"That where you got our number?"

"From a guy in the Republic of Georgia," I said.

Bradley's smile widened for a moment, almost to a laugh. "I hear that guy's a piece of work."

"To be honest, he kinda scared the shit out of me."

That earned a nod, and then Bradley sank back in his seat, apparently relaxing. I did the same, keeping one eye on what was outside the windows. We'd turned north, and, at first, I thought we were heading outside of town. We passed a New Paradise police car, parked outside of a strip mall Starbucks, then a school, then another strip mall. The driver, Mike, turned us east, onto a curving street called Oasis, and after half a mile we passed through an open gate, into a development of shiny new McMansions. Like the market in Vegas, the market in New Paradise had taken a hit. It was now dark, and I didn't see a single light burning in any of the homes.

We wound through the empty streets, finally entering a cul-de-sac with five of the largest homes I'd seen yet. Three cars were parked here on the street, a Lexus convertible, a Porsche SUV, and a large Ford 4x4. The garage door opened automatically as we approached, and Mike parked us within. The door was closing before he'd shut off the engine.

"Here we go," Bradley told me. "If you'll follow me, Mr. Twigg."

I followed him, and Mike followed me. Mike was shorter than Bradley, but with much the same look, maybe even the same age, though his hair was a light brown, not black. I also noted that Mike was wearing a pistol in a holster on his hip. He stuck with us into a marble-floored hallway that we followed into the front hall of the house. A wide staircase in the center of the room split the space neatly in half, with hallways running off on either side, and an archway leading to a sunken living room to our right, what would've been the left if we'd entered through the overlarge front doors. There was nobody in sight, and I wasn't hearing anything but a distant stereo, playing classical music, what was maybe Chopin.

Bradley took me down another hallway lined with framed black-and-white photographs, artsy pictures of children, some of them smiling, some on slides, some on swings, some simply staring into the camera. Wall sconces were placed regularly between them, throwing soft light up at the ceiling. At the end of the hall was a closed door, another sconce beside it. This one, I noted, was unlit.

Bradley knocked and opened the door enough to lean in, saying, "Mr. Twigg is here."

The voice that answered matched the one I'd heard on the telephone the previous evening.

"Send him in."

Bradley opened the door wide, closed it behind me as soon as I was through. He stayed outside.

The room was fairly large, half home-office, half library. A large wooden desk with a laptop and cell phone, one chair positioned facing it. A couch to the side, leather upholstery. Bookshelves filled with tomes of identical spines, the kinds of books bought by the yard and not by the content. Two more framed photographs, still black-and-white, but more erotically charged: one of a dramatically lit woman's bare back, with just enough neck to see the dog collar she wore; the other of a man's hips, angled so his erection was apparent, a drop of fluid falling from its tip.

The woman, Bella, wasn't what I'd expected. She might've been as young as mid-thirties, maybe as old as mid-fifties. Her hair was expensively styled in a way that made me recall Ia, Bakhar's wife, and similarly dyed, though hers was black, and Ia had favored blonde. She wore a navy blue blouse and long black skirt, and a string of pearls around her neck. Her shoes were black leather, low-heeled. Aside from the necklace, there was no other jewelry.

She moved to greet me, smiling, and offered me her hand.

"Matthew," she said. "Bella Downs, very nice to meet you in person."

"Thank you," I replied.

Bella Downs indicated the chair opposite the desk, then moved around behind it, taking a seat. Her hands stayed out of sight, and I thought of the unlit sconce outside. There was a switch, probably, something she could hit with a finger or a foot, that would turn that light on and bring Bradley and Mike running.

"No trouble finding us?" she asked.

"No, the instructions were very clear. Brad—Bradley?—has the money you told me to bring."

"It's Bradley."

"He searched me."

"Of course. We're an extremely exclusive business, Mr. Twigg. We can't allow just anyone to come through our doors, especially people we know next to nothing about."

"I understand. I just didn't think he'd search me. That's never happened before."

"We're required to be more careful here than in Eastern Europe." Bella smiled again, and I nodded, thinking that I hadn't told her that on the phone, that the car had to have been bugged, and that she must've heard our conversation on the way in. "So, what can we do for you?"

"I'm looking for a specific kind of girl," I said.

"I should hope so. What do you have in mind?"

"I'm not sure, exactly. I'd like to see what you have."

Bella Downs shook her head, still smiling, but it was less friendly, more remonstrative. "That's not how it works here, Mr. Twigg. This is a specialty location, not the Mustang Ranch. You tell me what you'd like, and I will provide it for you."

"See, I don't think I'm going to know what I'd like until I see her," I said.

The smile thinned. "That's not an option."

"I just want to see them."

"Our girls are not for display."

Behind me, I heard the door open.

"Mr. Twigg is leaving," Bella Downs said, and now there was no sign of a smile on her face at all, not even its memory. "Please take him back to his car."

"Mr. Twigg." I could hear Bradley approaching, his voice now almost directly over my shoulder. "If you'll come with me."

I looked at Bella Downs, and she stared straight back at me, and I realized I'd blown it. Somehow, someway, I'd stepped wrong, had violated protocol. I had pushed too hard, or had said yes when I should've said no, or had stayed silent when I should've spoken. I didn't know. It didn't matter.

"I'm sorry if I've offended you," I said. "I'm new at this and—"

"Obviously," Bella Downs interrupted. "And now you're leaving. Goodbye, Mr. Twigg."

I felt a hand on my shoulder, no squeeze, not very much pressure, even. Just its presence to let me know that my time here was up, and that if I wasn't willing to leave on my own, Bradley would be happy to assist me. Violently.

"My apologies," I said again, and got to my feet.

Bradley escorted me to the door, where Mike was waiting.

He hadn't drawn his pistol, but his hand was resting on its butt, the intention clear. With the right timing, I could probably take them both, but the fact was that I still hadn't recovered from Amsterdam, and I wasn't certain what it would give me, anyway.

I had more than I'd arrived with. I had the location. I could come back on my terms, in my time, and get what I was after.

CHAPTER
Thirty

Mike and Bradley drove me back to the Albertson's parking lot without a word, dropping me off exactly where they had picked me up. I watched the Town Car pull away into the night, then unlocked my rental and climbed inside. I retrieved the BlackBerry, tucked it away, then started the engine and pulled out.

On my way out of town, a New Paradise police car fell in behind me, holding maybe three lengths back. It held the distance for almost two miles, until we were securely into the desert's darkness, and then hit its lights. I pulled off to the shoulder, slowed, and stopped. The cruiser came in behind, maybe three or four meters back. I left the engine running, watching in the rearview, leaving my hands on the wheel.

The cop kept me waiting for almost two minutes, and I figured that was because he was running the plates. The interstate was quiet, very little traffic running in either direction. Then I saw another set of red-and-blues coming my way, flashing lights but no siren, another police car speeding out from New Paradise. This one pulled in close behind the first, and I could just make out an officer stepping out of the car in my mirrors.

Then the cop driving the car that had stopped me got out as well and, together, the two of them approached my vehicle. I got a flashlight beam in the face, a hand motioning me to lower my window.

"Problem?" I asked, already with a very good idea what that might be. As far as it went, I was running clean. I hadn't carried a weapon since I'd left Dubai, not counting Mesick's knife, and that was currently at the bottom of an Amsterdam canal. The papers for Matthew Twigg were watertight.

"License," the cop said.

I dug out my wallet and handed it over. When he took it, I caught a glimpse of the watch on his wrist. It was a Rolex, platinum, the same model that Bradley had worn. It occurred to me that I had yet to meet an honest cop wearing a platinum Rolex. I supposed there was always a first time.

I didn't think this was going to be it.

"Mr. Twigg," the cop said, handing my license back to me, "kill your engine and exit the vehicle."

I unfastened the seatbelt, following his orders. "What'd I do?"

"You were driving erratically, sir. Have you had anything to drink?"

"Nothing but water."

"Turn around, hands on the vehicle."

"I didn't do anything."

"Turn around."

The other cop was drawing his weapon.

I turned around, put my hands up, and immediately found my right with a cuff around it. The cop who'd stopped me yanked my arm around, secured my wrists together behind my back. He gave me a quick patdown, then began maneuvering me toward his car. He had the door open to the rear seat when I tried again.

"I didn't do anything."

"Mr. Twigg," the cop said, "shut the fuck up."

The second cop followed us, and we didn't go far, maybe half a mile from where I'd been pulled over, then off the freeway and into desert scrub. Both cars came to a stop, and the officer who'd pulled me over waited until his partner had exited his vehicle, then came around, and together they pulled me out of the back. We weren't so far from the interstate that I couldn't see the occasional light, hear the soft whisper of the traffic. The sky was clear and bright, and the moon had risen.

I was starting to get very worried. If their plan was to kill me, there wasn't going to be much I could do to prevent it. The only glimmer of hope I could find was, if that was their intention, they'd have taken me further from the road to do it.

"Ms. Downs asked us to give you a message." The one who'd pulled me over seemed to be doing all the talking.

"I think I've gotten it," I said.

They shoved me forward, hard, and I tried to keep my balance, but with the terrain and the force of the push, it was a lost cause. I managed to catch myself on my knees, started to turn my head back to them, and even though I was expecting it, even knowing it was coming, the pain of the blow exploded bright through my vision and sent me down on my side. The fleeting hope came and went that my glasses would somehow survive whatever happened next.

What happened next was a beating.

I tried to tuck up into a ball, to protect my left side and my right arm while both cops went at me using their sticks, but with my hands cuffed behind my back, there was no way to do it, and I was at their mercy. They worked my back and shoulders, hit me a couple of times in the head. My perception fractured, began dropping time. All I could do was lie there and take it.

After a while, they stopped. The one who did all the talking used a kick to flip me onto my back, then jabbed me in the sternum with his collapsible baton. I made yet another noise I wasn't proud of.

"It'd be a good idea," the cop said. "It'd be a very, very good idea for you to forget you ever came to New Paradise."

I groaned in agreement. He was making a lot of sense.

"You come back here, Mr. Twigg, and we'll have to have another talk with you," he said. "There's a lot of desert between here and Vegas. A lot of desert. It could be years before somebody found what was left of you. Are we clear?"

I tried to nod.

"Don't come back."

I tried to nod again.

He motioned for the other cop, and they rolled me onto my stomach, unfastened the cuffs. I didn't move, feeling fresh misery rush into my shoulders. One of them hit me in the back again, and then I heard them walking away, the sound of the car doors slamming closed on each patrol car. Their engines started, one after the other, and their tires ground the earth, then faded away into the night.

I rolled myself onto my back slowly, trying to guard my left side, checking the site of the knife wound with my fingertips. When I brought my fingers up to see them in the moonlight, I saw blood, but not a lot. Hopefully it was only a couple of torn stitches. I dropped my hand back to my side and just lay there, feeling the earth beneath me still hot from the day's sun, trying to get a grip on the pain, thinking.

Bella Downs had members of the New Paradise Police Department on her payroll. At five thousand dollars just to get through the door of her house of horrors, she certainly could afford it. A town the size of New Paradise, there couldn't be more than six, maybe eight cops on that force. It was possible she'd bought them all. That was her strength, how she guarded her home turf. Bradley and Mike inside, and the cops on speed dial should they ever be required.

She'd shown me her best cards, I realized, and I started to laugh, and kept on laughing, not caring how much it hurt, because I saw it then, saw what to do and the way to do it. Bella Downs didn't know who Matthew Twigg was, she couldn't be sure how I'd found her, and she didn't know what I really wanted. As far as she was concerned, I'd strayed off course and into her operation, and so she'd shown me her best cards to convince me to go away and not come back.

If I'd been a man named Matthew Twigg, I probably would've listened.

With effort, I pulled myself to my feet. The walk back to the rental was going to be a long and painful one, but I knew the car would still be there. The cops from New Paradise would make sure of that. The drive back to Vegas would be even longer, and probably hurt worse. But none of that mattered.

Tiasa was close, and I finally had a way to reach her.

CHAPTER
Thirty-one

There were three students at work in the RF lab at the Howard R. Hughes School of Electronics at the University of Nevada, Las Vegas, when I walked in during lunch hour the next day. Of them, only one looked up, a young Hispanic man in wire-frame glasses and a Green Lantern T-shirt, apparently mid-process of assembling some piece of electronics or another.

"Dude," he said. "What happened to your face?"

"Lost a bet," I said.

"Some bet. Can I help you with something?"

"I'm looking for Sharala Chandna. Professor Blackstone gave me his name."

The other two at work—another man and a woman, each perhaps in their mid-twenties—broke off from their respective tasks, listening. The man was Caucasian, and the closest to the cliché I'd walked in expecting, despite myself, in black cargo pants and white work shirt, pens and a calculator in his breast pocket. The woman looked to be Indian, wearing torn and weathered jeans, and a faded light blue T-shirt with the words *Big Blue Marble* barely legible beneath an iron-on Planet Earth.

"That would be me." The woman pushed the laptop she'd been working at to the side. There was a decal on the lid of the computer, a caricature of a girl in horn-rim glasses with a mop of black hair. The words *Flirty, Dirty, and Nerdy* had been printed beneath.

"Beg your pardon," I said. "He led me to believe I was looking for a guy."

"Yeah, Blackie does that." Sharala Chandna nodded. "Likes to poke holes in the stereotypes. He tell you to look for the one with a pocket protector, too?"

"Nerd glasses, actually."

Sharala Chandna approached, leaving her workbench and her laptop behind. Various pieces of equipment that I hadn't the first idea about populated the workshop, along with circuit boards, spare antennae, soldering equipment, oscilloscopes, voltmeters, and tools of every shape and size. The two men went back to their respective projects, and I didn't even try discerning what they were working on.

Sharala looked me over, and I had a good idea what she was seeing, and so didn't take it personally. Aside from my jeans, T-shirt, and boots, I had a new selection of bruises, including a cheerfully swelling one rising quickly on my right cheek. My lower lip had been split at the corner. In my short sleeves, the bandage covering the stitches on my forearm was clearly visible.

"I'd offer to shake your hand, but I'm afraid it'd fall off," she said.

"The right one works fine." I offered it to her. "My name's Matt."

She shook my hand briskly. "What can I do for you?"

"I'm looking for someone to build something for me, and to build it quickly. I'm willing to pay for the time and materials. Professor Blackstone said I should come down here and ask for you. He said you were a, uh, 'maker'?"

She grinned. "He said that? He'd know. What sort of thing are we talking about?"

I pulled the schematics I'd printed out that morning from my back pocket, handing them to her. I'd found them online, at a website that had offered the designs as open hardware. Once I'd found them, I'd brought up the website for UNLV, and in short order that had led me here.

"Oh fuck!" Sharala said. "Oh fuck yeah, it's Limor!"

Both men looked up sharply from what they were doing, immediately and visibly curious. The one with the pens in his pocket asked, "Which one?"

"The Wave Bubble! He fucking wants a Wave Bubble!"

"No shit?" This from the other one, the one who'd asked what had happened to my face. "Let me see!"

All three of them crowded around the schematic, and then Sharala handed them the sheets and grabbed her laptop, pulling it over to the worktable nearest them. She opened her web browser, typing in a URL from memory, then clicking once, twice, giggling to herself the whole while.

"Yeah, it's Limor's Wave Bubble, all right!" she said gleefully. "I made her Minty MP3 like a year ago, that was so cool."

"The POV—"

"On the bicycle wheels! Fuck yeah!"

"Excuse me," I said.

"Did you see the new Arduino stuff? Fucking awesome."

"No, the TV-B-Gone! The TV-B-Gone is genius, I fucking *love* that thing. You heard about Greenberg, right?"

"What'd he do?"

"He built one, took it down to the Strip. Started going through the casinos, hitting each of the sports bars, fried every LCD screen he could find. Got all the way to Caesar's before they caught him."

"Outstanding."

"Excuse me," I said again.

They all stared at me, seemingly having forgotten I was there.

"I assume this means you can make me one?" I asked Sharala.

"Oh yeah, hell yeah." She was almost dismissive. "Couple of weeks, sure. Limor lays everything out—she's fantastic, I love her, I would have her babies if I could, seriously."

"Thing is, I need it sooner. End of the week, if possible."

"That's harder. You gotta do the Gerber plots, then have the PCBs made. We can get those done in town, but it's more expensive. And some of the components, they'll have to be ordered."

"And I need it boosted."

That caught her by the curiosity. "How much?"

"It has to be able to blanket a house, a big one. Some of the exterior."

"But still this scale?"

"It can scale up," I said. "Just needs to be portable, something I can carry."

"Sure, yeah, you get a bigger battery, a power amplifier, that's one way to do it. Just factor up the math."

"Wait." The one with the pens in his pocket was staring at me. "Why?"

"Why?" Sharala asked.

"Why does this guy need a Wave Bubble, one that's stepped up?" He was still staring at me. It was a fair question, and I was a little surprised it had taken this long to be asked. "Why does he need to jam all forms of communication going into or out of a great big house running between eight hundred megahertz and two point eight gigahertz?"

All three of them gave me the hairy eyeball.

"I've got to do something," I told them. "And I don't want the people I'm doing it to making any phone calls while it's being done."

"Yeah, see," he said. "That kinda sounds like something maybe Sharala and Solomon and me wouldn't want to be a part of."

"What's your name?" I asked him.

"Augustyn."

"Auggie," said the one in the glasses. Solomon. "We call him Auggie."

"You guys mind if I close the door?" I asked.

"Why?" asked Sharala.

"Because I want to answer the question, and I don't want us being overheard while I do it."

"Go ahead," Auggie said. "But, man, you try anything and we'll shove a soldering iron so far up your ass you'll have smoke coming out your nose."

I nodded, turned to close the door. None of them had moved when I turned back, each of them watching me as if trying to determine how I myself was wired.

"Let me tell you about a girl," I said.

Sharala, Auggie, and Solomon, it turned out, were all "makers," and all of them were looking to change the world. By "makers,"

I learned, they meant those who actually built things, who tinkered and dinked and took apart and put together and built workshops in their garages. They differentiated themselves from "abstracts" and the "normals." The "abstracts" were the abstract thinkers, the ones who, as they put it, sat around all day dreaming about what could work, would work, how to make this more efficient and that more powerful and this more elegant without ever getting their hands dirty. Professor Blackstone, who had referred me to them, they said, was "abstract." Conversely, Limor Fried, the creator of the Wave Bubble, was, by their account, a Saint of Makers.

"And the normals?" I asked. We were at a restaurant a few miles from the campus that they had suggested, a place called Metro Pizza. So far, they'd worked their way through a cheese pizza and a pitcher of beer, and seemed eager to start on a second round of each.

"Normals are the ones who do it for a living," Solomon said, pouring a fresh glass of beer for himself. "They get their degree and then they go to work for The Man. But never mind that, this stuff about this girl, Tiasa—this shit's for real?"

"Yeah," I said. I hadn't told them everything, because there were things they didn't need to know to help me. But I'd told them about Tiasa, about how she'd been taken from her home, about how I'd been chasing after her for a month.

"Still doesn't explain the need for the Wave Bubble," Auggie said. Of the three, he was the most suspicious, not because he distrusted me, I'd realized, but because he was very concerned with how what he made might be used.

"Where she is now—where I think she is—the people who have her, they've got some police in their pocket," I said. "All of these people are using cell phones, they don't like landlines, they don't like anything that can be traced. I don't want them calling for help when I go to get her."

"How do you know they've got the cops in their pocket?" Solomon asked.

I indicated my face.

"Go to the feds," Sharala said. "Or the state police."

"And what if someone tips these people off first?" I asked. "Then I lose her. I can't take the risk."

"This one girl, she's there, maybe, but ... but there are other girls there, too. You're just going to leave them there?"

"No," I said.

"What're you going to do for them?"

"I'm working on it. Look, I've told you guys as much as I think it's safe to tell you. I'm dealing straighter with you than I've dealt with anybody in a long, long time. Are you willing to help me or not?"

"Of course we'll help you," Sharala said.

"I'll pay for the equipment, anything you need," I said. "I'll pay for your time."

"We'd do it for free," Auggie told me.

"But money's good, too," Solomon added.

"So what do we do now?"

"Now?" Sharala asked, with a grin that seemed almost too delighted for her face to hold. "Now we make shit."

CHAPTER
Thirty-two

I went apartment hunting that afternoon. I found my-
self a cheap place on West Cheyenne for six-fifty a month, and
had a rental agreement with Matthew Twigg's name on it by
four in the afternoon. That gave me just enough time to get to
the DMV before they closed at five. With the rental agreement
in one hand and my Washington State driver's license in the
other, I was able to provide proof of residency, and left just as
they were locking the doors with a brand new Nevada State
driver's license.

I raced down to Tropicana, jockeying through traffic and
watching the clock. My haste wasn't truly necessary, but the
more I got out of the way now, the less I would have to do later,

and the plan I was forming—such as it was—was going to keep me fairly busy for the next few days. According to the rental's clock radio, it was seven past six when I pulled into the parking lot of The Gun Store, and when I went inside I got eyefucks from just about everyone behind the counter, which is never a nice thing, and all the less pleasant when the people delivering them are also wearing firearms, as all of them were.

I made it easy on them, though, because I knew what I wanted, and they had it. I picked up a Glock 19 and one hundred rounds of nine-millimeter, and while I was at it I acquired a small Benchmade knife from their selection. They ran my brand new driver's license while I listened to the sound of gunfire in all calibers coming from the shooting range. They even had submachine guns and a Squad Assault Weapon available for rental. The check on Matthew Twigg came back, and nothing in it said I wasn't to be trusted with a pistol.

Next task was to find an electronics or, better, an office-supply store, but the hour had gone late enough that I didn't think I'd be able to manage it today. I headed back to the hotel, ordered up some food, and set about checking the pistol I'd purchased, fieldstripping it and reassembling its parts before loading it and stowing it deep in my messenger bag. I was sore and tired, and when I looked at the clock, I realized it was time to call Ballygar.

Alena answered this time, sounding miserable.

"What's wrong?" I asked.

"I've been sick," she told me. "Throwing up."

"Something you ate?"

"No, *sick.*"

"Oh."

"Yes." She sounded very far away, and small, and it made me miss her all the more. "I feel awful."

"I think I've found her," I said. "If everything goes well, I could be in Ireland in another seven days or so. Maybe less."

"When you reach her, speak in Georgian," Alena said. "That will help her."

"I'll remember that. Can you put Bridgett on?"

"Here she is."

"Bridgett?"

"She gets angry when she throws up," Bridgett said. "It's funny."

"Nice to know you two are still getting along."

"Things are better."

"That's good to hear."

"Yeah, she's been so tired the last couple of days she barely has the energy to insult me."

"Ah."

"I hear her right? You're close?"

"Think so."

"Good," said Bridgett. "I want to go home."

"You're not the only one," I told her.

Sharala, Auggie, and Solomon met me for breakfast the next morning at a greasy spoon close to the campus.

"We've got a design we like," Sharala told me. "Limor, when she did the Wave Bubble, it was a little thing, could fit in a cigarette pack. The power you're talking about, we need to scale that up. So we're thinking of a toolbox, one of those big metal ones, which'll give us some design benefits, as long as everything's insulated. It's gonna be heavy, though."

"How heavy?"

"Well, we're using a car battery for power, so, you know, that plus some."

"Doesn't sound like anything I can't handle."

"We emailed the Gerbers this morning, like, at three A.M.," Solomon said. "We're having the PCBs sent FedEx, like, warp speed, they should be here tomorrow."

"In English," I said.

"Gerbers," Sharala explained. "Think circuit diagrams, okay? PCB is printed circuit board."

"Gotcha."

Auggie slid a piece of notepaper over to me, a sketch of the design. The drawing was of a standard-sized toolbox, cutaway, notations all over it.

"With the car battery, this thing should go two, three hours before burning out," Auggie interjected. "And it's going to burn out, this much power, it's going to get hot, start melting components."

"That's more than enough time," I said.

"Cool. The other thing with the design, here, is that you'll need to attach the antennae yourself—we're using two of them, you can see here. You just pop the toolbox open, screw 'em on, then hit the Big Red Button and away you go."

"Big Red Button?" I asked.

The seriousness with which they regarded me made it seem as if we'd been discussing a nuclear bomb, and not a cellular jammer.

"There must always," Solomon told me, "be a Big Red Button."

After our meeting, I made my way to an Office Depot and dumped a couple hundred dollars on a printer, plain and photo paper, extra ink cartridges, and a spindle-stack of CD-ROMs. Next stop was a Walgreens, where I bought myself two packs of white cotton gloves, the kind used for dermatological care.

I'd checked out of the hotel before leaving for breakfast,

and so headed to the apartment, where I set up a workspace on the floor. I got the printer unpacked and communicating with my laptop, and then, wearing a set of the gloves, loaded the tray with photo paper. Then, one after the other, I began printing off multiple copies of all the photographs that Vladek Karataev had taken with his BlackBerry. While the printer ran, I opened up the word processor and began writing.

It was a long process. While the writing went quickly, the printing did not, and each time a sheet was finished, I had to don my gloves to remove it from the tray. It slowed an already time-consuming process immeasurably. I'd gone through most of the ink cartridges, and the world had shifted back into night, before I was finished.

Then, again using the gloves, I loaded the plain paper, and printed out sixteen separate copies of what I had written. I put each aside, with a set of the photographs.

Last, I began burning the CDs. On each one, I included digital copies of the photographs, and most of the video that Vladek had taken. As with the photographs, I left out all images of Tiasa Lagidze.

"Wow, you look wasted," Sharala said to me the next morning. "Have some coffee."

"Don't do coffee."

"You get any sleep?"

"I was up all night," I admitted. "Where are we?"

"You want the good news or the bad news?" Solomon asked.

"Bad news first."

"We're having difficulty tracking down the power amplifier," Auggie said. "All the normal supply houses we go to for parts like this, they're out of stock. Sharala and I must've gone to every RadioShack in the greater Vegas area looking for one, no luck there, either. We think we found a guy in Canada, but the earliest it'll get here will be tomorrow."

"Okay," I said. "And the good news?"

"The good news is that the yellow boards arrived just before we came out to meet you," Solomon said. "All four of them."

"Yellow boards are . . . ?"

"The PCBs, we told you this."

"You called them PCBs last time."

"They're the same thing."

"I see."

"We'll start assembling and testing today," Sharala said. "We get the amplifier tomorrow, we could have the box ready maybe tomorrow night, the day after at the latest."

I did a quick mental calculation, which wasn't all that quick given my lack of sleep. "That'll work."

"Then we'll see you tomorrow."

On the way back to the apartment, I stopped at the same Walgreens I had the day before, and then at a high-end photography store. At the Walgreens I bought first aid supplies, a couple of cheap towels, and a cheap cowboy hat; at the photo place I paid far too much for a Nikon digital camera, two lenses, an adaptor, and a sixteen-gig memory card.

Back at the apartment, I took a shower, shaved, and changed the dressings on my wounds. Where I'd torn stitches in my side, the flesh looked angry and red, but when I gave the laceration a gentle squeeze, nothing issued from the wound in exchange for the pain I inflicted on myself. If I was carrying an infection, I couldn't tell.

I finished tending my wounds, then I lay down on the floor of my unfurnished apartment and tried to get some sleep. I didn't think I'd be able to do it, but surprised myself when I awoke seven hours later, sore and stiff, but feeling marginally refreshed. I dressed and headed out, taking the car back to the rental service. I dropped it off there, caught a cab, and hit the first used-car lot I could find.

After forty-five minutes and some haggling, I purchased, in cash, a ten-year-old VW Jetta with seventy-eight thousand miles on it. It wasn't the nicest car I'd ever owned, but close examination of the engine and tires had given me faith that I could rely upon it to do what I required.

I drove my new used car back to the apartment, picked up my messenger bag and filled it with the Glock, the camera, and the lenses. Then I hit the interstate, heading east.

The drive to New Paradise took two hours, and it was still light enough when I arrived in the town that I only needed one of the two lenses. I parked on the main street, put on my cowboy hat, and, keeping an eye out for cops, took a handful of photographs. I made certain to get at least one of the big wooden "Welcome to New Paradise" sign. Then I got back in the Jetta and drove to a local movie theater, where I paid to see something loud, with superheroes in it. I didn't pay much attention.

By the time the film had finished, it had gone dark. I found the Albertson's I'd been directed to before, then followed the route Mike had driven for another mile, before pulling over at the strip mall with the Starbucks and parking. I took the messenger bag and went on foot from there, staying off the streets and out of the lights where I could. After twenty-three minutes I reached the stone wall bordering the Oasis housing development.

Following the wall, I worked my way around it to the north. Streetlamps burned along the empty streets full of empty houses, and the best I could manage from my side was a spot that wasn't in direct light. The fence was close to three meters high, but the stone made finding handholds and footholds relatively easy, and I scrambled up and over, dropping down and into cover as quickly as possible, ignoring the stabbing pain that shot from my side. I checked the BlackBerry, saw it was eleven minutes to midnight.

It was almost twelve-thirty before I found the cul-de-sac. Sneaking through the deserted streets had made me feel like I was traveling through a ghost town, and my paranoia certainly didn't help that. Every noise made me stop, ducking for cover. Twice I heard cars, and once I saw headlights, went prone beneath a line of untended and dying bushes. A New Paradise police car rolled past but didn't stop.

There was an abandoned—or never occupied—house opposite the mouth of the cul-de-sac, and I went around the back, began trying the doors and windows. Nothing on the ground floor was open, and while I could get up to the second floor, working my way around the building searching for an open entry was going to be risky. The houses, however, looked like they all had finished basements, and when I noticed that, I went around again, searching for an egress. Building code would've required a way out in an emergency, if the house, say, was on fire. I found one on the west side, a dugout with a short metal ladder, dropped myself the five feet down into it, then ran my hands along the edges of the window, trying to get a feel for how it opened, if it slid up or would swing out. Closer examination revealed, barely, the hinges on the inside of the window, on the right-hand side. I put my back to the wall of the dugout, and my boot to the side opposite the hinges, and started pushing. Hard.

It broke open with a *pop,* and I slid through on my belly into darkness, landing on a cold concrete floor. I righted myself, closed the window as best I could, then waited for my night vision to catch up with the rest of me. It wasn't doing very well, because there was almost no ambient light penetrating the house. I started forward carefully, feeling my way, and then stopped when I realized I was being a fucking idiot.

From the messenger bag, I removed the camera and one of my two lenses, hooked them together. Then I switched the camera on, heard it whine with power, and put it to my eye, seeing the world through night-vision green. With the camera to help me, I made my way through the finished basement, to a flight of stairs, and onto the ground floor, and then, from there, to the second story, moving with care the whole time, staying away from the windows.

There was a room on the second floor that was perfect for what I wanted, facing directly onto the cul-de-sac. I hunkered down, switching my lenses, then using the adaptor to thread the night-vision lens onto the telephoto. It made the whole thing ungainly and heavy, but when I looked down the viewfinder, everything was crystal clear, and zoom brought out the detail.

The same three cars were parked outside tonight, the Lexus, the Porsche, and the 4x4. I took multiple pictures of each of them, zooming in to catch their license plates. Then I took a good dozen more shots of the house itself, some in context, some zooming in close to pick out details, so that the pictures would aid in its identification. I checked my clock, saw it was now twenty-six minutes past one.

For the next hour, I sat with my camera, watching the house. Light leaked out from around drawn curtains, and sometimes I saw shadows, movement within, but nothing that would make a Pulitzer Prize–winning photograph. At two-fifteen, a New Paradise police car rolled lazily down the street, stopping directly in front of my house. After a handful of seconds, it started forward again, and I realized that the driver had been checking the cul-de-sac, had most likely never even looked in my direction.

At three minutes to three, the garage door opened, and the black Town Car began backing down the driveway. I brought the camera up and took another half dozen pictures, again catching the license plate. The car windows were tinted enough that I couldn't see the passenger, but just as the Town Car came onto the street, I saw Bella Downs race out of the house, carrying what looked like a small piece of hand luggage. I took pictures of her, too, as well as Mike, who was once again behind the wheel of the car, visible for a moment as he rolled down his window to take the offered bag. He was handing it to someone in the backseat as the window came up again, and I couldn't see who his passenger was, or even how many people might've been inside.

The Town Car pulled away, and, for a moment, Bella Downs stood in the driveway, surveying her domain. Then she put a hand to her hair, patting it back into place, and I got another three pictures of her before she turned to head back inside the house. I lowered the camera.

Then movement in one of the McMansion's windows caught my attention, and I brought the lens up once more, trying to zoom in on it. Someone had pulled back the curtains in a room on the second floor, and I adjusted the focus. Light inside the room threw off the night vision, created a bloom that obscured what I was seeing in a cloud of orange. I hastily re-moved the adaptor, tried to get a view inside again.

It was a girl, standing there, holding the curtain back. She was blonde, her hair past her shoulders, wearing a red camisole. She was crying.

I had to remind myself to take a picture, then a couple more.

The girl turned, alarmed at something inside the room, a sound, and Bradley entered the shot. With one hand, he took hold of the girl by the shoulder. With his other, he punched her in the stomach, and the difference in their sizes, their strengths, made me think of a child beating on a rag doll. The girl would've gone down, doubled over, but Bradley didn't let her, ready to hit her again.

Then I saw Tiasa.

She came in from the side, shouting, pushing at Bradley, and without letting go of the other girl, he hit her across the face with the back of his hand. She disappeared from view, and then Bella appeared, yelling, gesturing. She pulled Tiasa up from where she'd been knocked to the floor, slapped her, screaming at her. Then she shoved Tiasa out of sight and, still shouting, reached out and yanked the curtains closed.

Somehow, I'd remembered to keep taking pictures.

I lowered my camera, thinking that I had a gun. Thinking that I could march across the street right now and put a bullet into Bradley, Bella, and anyone else I didn't like the looks of. Somebody in that house had the keys to the Porsche SUV. I could break in, free Tiasa, and be in Salt Lake City by morning.

There were other girls in that house.

I had a plan. I had to stick to it, no matter how hard it was to remember that at the moment.

So I didn't move, waiting, watching. When the Town Car returned, parked itself in the garage once more, I lowered the camera, stowed it again inside my messenger bag. I left the house as I'd entered.

It was dawn when I reached the Jetta and started back to Las Vegas, and despite myself, I felt like I had abandoned Tiasa.

I felt like a coward.

CHAPTER
Thirty-three

I started printing out the new pictures I'd taken, all but the ones of Tiasa, as soon as I got back to the rented apartment. They were still printing when I fell asleep, but they'd stopped when I woke midafternoon, because I'd run out of ink for the printer again. I got myself sorted, then took my laptop and the unused set of cotton gloves with me when I went out.

With a little searching, I found a postal service store in a strip mall. I put on the gloves before leaving the Jetta. The store had ink cartridges, so I bought replacements, and then pretty much took their stock of FedEx packs and labels. I got some looks, and explained away the gloves to the cashier by saying that I had dermatitis.

Back in the Jetta the gloves came off, and I drove around until I found a coffee shop that also offered wireless access. I got myself a cup of mint tea, then got myself online, began searching up the addresses I wanted. I compiled a list, finished the tea, and headed back to the apartment. Before touching the envelopes or the labels, I made sure I was wearing my gloves.

The gloves stayed on my hands for the next two hours, as I resumed printing. When I finally took them off, I had sixteen FedEx packs loaded and labeled, each one containing a set of all the pictures I'd printed, the CDs I'd burned, and the narrative I'd written.

Then I settled in once more to try to sleep, and to wait for morning.

Sharala called at 10:17 the next morning.

"Congratulations," she said. "It's a monster fucking Wave Bubble."

"I'll be right over," I said.

I lied, but only a little bit. I had to get my things cleared out of the apartment and loaded into the car first. Having done that, I donned my white cotton gloves for what would be the last time, and took my stack of FedEx envelopes to a drop box I'd located earlier. I'd marked each of the domestic packs to be at its destination by ten-thirty the next morning. The internationals, of which there were four, would likely take longer.

With the envelopes on their way, I stripped off the gloves, threw them in the first trash can I could find.

That completed, I headed back to UNLV.

■ ■ ■

They were waiting for me in the RF lab, the same place I'd first met them three days prior. The toolbox was a large one, traditional bright red, resting on the worktable in front of them, and each of them beamed at me like proud parents. Auggie opened it up as I approached to allow me a look, removing pieces and explaining what each component was. I listened as if I understood, but for all his care in explaining it, to me it was simply a sandwich of yellow circuit boards with hand-soldered wires joining them together, all of them secured to a flat piece of wood. They showed me where the antennae would attach.

There was also, as promised, a big red button.

"Thank you," I told them.

"You kidding?" Solomon said. "We should be thanking you. This was a blast."

I shook my head, bemused.

"Nah, you don't get it," Auggie said. "This is why we got into this stuff in the first place. We all wanted to make the shit Batman carries around on his belt."

I laughed, then took out the envelope I was carrying in my jacket, handed it to Sharala.

"What's this?" she asked.

"Six thousand dollars," I said. "Figure that's two grand for each of you."

"That's too much. Maybe this was a thousand dollars parts and everything, shipping. This is too much to pay."

I just shook my head.

Six grand was nothing next to what I was hoping my new toolbox would buy me.

CHAPTER
Thirty-four

I left Vegas for the final time at four that afternoon, and was back in New Paradise before seven, just as the sun was starting to disappear over the desert. Then I had to make a choice, because what I needed to do next was kill time. My other option, one that I'd discarded, had been to leave Vegas later, much later, around one in the morning, to try to time my arrival closer to when I planned to hit the house.

The problem with that plan was that New Paradise wasn't very large, and a car driving down main street at three in the morning was more likely to attract police attention than one that did so at seven at night. It's why I had parked so far from the house on the cul-de-sac the night I'd made my surveillance;

the last thing I had wanted to earn was police attention. The Jetta had been purchased in Matthew Twigg's name, and the plates that had come with it led back to him. If the police knew I was coming, all my careful planning would be for naught.

So arriving earlier, when the town was still awake, seemed a better idea. The problem was it left me with time to kill, and time to kill brought with it nervousness. This was complicated by the need to find a place where I wouldn't draw attention while I waited.

For that, though, Nevada provided its own solution. Twenty-four hours, rain or shine, holiday or no, there is always a seat for you in a casino.

At three in the morning, I left Paradise Rollers and returned to my car. There were still enough vehicles in the lot that mine had remained inconspicuous. I was glad to get out. Cigarette smoke, lights, and noise had done nothing for my nerves. To top it all off, between blackjack and the craps table, I'd lost five hundred and thirty-seven dollars.

I hoped it wasn't an omen of things to come.

From the casino to the Albertson's parking lot took two minutes. From the lot to Oasis took another six, and I doused the headlights on the Jetta before I made the turn toward the still-open gates that led into the development. I slowed, lowering my window. The desert air had gone cool with the night, still dry. My stomach was already working its way through a Boy Scout's handbook worth of knots. During the entire drive I had seen only four other vehicles, none of them police, and all heading the opposite direction, and I thought that maybe I'd caught a break.

No such luck.

The spotlight hit me as soon as I was through the gate, coming from behind, its reflection in the rearview mirror blinding me for a moment. Then the other lights came on, blue and red, and the New Paradise police car that had been parked in the shadow of the wall as I'd passed pulled in behind me.

I stomped the Jetta's brakes, coming to an abrupt halt, and whoever it was behind the wheel of the cruiser had to do the same, surprised that I'd stopped so quickly. The light from the spot shifted, trying to scan the interior of the car, and I didn't turn around in my seat, staying still, furious with myself for not having counted on this, for not having a contingency.

The driver's door on the police car opened, followed immediately by the one on the front passenger side. Two cops, and I didn't need to check my mirrors to guess who they were. Again I cursed myself; I'd been so damn concerned with getting into the house, with what I'd do once inside, I hadn't considered the possibility I might not even reach the place at all.

A new light joined the glare from the flood, a flashlight beam, and I'd been right, it was the same two cops who'd stopped me before, the talker and his silent brother in corruption. It was the talker holding the Maglite, and he recognized me immediately.

"Jeezus, buddy," he said. "Can't you take a hint?"

I tensed my shoulders, tightened my grip on the steering wheel, set my jaw, still staring straight ahead, refusing to look at him. He read my body language, shifted further around toward the front of the car, now wary, pivoting to keep his eyes on me. One hand dropped to cover his holster.

"Out, asshole," he said. "Kill the engine and get out."

I hesitated, then snapped the engine off, put my hands back on the wheel.

"Get out of the fucking car, now."

"I didn't do anything," I said, and it came out as both petu-
lant and angry.

"You're trespassing."

"Bullshit, that's fucking bullshit."

"Get out of the vehicle, keep your hands where I can see
them."

I unfastened my seatbelt, shoved open my door. As soon as
I was out, the other one had me into the side of the car. I kept
my body tensed, pushed back, my hands on the roof of the
Jetta, and got shoved a second time, harder.

"There's no sign," I said. "There's no sign, there's nothing.
You can't do this."

"You want to make this hard?" the talker asked. "That what
you want to do? Because we can do that, we'd be happy to do
that."

I glared at him, trying to place his position behind the
flashlight in his hand. He was still covering his holster, still
keeping his distance. Behind me, his silent partner shifted, and
I heard the ring of metal on metal as he pulled out his cuffs,
and that was the cue I'd been waiting for. With an audible sigh,
I let myself sag against the side of the Jetta, let every muscle that
I'd been holding tense relax, let my posture shift from resistance to submission.

"I want a lawyer," I said softly.

The talker read my surrender, stepping closer, the Maglite
coming down, his other hand no longer covering the butt of his
pistol. He'd seen my behavior before on a hundred drunks
faced with the power of the badge, the moment when reality
sets in just before the cuffs go on.

"Tell you what, we'll go down to the station, sort this out."

I nodded slightly, thinking that all three of us knew damn
well there was no station involved in what they had planned.

The one behind me closed the cuff around my right wrist, pulled my hand from the top of the Jetta, bringing it down and behind me toward the small of my back, and that's when I moved, using my hips to pivot into him and away from his talkative partner. My right hand found his wrist, and I twisted, brought his arm up, straightening it and locking his elbow before slamming my left hand upward, into the joint. It broke and he screamed and I let go.

The talkative one had dropped the Maglite and was trying to index his pistol, but distance is everything, and I was too close to him already. I took his right knee with my boot before he could clear his holster, pounded my fist into the side of his neck even as he was going down. He landed on his side, and I stole the canister of pepper spray from his belt, gave him a faceful, then spun back and sprayed the rest of it at his partner.

Tossing the can, I took the cuffs off the talker and trapped his hands behind his back. He wore his keys on a lanyard, and I yanked them free from his belt, unlocked the set that dangled from my wrist, and reapplied them to his partner. He gurgled in pain when I twisted his arm behind him. I took his keys as well, along with his radio, then went back for his partner's. I let them keep their guns.

Both men were still mewling and gagging when I loaded them into the back of their cruiser. The residue of pepper spray was strong enough to make my own eyes water, and I was coughing when I locked them into the backseat, coughing even more when I slid behind the wheel and backed their car into the shadows beneath the wall. With the three of us in the vehicle, we sounded like a symphony of bronchitis.

I shut off the car, used the keys to lock it up, then climbed back into the Jetta. Without their personal radios, locked in the back of their cruiser, the cops wouldn't be able to call for help.

From what I'd seen behind the wheel of their car, the New Paradise PD tracked their units via GPS, which meant that somewhere, someone would eventually notice that they hadn't moved in a while. How long a while that would be, I had no way to know.

But somewhere, a clock was now running, and I had no more time to waste.

I crept the Jetta through the barren streets, using only the accelerator, afraid that brake lights would give me away, afraid of more of Bella Downs's bought-and-paid-for police lurking in the darkness. My visit the night before last had given me a good lay of the land, but now I had another decision to make. The cul-de-sac was a problem, because cul-de-sac meant dead end. That would leave only one route of escape. But the car would provide protection and speed.

In the end, I parked the Jetta behind the house I'd used for my surveillance, leaving it unlocked. The entire time I'd kept watch on the McMansion, I'd seen police come through the area only once, and that had been almost an hour earlier than it was now. Unless Bella had the entirety of the New Paradise Police Department patrolling her neighborhood, no one would notice the car.

I killed the dome light inside the Jetta so it wouldn't switch on when I opened the door, then checked the Glock a final time, making it ready. I got out, tucked the pistol into my waistband, at the front. Then I pulled the toolbox and the tire iron from the trunk. The toolbox was heavier than I remembered it being.

I made my way to the cul-de-sac, using every shadow I could find. I didn't know if there was a security system on the house, if there were cameras. I hadn't seen any during my visit, nor on my surveillance, but all that meant was that I'd missed them, not that they didn't exist. It didn't much matter. There was no way in hell that Bella Downs had sprung for an alarm system that would route through a security service; the risk of cops she didn't own crashing the party would've been too great.

I closed on the building from the west rather than straight on and, when I reached the side of the house, crouched and opened the toolbox. The two antennae screwed easily and quickly into place. I double-checked that I was on power, then hit the Big Red Button, and there was no noise, and for a moment I wondered if anything was happening at all. I put my hand on the side of the case; heat was beginning to radiate through the metal.

When I checked the BlackBerry, I saw that I had no signal.

God bless and keep the engineers, I thought.

I went to the cars next, opened up my knife. I punctured all four tires on the vehicles. The Town Car, hidden in the garage, I'd have to take care of on the way out.

I headed to the front door. The double doors weren't going to yield to anything my Glock could do, I knew, but that had never been my plan of ingress. Two curtained bay windows flanked the entrance at either side, and either one of them would do quite nicely. Since my plan was to surprise the hell out of them, and since making a lot of noise would aid that, the windows were going to be my primary entry. Ideally, the crashing glass would throw them into a panic, and naturally enough, they'd then try to raise their pet police. Once inside, I'd rely on my speed and their confusion, and hopefully the combination would do the trick.

With my windbreaker wrapped around my arm, my left hand up to shield my face, I shattered the left window, three vicious blows with the tire iron that brought the sheet crashing down in pieces that rang and burst all around me. I dropped the bar, swept the glass away from the frame with my protected arm, then pushed the curtain back and vaulted up and over, into the entry hall, drawing the Glock.

Mike was the first one to respond. He came out of the hallway to my left, bleary-eyed, wearing boxer shorts and a T-shirt. I'd counted on the bleariness; it was why I'd picked the hour. Nonetheless, he'd had the presence of mind to arm himself, a solid, traditional Remington pump-action shotgun, police model, in his hands, and I wondered if he and Bradley were also cops.

He saw me and he saw my gun, but, in relative terms, I had all the time in the world and he had none. I picked my shot, gave him the same one I'd given Vladek Karataev back in Batumi so many weeks ago, shattering his pelvis with a round and stealing his legs. He dropped face-first, his momentum carrying him forward on the marble floor, smearing blood.

"Bella!" he screamed.

I closed on him in two steps and then turned the third into a kick to the face. I kicked him hard, and he lost teeth. He also lost consciousness.

I started up the stairs, shouting in Georgian.

"Tiasa! It's David! David Mercer! Where are you?"

A door opened on the second floor, I couldn't see where, but I could hear it, then heard another one slam closed. Someone was running down a hallway, away from me. I kept moving, shouting Tiasa's name, racing up the steps. The hallway ran left and right, and I heard noise to the left, went that way first, stopping at the nearest door. I took the entry hard, kicking it open, the Glock ready in both hands. The room was empty. I pivoted, moved to the next one, this across the hall, a meter down, kicked it free the same way.

The door hit Bradley in the face, where he'd been about to open it, sent him staggering back. He had a pistol in his hand, but no shot, and I put one from the Glock in his knee before he could acquire one. He screamed and dropped.

That's when I saw he was naked, and that the girl in the bed was the same small blonde I'd seen while surveilling the house through my camera's lens.

God, I wanted to kill him.

I wanted to kill him all the more when he begged me not to.

He'd dropped his pistol, a Sig, the same model that I'd found in Bridgett's apartment. I kicked it away, and he clutched his knee with both hands, looking up at me.

"God don't please don't," he sobbed. "Please don't!"

The girl in the bed was staring at me, sheet pulled around her frail body. Her expression was blank, no trace of horror or pain or anger, nothing at all.

I kicked him in his wounded knee, and he screamed and flailed back, and I kicked him again, this time in the groin, then in the stomach, and then, finally, in the face. He lay bleeding on the navy blue carpet, skin torn, semiconscious. I stepped over him, grabbed the Sig from where it had fallen on the floor.

"The only reason you get to live," I said, "is because I want you to suffer."

Then I used the Sig as a hammer and hit him in the back of the head with it. The crack it made as metal met bone was nearly satisfying.

Tucking the Sig away at the small of my back, I asked the girl, "English?"

She nodded, slightly, staring at Bradley on the floor.

"People are going to come here," I told her. "Good people. By morning."

Her expression didn't change, and she nodded again, as small an acknowledgment as before.

"Tiasa," I said. "Which way?"

She pointed, indicating the right-hand hallway, the direction opposite the way I'd headed off the stairs.

"Good people will come," I promised her, and stepped back into the hall.

The house seemed to have gone silent, remained that way as I retraced my steps. Glancing down to the bottom of the stairs, Mike lay just as before. I moved into the new hallway.

"Tiasa! It's David!"

From behind one of the closed doors on the hall, I heard a rustle, a thump. I made for the sound, but this time took the entry softer, putting my body against the wall and reaching over for the handle. It turned without resistance, and then the shots came, piling one atop another, wild fire, until five holes punched through the wood, each round planting itself in the wall opposite me.

In the silence that followed, I heard someone whimper.

I pushed the door open and stepped around, raising the Glock.

Bella Downs stood in the bedroom. She was dressed in dark purple silk pajamas, a revolver in one hand and her cell phone in the other. The gun had been pointed at the door, but when she saw me she started to move it, to point it at the head of the girl huddling in the corner.

"Go away," Bella shouted at me. "Go away!"

"You stop!" I shouted back. "You point that at her and I will shoot you dead!"

The gun froze midway in its travel. Then her hand opened and it fell to the floor. I stepped in enough to catch it with my toe, pull it away from her, then went down far enough to scoop it up in my left hand. I pulled the release, swung out the cylinder. The revolver had carried only five shots. She'd used them all on the door.

"Take her," Bella Downs told me. "Just take her and go away and never come back."

"That's pretty much my plan," I said.

Then I hit her hard, across the face, with her revolver, shattering her jaw. She dropped, trying to scream, then discovered that made the pain worse. Blood gushed from her nose and mouth.

"Tiasa," I said, switching back to Georgian. "It's David, David Mercer. Yeva's husband. I'm taking you away from here."

The girl in the corner didn't rise, instead trying to make herself smaller. Bella Downs, on the floor, made sobbing sounds.

I tucked the Glock away, then knelt down, putting the revolver on the floor between me and the girl.

"Tiasa," I said. "It's me. We're leaving now. Let's go."

She raised her head slowly, afraid of being betrayed again, lied to again, used again. But when her eyes found mine, there was no relief in them, no joy on her face, no recovery to be found at all.

"Let's go," I said again.

In silence, she got to her feet, and I put a hand on her shoulder. I expected a physical response to that, a tensing of muscle, a pulling away from my grip, but neither came, and she let me guide her from the room, then down the hall, then to the stairs past Mike, still lying and bleeding on the white marble floor. We went out the front, to the Jetta, and I put her inside.

Tiasa never made a sound. Tiasa never said a word.

And Tiasa never looked back.

CHAPTER
Thirty-five

The first hints of the story were beginning to break when we stopped in Salt Lake City midmorning, after almost five hours of driving. In the motel room, while Tiasa bathed and changed into the new clothes I'd bought her, I snapped on the news, bouncing up the dial to first CNN, then MSNBC. The only item I found was on the latter.

"Acting on anonymous information, federal authorities raided a house in New Paradise, Nevada, this morning, as part of an ongoing investigation into human trafficking. More on this as it develops."

That was it. That was all.

I turned the television off and the BlackBerry on, called Alena.

"You have her?" she asked.

"I have her."

"How is she?"

"She hasn't said much. She hasn't really said anything."

"May I speak with her?"

"Hold on."

I moved to the bathroom door, tapped lightly on it. The water had stopped running over ten minutes ago.

"Tiasa," I said.

She opened the door, wet black hair and jeans and a dark green T-shirt. She didn't look at me; she hadn't much looked at me, at least when she thought I was looking at her, since I'd put her in the Jetta back in New Paradise and started driving.

"Yeva wants to talk to you," I said, and handed her the phone, then moved away, giving them privacy. For almost two minutes Tiasa said nothing, listening.

Then, her voice hoarse, she said, "I understand."

She brought the phone back to me, then sat on the other bed in the room and began to put on her new sneakers. I put the phone to my ear.

"I'll contact you when we get to New York," I said. "Ask Bridgett to call her sister, let her know we're coming."

"Don't rush," Alena told me, switching to English. "It would be stupid to die now because you were speeding."

"I miss you," I said.

"I miss you, too."

In the background, I heard Bridgett make a gagging noise.

We were back in the Jetta and heading north, into Wyoming, before afternoon. Mostly, Tiasa slept, or appeared to. We stopped in Cheyenne to eat, and she didn't have much of an appetite.

After dinner, we got back on the road, following Interstate 80 into Nebraska. Again, Tiasa seemed to sleep, or to try to. Sometimes, I thought she was talking to herself, her voice so soft I wasn't sure I was hearing it at all. I didn't know what to tell her, what to say, and so I drove and told myself that she would talk to me when she was ready, when she had something she wanted to say.

We were some eighty miles west of Omaha, past one in the morning, and I was thinking we were going to need to stop soon, when she finally did. The car was dark, the only lights from the instrument panel, the occasional splash from head-lights passing us in either direction. The farmland spread out forever on all sides.

"Yeva," Tiasa began, then stopped. She was speaking softly, in Georgian, and I almost lost her voice amidst the engine and road noise. She coughed, cleared her throat. "Yeva told me that she was raped."

"Yes," I said. "When she was young, younger than you."

"Oh," Tiasa said, and then lapsed back into silence.

We stopped for the rest of the night in Omaha. Tiasa went to take another shower before sleeping, and again, I turned to the television for an update. Since MSNBC had done well by me the last time, I went with them again.

The story had expanded. Six girls, between the ages of twelve and sixteen, had been rescued in the raid on the house in New Paradise. Footage showed them being led from the build-ing as men and women in FBI jackets fluttered around them. Authorities had three people in custody, one found at the house, the remaining two arrested at the local hospital. They were said to be cooperating. Authorities were also, apparently, searching for a fourth individual, who they stressed was not a suspect, but rather a person of interest. There was no mention of any part the New Paradise PD might have played in the business.

I turned the television off, removed my glasses, rubbed my eyes. My side ached, and my arm. From the bathroom, I could hear the shower still running. The sound of Tiasa trying to wash away shame and humiliation and pain.

She was in there a very long time.

A day and a half later, outside of Cleveland, making our last push toward New York, Tiasa spoke again.

"What am I going to do, David?" she asked.

I thought of the many ways to answer that, all the things the question could mean. Finally, I said, "You're going to be a dancer, Tiasa."

"No," she said. "No, I mean...I mean..."

She faded into silence again. I glanced over at her. She had her head leaning against the window, staring at the dashboard. She was biting her lower lip, hard, one hand wrapped around the handle of the door, the other in a fist, pressed into her thigh.

"I don't know what you're feeling," I said, after another couple of miles. "I can imagine it, but I don't know, not really. But I've lost people I love, Tiasa, had them taken from me, and there have been times when I didn't want to go on without them. And it's hard, and it is going to *be* hard for you for a long time. But you will survive this. You will survive this, and someday it won't hurt quite so much, and one day you'll smile again. One day you'll laugh again.

"And then you'll want to dance again."

Her voice was thick. "Yeva told me to be strong. That she knew I was strong."

"Yeva knows what she's talking about. Yeva's stronger than I'll ever be." I took another glance at her, saw that she was as before, but had shut her eyes. I looked back to the road. "Yeva's going to have a baby."

"Yeva is?" Tiasa asked, slowly.

I nodded.

"You're going to have a baby?"

"Yeah."

She thought about that.

"I hope you have a boy," Tiasa said.

The New York Times had the full story on the front page the next morning, below the fold, listed as part one of a series. The article seemed to work extensively from the material I had sent anonymously to the paper, supplementing it with information from the State Department's annual Trafficking in Persons report. It began with a description of the house in New Paradise, what it had been used for, the people who had maintained and managed the location.

Then it went on to talk about the girls who had been held there, where they were from, and how they had come to the United States, to the Land of Opportunity. It described the supply chain, how a girl in Ukraine would be sold to a man in Turkey; how that man in Turkey would offer that girl for sale; how, upon receiving payment for her, a "coyote," or middleman, in Amsterdam would bring her to the U.S.

The article pointed out that, according to the International Labor Organization of the United Nations, 12.7 million people were, at this moment, bound in one form of slavery or another around the world. Either in forced or bonded labor, or in sexual servitude. The majority of these slaves were women and children.

Some NGOs, the article stated, claimed the ILO estimate was exaggerated, that the number was closer to 4 million slaves. As if that made it better.

The piece concluded by saying that other organizations put the estimate as high as 27 million.

Three days after leaving New Paradise, Tiasa and I met Sister Cashel Logan in a park on the southeast edge of the Bronx, a place called the Half Moon Overlook in the Spuyten Duyvil neighborhood. It was the last Wednesday of July, hot and humid, and the sun was bright off the water where the Hudson and Harlem rivers met.

She was already waiting for us when we arrived, sitting on a bench near the wrought-iron fence marking the border of the park, and when she saw us coming, she rose to her feet, smiling. She was wearing a cream-colored blouse and black pants, and as ever, the pin of her holy order was in place on her lapel.

"Hello, Tiasa," Sister Cashel said in practiced and poorly accented Georgian. "My name is Sister Cashel."

Tiasa, walking at my side and not touching me, stopped, so I stopped with her. Cashel's presence wasn't a surprise; I'd told her who we were meeting and why, and Tiasa had nodded and kept her silence. Now, it seemed, the silence wasn't going to be enough.

"I have English," she told Cashel, in an accent as bad as Cashel's had been in Georgian.

"Atticus told you about me?" Cashel hadn't moved, still smiling, still calm and reassuring.

Tiasa's brow creased, trying to translate, and after a second, I did it for her, adding, "She calls me Atticus."

"Why?"

I debated, then said, "It's my name."

"Your name is David."

"David was my name in Kobuleti."

"I don't understand."

"It's all right. It's complicated. I promise I'll tell you about it sometime."

Tiasa looked at me, then to Cashel. "Yes, he tells me."

"I think I can help you," Cashel said. "I want to help you."

"Yes. He says this."

"Do you want my help?"

Tiasa nodded, just barely.

"I'm glad," Cashel said. "I'd like it if you would stay with me for a little while. I'd like you to meet some people, maybe have a chance to make some new friends. Some of them are your age. Some of them have been through bad times, the way you have. They might understand some of what you're feeling."

Tiasa looked confused, and again I translated.

"How long?" Tiasa asked me. "How long will I stay with her?"

"Only as long as you want," I said.

"I don't want to. I want to stay with you. I want to see Yeva."

"Yeva and I can't give you what you need right now, Tiasa. Sister Cashel can."

"I don't want you to leave."

"I'm going to come back," I said.

"What if you don't?" The question came quickly, as if she had been waiting to ask it, as if desperate to be let out. "You can't promise, you don't know what will happen. What if you don't come back? If you go away and you never come back? If you go away, like Papa and Mama and Koba?"

"You're right," I said. "I can't make you a promise and guarantee that I'll keep it. You're smart enough to know that. You're smart enough to know that no one can. I don't know what will happen, Tiasa, not tomorrow or next week or next year. All I know is what I will try to do. I followed you all the way from Kobuleti to find you. You know I mean what I say."

She closed her eyes, pained, nodded. Then, to my surprise, she threw her arms around my middle, pushing her face into my chest, the hug tight enough to hurt where the wound on my side was still struggling to heal. I didn't move for a moment, and then, very carefully, very lightly, I returned the hug.

When she let me go, she wiped her nose with her fingers, then turned to Cashel.

"Okay," she said in her fractured English. "I go with you."

CHAPTER
Thirty-six

I was in New York another two days, and saw Tiasa on each of them. Cashel had arranged for her to stay at a shelter for abused and battered girls in the North Bronx, one of three her order ministered to. It was the kind of place that didn't advertise itself and relied on anonymity and secrecy for security, rather than guards and alarms, which was a good thing. Guards and alarms were likely to bring back bad memories for Tiasa.

The first day, I went with her and Cashel to visit a doctor. Cashel had prepared her for the visit as best she could, but Tiasa was miserable all the same; she knew why the examination was necessary, but honestly understanding the need for it didn't diminish the fact that she was being asked to, quite literally, open her legs to another stranger, even if the reason for it this time was quite different. Cashel hadn't yet been able to arrange for a translator, and as a result, I had to remain nearby, which I'm sure didn't help things.

The initial results came back quickly, and were as good as could be expected. She wasn't pregnant, and had scored negative on a broad spectrum of tests for venereal diseases. Blood had been drawn for an AIDS test, as well, but it would be another day at least before we knew anything there. The doctor confirmed that Tiasa had been abused, physically and sexually, and while all the news was delivered with clinical precision and professional compassion, it was very hard for me to hear. Somehow, Cashel didn't seem to have the same problem, and I envied her practiced serenity.

The next day, in the afternoon, I took them to lunch at a Chinese restaurant Cashel suggested, near the shelter. Tiasa ate some rice, and a lone steamed dumpling, and that was all. She didn't offer much in conversation, so I did most of the talking, alternating between Georgian and English, trying to keep Cashel in the loop.

Cashel told me that they'd located someone to help with translation, a woman who would be coming by later in the afternoon. I shared that information with Tiasa, and she shrugged. The only emotion I was reading off her was anger, and that just barely.

Men weren't allowed inside the shelter, so after the meal I drove them both back to the house, and made my goodbyes in the car.

"I'm leaving tonight," I told Tiasa. "To check on Yeva and Cashel's sister."

Tiasa stared at me, and I saw that the anger I'd sensed was now, at least for the moment, being directed my way. She unfastened her seatbelt and got out of the Jetta.

"Fine," Tiasa said, and then she slammed the door.

Cashel, in the backseat, leaned forward slightly. "It's going to take time."

"She thinks I'm abandoning her."

"I think she knows you're not. She hasn't even begun to talk about what happened to her. As I said, Atticus, it's going to take time."

I sighed. It wasn't that I didn't believe her. In addition to her holy vows, Cashel had a degree in social work, and far more experience dealing with the survivors of abuse and addiction than I. It was one of the things that had drawn her to become a nun, a calling that had come about as a direct result of witnessing the damage caused by her sister's addiction to heroin back when Bridgett was a teen. I trusted that she knew what she was talking about.

"You have to tell me," I said. "Is visiting going to do more harm than good?"

"I think it would be wise if you stayed away for a little while," Cashel replied, carefully. "You have confusing associations for her, and it may complicate things."

"Great."

"Keep in touch. And tell Bridgett to call when she gets back in town."

"I will," I said. "Thank you, Sister."

"You're a good man," she told me, then got out of the car and followed Tiasa into the house.

I sold the car at a lot in Jersey City, got maybe a quarter of what I paid for it back, and used some of my new cash to take a cab out to Newark Airport, where Matthew Twigg was booked on a Lufthansa flight to Dublin via Frankfurt that evening. I'd made a point of divesting myself of anything incriminating earlier in the day, sending the weapons I'd collected into the Hudson River along with the keys and radios I'd taken from the New Paradise PD. After a moment's deliberation, I'd sunk Vladek Karataev's BlackBerry, too.

It had confusing associations for me.

Before the flight, I used an international calling card to reach Bridgett and Alena in Ballygar. I gave them my flight details, told them they could expect me the following evening. Both were happy to hear the news, I thought, each for her own, separate, reasons.

The flight was long and uncomfortable, and the connection through Germany only made it worse. I tried sleeping, couldn't much manage it, and after three hours the battery on my battered and much-abused laptop gave up, leaving me alone with the in-flight entertainment and my thoughts. Mostly, I was worried for Tiasa, if I was doing right by her.

It was just past five in Dublin when we touched down, and by the time I'd cleared customs it was a quarter to seven and already dark. When I emerged into the baggage claim, I was surprised to see both Alena and Bridgett waiting for me.

"She thought we should come to get you," Bridgett said as I approached.

I made a beeline for Alena, feeling the smile come onto my face unbidden. She looked, to my eyes, great, better than when I'd finally caught up to her in Odessa. Maybe it was just the light, but I thought that the cliché about how pregnant women glow had to have some merit to it, because she certainly seemed to be doing so to me. She was also beginning to show, and my reaction to the sight of the slight bump at her belly took me by surprise, delighted me.

"Hello," Alena said.

I didn't bother to drop my bags, just wrapped my arms around her and kissed her.

"Oh Christ," Bridgett muttered. "Should I get you two a room?"

I ignored her, told Alena, "I missed you."

"I missed you, too," she said, and actually smiled at me, then followed it with another kiss, this one even sweeter than the first.

"Please, please, please stop doing that where I can see it," Bridgett begged. "For the sake of my stomach if not my sanity."

"One wonders what she would do if forced to watch us fuck," Alena murmured.

"Gouge my eyes out, to start. The car's this way, come on," Bridgett said, then turned and began threading her way out of the airport. I took Alena's hand, held it as we followed her to where their rental was parked, the same Ford Focus that Bridgett had been driving last time. We shoved my bags in the trunk, and Alena insisted on my taking the front passenger seat, I think mostly because she didn't want to be that close to Bridgett.

It was a two-and-a-half-hour drive back to Ballygar, and the first half was spent with me relating what had happened since I'd left Ireland. For once, I didn't feel the need to spare any details. When I told them about the drop site in the desert, the concrete building with its jerry can and galvanized bucket, each of them swore under their breath, muttering the same curse, but in different languages.

By the time I was finished, we'd reached the N61, the road all but empty, the night sky clear and full of stars. For a while, none of us said anything, and there was only the expanse of Ireland's fields and the sound of the road and the engine.

Then Bridgett asked, "So am I finished here?"

"You could head home tomorrow," I said. "Cashel wants you to call when you get back into town, by the way."

"Of course she does. Tomorrow?"

"Sure."

"You don't need me around for another day or two?"

"I'd welcome the company," I said.

Bridgett lifted her chin, indicating Alena's reflection in the rearview mirror. "*She* wouldn't."

I expected Alena to offer a retort, or at least a confirmation, and when none came turned my head to see that the reason she'd become so silent was because she'd fallen asleep. Either that or she was avoiding participating in the conversation by pretending to fall asleep. I brought my attention back to the road.

"Maybe not, but she appreciates what you've done for us. I do, too."

"Good, you should." She sounded satisfied. "You know where you're going next?"

I shook my head. "Haven't had much time to think about it."

"You could come back to the States. It's a big country, I'm sure you two could find a nice quiet corner to hide in for happily ever after."

"You think?"

"Like I said, it's a big country."

"No, the 'happily ever after' part."

Bridgett grunted. "Fuck if I know. You two and baby makes three."

I thought about that, didn't speak. Thinking about the future, at least outside of the immediate future, wasn't something I'd devoted time to in years. When we'd lived in Kobuleti, the days had all seemed alike, and even as they passed, time felt like it was standing still. That was until Bakhar had died, until Tiasa had been taken, and in that, it seemed, our life there had been revealed for the purgatory it had been.

I was still thinking about it, lost in my thoughts, when the headlights burst into the car, shining much too close and much too bright. They appeared suddenly, no warning at all, and whoever was behind the wheel had been driving with them off, and as I realized that, I realized we were in trouble.

Bridgett knew it, too, managed to say "What the fuck?" and then followed it with an emphatic "Shit!" as the car behind us tried to clip our rear bumper. The Ford swerved, and she fought it back into line, accelerating. The road stretched straight and thin ahead of us as far as the headlights could see, no turnoffs, no buildings, just field on either side. From the backseat I heard Alena start awake. I twisted in the seat, got rocked a second time as the car following collided with us again.

"Stay down," I told Alena. She was wearing her seatbelt, which reassured me somewhat.

"Who are they?" Alena demanded.

"No fucking idea," I said. "Don't suppose either of you have a gun?"

"Talk to her," Alena snarled.

"I told you, it's Ireland," Bridgett snapped back, her eyes dancing between the view out the windshield and the view in the mirrors. "They don't like people having guns here!"

"Let's hope whoever's trying to drive us off the road had the same problem," Alena said.

"I hate you," Bridgett told her.

Behind us, the car was coming up for another try. As it swung out, I saw a new set of headlights revealed behind it, a second car, following close on the first.

"Now there are two of them," I remarked.

"I can see that!"

"Don't you think you should lose them?"

"The fuck you think I'm trying to do?"

The Ford rocked again, and I heard something crack on either our car or theirs, and suddenly our wheels broke with the road and we were spinning and sliding. Headlights seemed to flash from impossible angles, Bridgett swearing a blue streak, and I heard the engine scream in agony as she tried to treat the automatic transmission like it was a manual. We flipped around, facing the opposite direction, still moving, now in reverse, and the motor was shrieking like it was about to burst.

"Try to PIT me, motherfucker?" Bridgett said, and wrenched the wheel again, stomping pedals and yanking on the shifter. The Ford flipped around in a J-turn, once more heading the right direction, and then there was a gunshot, and just as suddenly, instead of being on the road we were off of it. The suspension bounced us like kernels in hot oil, and I realized we'd lost a tire to a blowout. The car slewed crazily in soft earth, and both pairs of headlights were still coming after us.

Whoever it was, they had demonstrated their sincerity, even if they lacked skill. The PIT—precision immobilization technique—as Bridgett had called it, was used mostly by law enforcement to immobilize a target vehicle during a pursuit. When executed properly, the fleeing car would be nudged just enough out of line to force a spin that would bring it to a halt. When executed improperly, any number of things could happen, normally beginning and ending with the word "crash."

Which was exactly what happened to us next.

CHAPTER
Thirty-seven

There was an air bag in my face when I came back, the dust from broken safety glass in my eyes and nose and mouth, and I didn't understand why. Then I did, and I started, felt pain in my right knee and lower back and head. The car was at an angle, its nose tilted down, and Bridgett groaned behind the wheel. I pushed at my door, got it open, but couldn't understand why I was having such trouble getting out. Then I remembered my seatbelt.

"Out," I said, and then, louder, "Out, get *out*!"

The soil beneath my shoes was soft and wet, and I went for the rear door, but Alena had already kicked it open. The back tires were in the air, the whole car canted like a javelin thrust into the earth, and as I pulled her free, the headlights found us again, both sets of them. I turned, keeping a hand on Alena, and with the light from the approaching cars could make out the field ahead and around us, sheep bleating and scattering in fear. The Ford had gone front-first into a creek, a four-foot drop, maybe ten feet across.

"Run," I told Alena, but I needn't have bothered; she'd read the terrain the same as I had, and was already moving.

I rushed around to the driver's door, met Bridgett as she toppled out of the car. Headlights made the blood on her face shine, where it was flowing from above her right eye and her nose. She was unsteady as I helped her to her feet, and she managed two steps, then went down to a knee. I pulled her up, got an arm beneath hers, and dragged her with me down into the water. It was cold and moving fast, and the first part, at least, seemed to revive her, so that by the time we'd crossed to pull ourselves up the opposite embankment, she was shrugging me off, saying she was fine.

I made it up before her, then turned back to see the two cars were still closing, but slowing. Bridgett pulled herself to her feet beside me, and together we ran after Alena, trying to make for the deeper darkness. Whoever was behind us, the creek would stop them as it had stopped us, force them to follow on foot.

We'd covered maybe twenty meters when they started shooting at us, two short bursts from automatic weapons. I didn't look back and I sure as hell didn't stop. Unless they were exceptionally talented marksmen, there was no way they were going to hit us at this range, certainly not with submachine guns, and if they were using assault rifles, we'd have been shot dead already.

We kept running, and the light behind us ran out, and out of the darkness ahead, I could see Alena, and she had veered off

to the left, and after another second I saw why. An old barn resolved out of the night, ghostly pale stone and wood. By the
time we'd reached it, Alena had already managed one of the two
doors on the side, and I followed after Bridgett, again turning
to spare a look at our pursuers. They'd left their headlights on,
and now I could see there were only two of them, silhouettes
making their way patiently toward us.

I pulled the door closed behind me, feeling along the wood
in the deeper darkness until I found the locking bar. It resisted
me, and I had to force it free before it would slide into place.

"Yeah, this is *so* much better," Bridgett muttered from
somewhere to my left.

"There are two of them," I said. "Submachine guns. We've
got maybe a minute before they reach us."

I heard motion off to my side, the sound of metal clattering
on metal. Alena cursed. There was absolutely no light in the
barn, nothing coming in from above. After another second, I
heard metal on stone, knew that Alena had found the bolt on
the other door and thrown it.

"Light," I said. "Matches, lighter, anything."

Bridgett laughed bitterly.

"Start feeling around," Alena said. "There must be something here we can use. A tool, something."

I put my hand out to the wall, feeling the stone cold beneath it, using it as a guide, fumbling like a blind man. My left
foot hit something hard and I reached out with my free hand
for it, was rewarded with the feel of cold metal, thinking of the
old joke about the five blind men trying to describe an ele-
phant. Behind me and to the side there was another clatter as
either Alena or Bridgett knocked something over. I tried getting
a grip on whatever it was I was feeling, found an opening at the
top, managed to lift it up with one hand. It felt heavy and un-

gainly, and I couldn't imagine what it was. Maybe a milk can. Too awkward to use as a weapon. I let it go.

"Got something," Bridgett whispered. "Tools, I think."

"Keep talking," I said, coming off the wall and trying to find her by sound alone.

"Wooden handle, two wooden, no, three, four wooden handles...rake, one's a rake, think I've got a shovel, too, feels like it...maybe an axe. Something else."

My outstretched hand touched her body, and I felt her own hand take my arm, guide it to what she'd been feeling. It was, as described, a wooden handle, worn and smooth, and when I lifted it, the weight on the end was solid and familiar. With my other hand, I felt for the axe head, found it. The edge was dull. Not that it would matter if I got the chance to use it.

The handle on one of the doors rattled, checking it, then stopped. The darkness was disorienting, but I guessed it was the same one I'd locked.

Then a voice came floating in from outside, muted by the stone and wood, speaking in Russian.

"I know you're in there, David."

It was Arzu Kaya.

"I've been waiting for you, watching your women," he said, switching to English. It was the first time I'd heard him speak the language, and he spoke it well, and I wondered why he was using it, until he continued and I realized it was for Alena's and Bridgett's benefit, as much as my own. "You have very pretty women, David, even if they are too old to be worth anything."

His voice seemed to fall and rise irregularly, bouncing between soft and loud as it was deflected by the stone. None of us inside our darkness moved, each of us trying to get a fix on his position by sound.

"The redhead," Arzu said. "The one you were kissing at the

airport, she's pregnant, isn't she? Your wife, David? I know a few who pay extra for pregnant."

Carefully, I started sliding my feet forward, back toward the door I'd locked when I'd entered, hoping I wasn't heading straight toward it, and hoping more that Arzu didn't just decide to open up and spray the wood with his submachine gun. Behind me, metal scraped stone as one of the women took up another of the farm implements.

"Who is the other one, the dark-haired one? Some bitch to fuck when your wife says no?"

I half expected Bridgett to respond to that, but she didn't. One of them was moving, though, I could hear her, but with Arzu's voice outside and the acoustics inside, I was having difficulty fixing her position.

"Don't you have anything to say, David?"

I had a lot to say, but I wasn't going to say it right then. My foot hit the wall, and with my free hand I reached out, feeling for the edge of the door. I'd come in close to it, within a foot, and used that as a guide to get my back against the stone wall. I took the axe in both hands, wondering who in the world I was trying to kid. Unless I could get around behind him, by the time I had managed to raise and swing it, Arzu would have shot me a dozen times.

"Then I will say it." Arzu's voice seemed closer now, as if he was just outside the door. "You and your bitches locked in an old barn, and I am outside. If you had a gun, you would have used it already, so you have no gun. So you have no defense. But I have a gun, and if you make me come inside for you, David, not only will I kill you, I will kill your women, too. I will kill your child. But if you come out, I will let them live. You understand me?"

"You should have let it go," I said.

"Let it go?" Arzu's voice crackled with anger. "How do I let it

go? The Russians, the Americans, everyone is looking at me because of you! They think I'm Bakhar, now, just like Bakhar! You
did this, not me! You made this!"

"You'll let them live." I made no effort to hide my contempt.

"Yes, I will," Arzu said. "Or maybe I keep you alive long
enough to watch what I do to them. Make you watch when I
carve your baby out of the bitch's belly."

He went quiet, and the silence inside the barn weighed like
lead. Then, just as emphatically, it broke.

From the opposite side of the barn came the sudden sound
of wood snapping, and a door I hadn't known was there flew
open, and a silhouette filled it, large and lean. Theunis Mesick
from Amsterdam with a submachine gun in his hands, and
whether he could see me or not I didn't know, but he had his
weapon pointed straight at me, and I had nowhere to go and no
move to make.

The sub came up to his shoulder, and then Alena slammed
him in the face with the shovel she'd found, and Theunis
Mesick staggered backward, finger heavy on the trigger, muzzle
flash as a strobe light as bullets whined wildly off the stone
walls and pierced the roof above us. She hit him a second time,
knocking him to the ground, then brought the blade of the
tool down and into the back of his neck.

I grounded the axe as Alena scooped up the submachine
gun, caught it when she threw it to me, pivoting in place. It was
an old Sterling, and I tucked it against my side. Arzu was shouting Mesick's name, trying to figure out what had happened,
and when no response came, he threw a burst at the door he'd
been standing outside, and I stepped away from the wall and returned it with one of my own. The sound of gunfire echoing inside the barn was ferocious.

With the light from the now-open door opposite, I could
make out more of the interior. Alena was searching Mesick's

body, and Bridgett had some tool of her own in her hands, was moving to her side. I turned from the door Arzu and I had just perforated, made for the other one along the same side, the one Alena had locked. Everything was down to speed now, the same as it had been for Tiasa.

I threw the bolt back and opened the door, exiting hard and twisting to my left, the Sterling ready, thinking that planting four or five rounds in Arzu's chest would end this once and for all. I would've been right about that, too, except for one small thing.

He wasn't there.

I'd started to turn when I felt the muzzle press into my right shoulder from behind, and I lost the sound of the shot as a bullet exploded out of me from in front. I dropped the Sterling and found myself following it to the ground. My right arm absolutely failed to support me, and I went face-first into mud. I couldn't get my breath, tried to raise my head, thinking that it would be better if the last thing I saw in this life was the sky. The muzzle returned, the metal hot, jammed into the back of my neck, but the shot didn't come.

"I *told* you," Arzu shouted at me, rage and glee commingled. "You should have taken care of your women!"

I managed to lift my head enough to look around and up at him, and he was leaning over me, the barrel of his Sterling still digging into my neck. I saw him, and I saw beyond him, and despite his gun and the bullet and the mud and pain, I had to laugh.

"The women can take care of themselves," I told him.

Then Bridgett Logan buried a pitchfork into his back.

CHAPTER
Thirty-eight

In mid-August, Alena told me that she wanted to visit Tiasa. We had resettled in Vancouver, Canada, and she was well into her second trimester. She was in New York a week, leaving Miata and me alone to continue our respective convalescences and to pursue our slow search for a more permanent home.

The night she returned, Alena said, "She wants to come live with us. She doesn't want to go back to Georgia."

"What do you think?"

"I think it's a good idea."

"You talk to Cashel about it?"

"Yes."

"What did she say?"

"She thinks that Tiasa will need counseling, therapy, for a long time to come. That she needs stability. Safety. Love. She wonders if we can give her all of these things."

"We can," I said.

"Yes," Alena agreed. "We can."

In early October, Cashel and Bridgett brought Tiasa out from New York, to the house we'd purchased in Victoria. Alena and I met them at the airport. Tiasa hugged me when she saw me, and my right arm had recovered enough strength and mobility that I was able to hug her in return. She looked like a different person than when I'd last seen her in July. Somewhere along the way, somehow, she'd rediscovered her ability to smile.

Bridgett and Alena kept their mutual hostility almost cordial, more for Tiasa's benefit than mine. Bridgett stayed with us for only two days, but Cashel was with us a week. With her assistance, we were able to set up counseling and further treatment for Tiasa.

None of us had any illusions.

On the last day of the year, at thirty-six minutes past three in the morning, Alena gave birth to a healthy baby girl.

We named her Natalya, in memory of another lost friend.

All the while, even into the new year, I'd been following the news, trying to keep an eye on the various outlets I'd sent my FedEx packs to.

Some ran further with the story than others, and some ran with it not at all. Of the European outlets, *Der Spiegel* did the most with the material I'd sent, followed by *The Guardian*. In the U.S., as I'd seen, *The New York Times* took the lead, but in early October, *The Washington Post* began its own series.

It was, I knew, a drop in the bucket.

All I had to do was look at Tiasa, holding her baby sister as she sang Natalya to sleep, to see the memories still fresh in her eyes, to know the truth.

Acknowledgments

The research for this novel was some of the most painful I've undertaken, and the efforts of everyone who assisted me is greatly and sincerely appreciated. Of the many who offered their time, observations, knowledge, and assistance, the following are but a handful.

My thanks to both Eric Trautmann and Timothy O'Brien for research assistance. For an insight into the world of engineers, Andrew Greenberg—who really *is* a rocket scientist—was invaluable.

As he has done on almost every novel I've written, Jerry Hennelly provided firsthand tactical experience, professional know-how, and a deeper understanding of everything from surveillance technology to firearm techniques. I remain, as ever, in his debt.

My agents, David Hale Smith and Angela Cheng-Caplan, continue to supply moral and creative support, and consistently provide that most crucial of aid: they know how to listen, and they do so exceptionally well.

Christina Weir took time from a busy schedule and an insanely difficult year to read the manuscript in progress and offer comment, constructive criticism, and encouragement. Mine's finished; where's yours?

A special note of gratitude to E. Benjamin Skinner, a man I've never met, but whose book, *A Crime So Monstrous: Face-to-Face with Modern Day Slavery,* reveals one of the greatest evils of our time, and our failings in combating it. In combination with H. Richard Friman and Simon Reich's *Human Trafficking, Human Security, and the Balkans,* as well as Kevin Bales's remarkable book, *Disposable People: New Slavery in the Global Economy,* these works formed the foundation for this novel. Not a single scenario as presented herein was fabricated from whole cloth: everything is based in fact to a greater or lesser extent, gleaned from publications, testimonials, interviews, and documentaries.

Finally, to Jennifer, who listened when she would rather not have done, and who lived with me as I went once more to the dark places; thank you, again, for being there when I came back into the light.

ABOUT THE AUTHOR

GREG RUCKA resides in Portland, Oregon, with his wife and two children, where he is at work on his next thriller, which Bantam will publish in 2010. He is the author of nine previous thrillers, as well as numerous graphic novels, including the Eisner Award-winning *Whiteout* series, now a major motion picture starring Kate Beckinsale.